Awakening of the
Dragonfly
'A Legend Forgot'

By
I.A.W. Offor

First paper back and ebook edition June 2019

ISBN 978-1-9161713-0-5

INTRODUCTION

Welcome curious reader. You join this story many thousands of years from its beginning. Although you join it today, in fact this particular chapter will not start until tomorrow! Before we can get to that, you must understand that tomorrow's chapter, will start at the end of a chapter that has lasted for more than three hundred years of yesterdays. Tomorrow at last brings to us all hope, a hope that we had forgotten we could have even hoped for. A friend will be brought back to us, a protector of us, 'a legend forgot'. Tomorrow brings to us 'the awakening of the dragonfly'.

Today, let's begin with a most important, truthful and wonderful fact. In every village, in every town, in every city, in every country, on every island on our wonderful planet Earth, exists the most unexpectedly, splendidly, wonderfully perfect home. This most unexpectedly, splendidly, wonderfully perfect home, although being different in appearance in every village, in every town, in every city, in every country, on every island on our wonderful planet Earth, is in fact the same.

Every unexpectedly, splendidly, wonderfully perfect home, greets you with its lovingly made, red iron flower covered decorative garden gate, the same gorgeously red, wobbly cobbly footpath. Each wobble and cobble are framed by the most unexpectedly, splendidly, wonderful display of flowers, with every shape, colour and smell your mind could conjure up. Each home has the same friendly, perfectly formed, incredibly inviting bright red front door, with its completely oppositely crooked windows that give this unexpectedly, splendidly, wonderfully perfect home its most inviting of smiles. With all the quirkinesses that simply shouldn't work on any home, it simply does. And by simply working, each Dragonfly home is the most unexpectedly, splendidly, wonderfully perfect home. Oh and if you are lucky enough to be invited in, well, actually that's a story for another day, but all you need to know, is the real magic about all Dragonfly homes is hidden inside that most unexpectedly, splendidly, wonderful red door.

Sadly, the last three hundred years of yesterdays have taken their toll. From what was once a home that all knew in every village, in every town, in every city, in every country, on every island on our wonderful planet Earth, they have, over the last three hundred years, slowly been forgotten. Although they have moved from fact to fairy tale and legend, to fiction then forgotten by all, the magic splendour and purpose, today in no way recalled, they still however exist. There will indeed be a Dragonfly house very close to you. You will have to look hard, as sadly your Dragonfly house may not look as bright as it once did, or resemble what it once was. Over the last three hundred years, the keepers of these homes have been disappearing as quickly as our memories of such magical places.

There have indeed been no stories told or pages written about these homes, in far too many yesterdays, however tomorrow is coming…

CHAPTER 1

Another home, another town, another school, another bully. A week had passed and the sixteen year old Alex feared his previous bad experiences of change, were going to repeat until the day he died. It is said 'change is as good as a rest', that is not how Alex felt. He never had a true place to call home - he had never been able to make a true connection with anyone, never been able to be a local. No, change was dreadful - anything but a rest.

Every year or two Alex was shunted from one end of the country to another. He dreamt of making true lifelong friends, but it seemed that it was not meant to be, he always found himself alone. Alex had become a young adult, turning sixteen before arriving at his latest new home. He so wanted it, along with his new school and the new people he would meet, to be different.

A sweet looking boy, Alex had bright blonde hair with natural, romantic curls and the brightest of blue eyes. Those who actually spent any time looking into his eyes, could not only see the pureness of his soul, but in certain lights, they could also see a most unusual hint of the colour purple. Alex wasn't the smartest, but common sense made up for any lack of intelligence. His ability to take on any physical challenge without hesitation or failure seemed almost supernatural, and generally made him unbeatable at any physical task he faced. With all the qualities he had, the usual rules governing social interaction and acceptability should find Alex in any of the popular crowds. Sadly to this point in his life, it had not been the case. His negative experiences and memories from the years of torment, continually haunted Alex. He had become impressive in his ability to block them in his waking life. However, as hard as he tried to keep them in the dark forgotten parts of his mind, the haunting memories, plentiful, would seep out into his nighttime dreams.

There was one particular memory that found its way, almost nightly, to the front of the line of the many painful, nasty, horrible, sad, lonely, despair ridden memories. In this reoccurring nightmare Alex was twelve. It was a replay of a reality he had lived. Arriving at yet another new school, the young Alex was welcomed by a boy, the head of the elite popular clique. The boy's arrogance and popular status blinkered him to the reality that the majority of the pupils actually had a strong dislike for him. His rowdy clique of intimidators gave him more power than he should have had or deserved.

Four weeks passed with relative calm. Having not learnt the lesson from starting new schools in years gone by, Alex found himself sucked in, once again. The cycle was in full swing - welcome the new boy, learn about the new boy, use everything learnt against the new boy, make the new boy the focus of all abuse and mockery. Rumour spreading, laughing at, making a fool of at every opportunity, was this bully and his cliques modus operandi. Too much of a coward to get physical with Alex, he tore at his heart and soul on a daily basis. With a blink in his dreams eye, Alex found himself a year on - thirteen years old. Every time he found himself in the dream, he tried to change it. He couldn't, so again he found himself in the same place, doing the same thing, in the same nightmare his mind refused to let him forget.

The lunch time bell had sounded. Alex found himself standing in a familiar doorway, that of the school canteen. He made his way to join the line of young people, carefully avoiding eye contact with anyone. The smells of unappetising food filled the room. Having escaped their classes for a short period, the two hundred children shuffling about, laughing and talking, would fill many with happy memories. This was not the case for Alex. He collected his food, turned and for the first time looked up. Usually he managed to find a table hidden away in a corner. But on the day that he replayed over and over in his dreams, he couldn't see any seats available amongst the battlefield of tables, chairs, food and loud young people. Rather than standing in one spot for too long, which was sure to attract attention, he began his search. As he passed the first full table, Alex, scanning the room, saw the perfectly dressed, clean cut, popular, most evil child he had ever met. He was directing people, pointing, sniggering and finally with one signalling clap of his hands, the room fell silent. All attention was now directed at the battle weary Alex.

Not visible to the onlookers, Alex felt a heat build up inside - a rage like he had never felt before. Fighting hard to keep control of his usually calm self, he took four deep lung-filling breaths. He knew that if he let out what he was experiencing within, whatever would have happened would have marked him for the rest of his days. His heart slowing, the red mist that had fallen over his wide open eyes fading, Alex was pleased to be getting control. However like every other night when he relived the same day in his dream, his nightmare, calm was not to last. Like a twenty foot boiling wave crashing over him, he was engulfed. Not by his own memories or emotions, but by those of every single person staring at him, by every person who was sitting or standing in the room. He was living each one of their lives in an instant. Happiness, joy, family, fear, depression, death. The voices in his head got louder and louder. The visions getting more intense and vivid with every passing second. Each scream, each scene from the minds and souls of every person in the canteen, flashed through his mind. Alex was no longer conscious of the physical presence, of any pupil or member of staff watching him. The heat he was experiencing was causing a most unnatural reaction - his tight grip on his tray was causing it to warp. Finally as a final wave of visions soaked him, the bent out of shape tray could take no more. With a loud crack and an ear piercing scream from Alex, the food flew in every direction as it snapped in half. The audience screamed as they were covered in what had been collected by Alex from the dinner ladies. The noise brought the thirteen year old Alex back to his unpleasant nightmare reality. Composed beyond his years, Alex made his way back to the food counter, placed the remnants of his tray on it, turned and left the canteen.

As the door shut behind him, he could hear the sound of the two hundred young people burst into unified laughter. The heat from his body was cooling, but a pain was growing deep inside his soul. Having walked calmly out of sight, Alex heard an angry voice shouting after him. It was one of the responsible adults, who sat and did nothing in his moment of persecution. Alex ran, he ran as fast as he could, away from the place of torment. His run, which left the unhealthy teacher far behind, took him to a deserted corner of the school grounds. With every ounce of strength he had left, Alex fought to keep the pain inside. He was embarrassed at his scream in the canteen, he wasn't about to let that happen again. He had learnt over many years, that showing any kind of emotion on the outside, did not end well for him. No one in sight, resting his back against the old school wall, Alex looked up at the sky. Quite some time past before he finally got control of himself. Mother Nature did her part, using her passing brilliant white clouds to hypnotise him, to give him focus on the beauty that was beyond the place he stood.

Finally, tearing himself away from the fantasy life of the dancing clouds, his gaze returned to the dull grey surroundings of where his run had taken him. Alex looked out from where he was hidden, towards where he expected someone to appear - teachers, although more likely, the classmates who wanted to torment him further. Nothing, no one. As hard as he tried, he could not even hear the sound of distant voices or footsteps that may be heading his way.

Alex was comforted by the fact that it appeared no one was looking for him. He went to look back up at the sky, but as he did, something in a small window caught his eye. It was his reflection, as expected, but his reflection wasn't alone. In the window behind him he could see a silhouette. He went to turn and see who it was but before he could, he felt a pressure on his shoulders. He glanced to his right. The pressure felt like hands, but he could see nothing. The ghostly hands made their way down each of his arms. The escaped tears he had been trying to hold back were blurring his vision, so he shook his head and wiped them away. Looking back to the window the silhouette was gone, as was the pressure from the ghostly arms. Alex as always in his nightmare was completely confused. He looked around, hoping to find some sort of sensible explanation for the pressure he had felt. Strangely in that moment, he felt a calmness.

Sadly the moment was simply that, a moment. The feelings, emotions, pain, visions he had managed to take control of from the canteen experience were back, but bigger. They were not only from those nearby, they were from strangers far away. Something had been awoken in him. Alex had come to believe that the ghostly calming touch he had received, was preparing him for what was to come. Tears poured from his eyes. Within his nightmare the pain took over completely, as it did on the day it was reality. Alex felt as though his mind was being lost, that his body could take no more. His ability to keep hold of his conscious self was lost.

That was the point Alex woke up from his nightmare, every time, without fail. On the actual day three years earlier, when he had lived his nightmare, he in fact did not wake up. The teacher who had chased him from the canteen, who had failed miserably to care for his student, finally found Alex slumped in the dirty, damp corner where he had ended up. Finding the lifeless Alex, the useless teacher actually acted - he raised the alarm. An ambulance crew arrived quickly. They had no answer for Alex's state, his vital signs so weak. With a thirty minute drive to the nearest big hospital, they had prepared themselves and the school, for the worst of losses - the loss of a child. The worst did not happen, however it was two weeks before Alex eventually woke up. He never did return to that horror filled place again, in his real life anyway, just in his torturous nightmares.

Not all thoughts filled the sixteen year old Alex with dread. Somehow with all he had been through, he still found the strength to daydream. Lost in a stare, he would think about the perfect life. A place where he would grow up living in one place, be surrounded by family, have good friends, feel accepted, be at home. A place where being himself didn't create envy, fear and uncertainty in all who met him. His daydreams - they were key in giving him the strength to make it to the end of his first week at his new school.

As he walked out of the gates Alex was pleased with himself. At last, some of the lessons he had learnt over the years of new school after new school, were starting to pay off. He had not answered any questions, he had not got involved in any groups. He had in fact gone into this new social world keeping his head down and acting disinterested. Success, he had been left alone. On the bus and having made his way past the first three rows of seats, Alex was about to find out, the hard way, that actually no tactics, let alone his new tactics from his lessons learnt, would make any difference. From row number four on the drivers side a foot appeared. Too late to make any change in direction, Alex found himself lying face down on the wet, smelly, sticky, grit-covered floor of the school bus.

As quickly as he fell, Alex was back up. Not saying a word, not making eye contact with his comedian attacker, he made his way to the nearest vacant seat and sat down. After such an event, the familiar sound of laughter erupted, affirming his thoughts that generally, people are unpleasant. After a good week, today was going to be different. As quick as Alex found his seat, he was back up. A strength that surprised even him, welled up inside. For once, not thinking about others feelings, opinions or indeed consequences of his own actions, he made his way back to the fourth row of the bus. Once there he stood motionless, not making a sound, not making eye contact with a single person, he just stood. The bus fell silent. The anticipation of all the onlookers filled the air with an electric energy, sparking invisibly with the slightest movement or sound from any part, person or object. With the stops, with the starts, with the bumps, with the bends in the road, Alex did not move his feet from the spot. His apparent supernatural physical abilities, defying science and its understanding of gravity.

Ten minutes past, stops came and went, the bully was as motionless as Alex. The occupants of the bus seemed to have got bored with the stand-off. The ripple of quiet conversation could be heard. Of course most of the quiet voices were talking about Alex, but he did not care. Finally Alex's stop arrived. As he walk forward, the occupants of the bus once again fell silent. His senses heightened as he made his way to the exit. Alex was alerted to the sound of movement from behind. He didn't know if it was or was not the bully, either way he stayed focused. Purposely he placed each foot firmly on the dirty bus floor, the floor he had known intimately just ten minutes earlier.

As Alex placed his foot onto the last step of the bus, he heard a muffled thump followed by laughter. He did not look back. He continued his slow, but purposeful walk off the bus. He was so relieved to have made it. No further aggression had been directed at him, it really was a good first week.

Stepping from the bus, Alex's ears were pierced by the sound of the frozen pathway crunching beneath his feet. The sound echoed between the bus and the old stone wall opposite. In that moment Alex did something most unusual. He did something he hadn't done for many years. He did the very thing that had brought him back from the brink of despair three years ago in the damp, dirty part of the school he had found himself in. He took his gaze from the slippery floor and looked up.

The sky was beautiful. The cloud-free blue daylight sky was turning into the deepest of blues, as the sun was vanishing over the rooftops to the west. A glow from the distant cities' lights, looked as welcoming as returning to a freshly lit open fire after a cold winters walk. At that very same moment the street began to dance into life, as the houses with their curtains not yet closed and the street's Christmas decorations awoke, bursting into life with every colour imaginable.

Alex took in a long deep breath, his throat freezing from the cold air that seemed more full of life-giving oxygen than ever before. He couldn't explain it, but he had a sense that something had changed in the world. He felt it, he knew it. He didn't know how, but something, just something was new. Taking yet another deep breath, Alex felt one single tiny electric pulse come from somewhere inside him. Although the pulse was singular and gone as quick as it came, he was left with something, a point of energy, a dot of light deep inside the place of darkness he had lived every day.

As the bus moved off, taking the location of his little victory away, the old diesel engine roared. The noise snapped Alex back to reality. His head held high for the first time in far too long a time, Alex smiled.

The bus stop was only a few hundred yards from his new home - a square filled on both sides with old character-full red brick houses. Sitting at the far end sat the most impressive church. In the middle, being looked on to by all the houses, was the grassy communal area, where fetes and games would be played in the summer months. On this winter's day however, no grass was visible, just undulations of frozen snow and the snow creations of the squares' residents. The snowmen built the night before had grown a little, thanks to the help of Mother Nature. The new snow gave them a more natural, less human-made look. It was as though they could get up and walk off at any moment. The roads were far from smooth, they hadn't been cleared effectively over the weeks of snow and ice, so there were frozen impressions of the residents car tyres criss-crossing over each other. The cars that hadn't left the square sat with their hats of snow, sparkling from the reflection of the street lights and the Christmas lights that hung from them. Alex was happy to be walking home that particular day. He was happy that for the first time in his short life, he didn't back down, or react in any other way than what he perceived to be strong.

Almost across the main road and heading into the square, his smile still lighting up his face, he was knocked from behind. Struck by a stranger, a young girl clearly in a hurry. Alex shook his head disapprovingly and watched the wavy, fiery, red-haired girl disappear into the distance. His confidence having grown from the bus journeys events, meant the new Alex had a few words for the young whirlwind. However he didn't have time to get them out, as quick as she had bashed past him she was gone.

The mild assault forgotten, the smile having returned to Alex's face and a short walk later, Alex was home. He paused at the bottom of the drive and even though the windows were in darkness, his new home seemed brighter somehow than it had in the few short weeks since he had moved in. As bright as the house now seemed, he was aware that it did stand out from the rest of the street. It had a severe lack of Christmas decorations. Reflecting on what had gone before, Alex felt it quite simply did not matter.

Having made his way up the drive and up the four slippery steps to his front door, he took hold of the large cold brass handle. As he went to turn it, Alex was distracted by a faint sound. It wasn't the sound of distant traffic, industry, wind, rain or voices. Tilting his head towards where he thought the sound was coming from, he tried to focus his hearing. A slight momentary lowering in volume of the usual evening's sounds, clarified what Alex thought he had heard - the sad sound of despair. The sobbing sounds were coming from the direction of a house one garden away. His evening had filled Alex with such warm positive feelings, the sound he was hearing was a reminder of his usual reality. Could it be that his victory had been the cause of someone else's loss? Was Mother Nature creating balance and should he accept it? Ultimately Alex was hearing someone in distress and he could not ignore it, that just wasn't him.

Having shaken the questions from his mind, confirming where the sobs were coming from, Alex turned away from his new home. He dropped his bag from his back leaving it where he stood, and made his way back down the slippery steps, ran down his drive, back along the slippery snow-covered footpath and towards the heartbreaking sound.

Arriving at the gate to the garden he had decided the sounds were coming from, Alex attempted to slow his fast and loud breath so he could hear clearly. The sobbing that had taken him to where he was, had stopped. Alex stepped closer to the gate. Looking beyond the gate he could see an overgrown garden. It should have been as sparkly and light as the rest of the square with its white fresh snowfall, but it wasn't. It was dark, a darkness that wasn't helped by the properties imposing six foot high stone walls that towered above him, each side of the iron gate. Alex, still curious as to where the sobs had come from, gently pushed the gate to go in. It didn't move. He pushed harder, still it did not budge. Beyond the uneven snow, Alex could see the start of a small cobbled pathway clear of snow. It wound its way out of sight, through a very overgrown canopy of ivy covered trees and holly bushes, giving a thickness impenetrable to the naked eye.

Standing motionless for a few moments, as much as he tried straining to hear what he thought he had heard, he heard nothing, the sobbing had stopped. Had he been imagining it?

Not sure what had happened, what he had heard and why he had dashed to the rescue of apparently no one, Alex turned to head back home. As he did he lost his footing. Slipping slightly, he grabbed the gate to stop his fall. His legs spread apart to get balance, his body bent forward as his hand held on tight to the immovable gate, he found himself looking at the floor. Something caught his eye. There was a small dark patch. It did not in any way match the bright sparkly snow that covered every other part of the footpath. On closer inspection, directly below the handle of the gate Alex could see that in the snow, a vertical tunnel had been created, within which could be seen a warm, shining liquid in the deepest shade of red. The liquid's warmth had melted the snow as it passed through to its resting place - blood!

CHAPTER 2

Sophie dreamt often. Not every night, but when she did she would wake in a sweat from what were the most vivid of dreams. Dreams that often seemed more real than reality itself. She would find herself in places, with people, adventuring around buildings, worlds that she thought could not exist. Many a waking hour was spent trying to find meaning within her fabulous dreams. Her conclusions were always the same, they were just dreams.

Not all were happy, adventurous and fun. The dream that woke her that morning was one of the terrifying ones. Having left the beauty and lush green of a beautiful unknown outside world, she found herself in the darkest, dampest, of narrow rock-walled corridors. There were no doors, no windows. As she walked through the dark, she could see no way out. Her heart, in her dream, was racing, just as it was in her motionless sleeping real self. Having walked for some time through the darkness, she found herself unable to go any further. A smooth black wall faced her, she had reached a dead end. Then the familiar sound began. The sound was of pounding feet, too heavy and too many to be human. What must have been a large animal was fast approaching. The loud pounding feet slowed, this allowed Sophie to hear whatever it was breathe. It was getting closer and louder. Panic setting in, she had to get out, she had to escape. As terrifying as it was, there was a way out, she was only dreaming. All she had to do was wake herself, before the terrifying unknown creature found her. She had managed to train herself over the years to do just that. It wasn't always the easiest thing to do, but she always managed. Until that is, this night. As much and as hard as she tried, she could not leave the place or wake herself up. The terrifying sounds of the approaching beast got ever closer with every heart-racing, sweaty moment that passed.

With no escape, pure terror filled her completely. Her body prepared for the attack that was about to happen. Strangely it wasn't getting ready to fight, in fact it submitted to the unknown. She let the terror go, she relaxed into the moment and calmly waited for the end. Turning away from the dead end she had frantically been looking at to find some sort of escape through, Sophie looked into the dark, towards the sounds of the bounding paws and heavy breathing that was fast approaching. As she did, a familiar set of the brightest, colourful, light-producing eyes appeared. They shone from the silhouette of a figure. From its stature, it was a male figure who had appeared in many of her dreams before. She tried to focus beyond the eyes, hoping to make out features on the visiting silhouette. Before any slight detail could be seen, Sophie was suddenly awake.

"Damn it!" she exclaimed out loud. He had appeared in her dreams for so many years but only in the ones full of fear and dread. Sophie had become fascinated, almost obsessed by him. As scary as they were, she had begun to hope for the scary dreams where he may happen to appear. Every time, she would hope to stay asleep long enough, to give her that one chance to actually meet him. Much to her frustration, her attempts to see more than just the bright eyes and silhouette failed. She, frustratingly, was just unable to get enough control in her dream state, to hold back the fear in the moment long enough to make contact with her shadowed saviour. Of all the nights, she thought tonight she was actually going to meet him. He was so close, closer than he had ever been. She did everything perfectly, she had submitted to the inevitable, she was calmer than she had ever been, but alas it was not to be.

Out of breath, her heart racing and her body dripping with sweat, Sophie decided no more sleep would be the preferred option for the remainder of the night, bright eyes or not. Slowly turning on to her side, she slowly opened her eyes to take a look at her alarm clock - 4am. She knew it would be a long tired day at school. From experience, she knew she wouldn't be able to get a glimpse of her silhouette for a second time in one night, so she decided, as she often did, staying awake was the way to go. Time on her own, time away from people. Three hours of reading, three hours of quiet, three hours of spending time with her thoughts, with no exhausting dreams and no dread of having to be at school.

School wasn't her most favourite of places. There wasn't anything in particular she didn't like about it, she just preferred not to be there, or to be around people. Sophie was a studious and quiet young woman. If she wasn't in class, she was in the library. If she wasn't in the library, she was hiding in a corner reading. Her life experiences had made her into the person she was. That person was someone who was overly protective of herself and generally happier alone. She would never make eye contact with people, she didn't take any interest in anyone. If a teacher asked her a question, which they often did as Sophie always had the answer, she wouldn't even look up from the desk to answer. Her younger years of neglect had taught her that the only person she could rely on, was herself. Sophie was happy living in her world of self-inflicted loneliness. She was sure she could have made friends if she had wanted to, she just didn't. Time alone in her bedroom sanctuary in the early hours of the morning, away from anyone who may be looking at her, was a wonderful place for her to be and she took full advantage.

For a few moments, before reaching for a book, Sophie lay motionless staring up at her star covered ceiling. She had spent hours putting each one of the sticky illuminous stars in place, in an effort to bring her dreams to life. She took great pleasure in enjoying the recreation of the skies, from the worlds in her dreams. Quite some time passed. Finally she put on the lamp which sat on her cluttered bedside table. It was time to read, time to lose herself in a world not quite so scary as her dreams. Time to live a new life within a book, to experience love, fantasy, heroism, honour.

Laying close enough to the light to read the words in her chosen book, Sophie could feel the heat from the coloured glass of the lampshade. The shade was being warmed by the radiated heat of the light bulb. The heat waves from the bulb caused the glass gems, which hung on threads around the shade's edge, to move. As they swayed backwards and forwards, they sent playing, dancing shadows around the walls of her room.

She wasn't the tidiest of people. Her clothes were strewn all over the floor, mixed up with her many books and drawings. She spent many an hour recreating images of the places she had found herself, in her dreams. As messy as it was, it was her sanctuary, it was her room.

An hour passed. Sophie was totally immersed in the world created by the author of her book. So lost in the story, she hadn't even noticed the sound of the house's old pipes creaking, as the heating fired up and began pumping its almost warmth around the big iron radiators. It was winter, the old house really needed all the help it could get to take the chill out of its thick, stone walls. Lost in the white sand beach and clear blue sea in the pages of her book, the alone time hours vanished far too quickly.

Truth be known, Sophie, although happy to be by herself in a crowd, was not a big fan of feeling like she was alone in the house that was her home. No matter how much heat was produced by the old heating system, there was an eerie coldness to the place. Thankfully those times were rare, only happening on mornings such as this. That is to say, Sophie waking early and the one other occupant of the house being fast asleep. The other occupant, full of love and life, brought warmth and light to the old house - her grandmother.

'Wakey, wakey my little princess.'

The bedroom door flew open. Grandmother in her flowing pink dressing gown, rollers in her hair and smile on her face, greeted Sophie very excitedly. Her dressing gown was crumpled up on the floor, as all four foot ten inches of her couldn't lift it any higher. The eighty year old's face showed signs of having a very well used smile. Her eyes had a youngness about them. With the curtains having been thrown open without warning, the soft gentle light from Sophie's lamp was lost in the brightness of the low morning sun.

'Grandmother! I was reading,' Sophie said.

'Yes princess but today is a special day, not one

minute should be wasted,' was grandmothers
response. Sophie couldn't be cross with her, she never
could. Sophie had lived with her grandmother from
the age of eight. She had been abandoned by her
parents, who were happy to have been forced into
acknowledging that parenthood was not for them.
From the moment Sophie's parents fell accidentally
pregnant, their unsuitableness as caregivers was clear
to the rest of the world. The pregnancy, then birth of
Sophie was met with annoyance by them both. Sophie
was a hinderance to the career and life of both her
mother and father. Both lawyers, both incredibly self-
centred, both having a focus that was always about
bettering themselves, no matter what the cost.

From birth, Sophie was left alone in her room far
too often. Shown no love, her loud cries became
silent tears when after so long, no one would visit.
There was not a maternal or paternal bone in either of
their bodies. As Sophie got older, not only was she
left alone in her room, she would be left alone in their
big city top floor apartment. Her parents were far too
wrapped up in climbing to the top of their legal
business tree.

Sophie's move and ultimate life change that came
about at the age of eight, was thanks to a nosy
neighbour. She became increasingly concerned about
the pretty young girl who never said a word. She
would pass her in the flats' corridors, in silence and
usually on her own. The nosy neighbour also had
children. They were of a similar age and attended the
same school as Sophie. They would come home
laughing about Sophie and her silence. Yes the
neighbour was nosy, but her heart was in the right
place. Choosing not to just curtain twitch and gossip,
she confronted Sophie's parents. In a sad reflection of

who they were, Sophie's parents were very happy about the confrontation, and its conclusion. Before any negative press that may have affected their careers got out, mercifully and without hesitation, Sophie was taken to and left with a family member - Sophie's wonderful grandmother. She was loving, caring and the most eccentric lady. She lived her own life, in her own way and in her own time. Full of stories, full of support for Sophie. Full of the kind of love that Sophie, like every child, deserved. So, being disturbed by the curtains being flung open that morning, she couldn't stay cross with her.

'Eh?' Sophie responded, unsure why the day was so special.

'Let me give you a hint.' She began to sing 'happy birthday to you, happy birthday to…'

Before the song could get any further, Sophie was out of bed, dancing around her room and singing her own version 'happy birthday to me…' Just as the song was reaching its finale, Sophie totally lost her footing on the mess that covered her floor. Her legs in the sky, her arms flailing about, her hair falling all over her face, with a thud, she landed on top of a pile of clothes.

'Oh, oh, oh are you all right?' grandmother asked. Sophie burst into hysterical laughter. Through the high pitched laughing, she managed to spurt out,

'Yes, I am fine.' Grandmother tiptoed round the mess to where Sophie was lying. As she took hold of Sophie's hand to help her up, she also lost her footing. She had accidentally stood on Sophie's foot - it was hidden under the pile of clothes that had broken her fall. Within a split second, the two of them were lying side by side, looking up at the same star-covered ceiling. The laughter calming down, they turned to look at each other. As quick as eye contact was made, the two of them burst into another fit of laugher. Neither could talk, neither could breathe, neither made any attempt to move. Just as Sophie thought the laughter would never end, she would never catch her breath, her sides would ache forever, something caught her eye.

'Grandmother, what is that?' Sophie asked sitting up. Her question wasn't answered. She looked over to her grandmother to find out why. As she did, she saw something she had not seen from her before. For the slightest of moments there was fear in her eyes.

'What's what princess?' grandmother asked. She put on her happiest of voices sensing that Sophie had picked up on her lack of response.

'That there!' Sophie replied, pointing to the corner of her doorframe. Sophie swore she saw something moving, a shape in the frame of the door itself.

'I see nothing,' grandmother said dismissively.

'But grandmother!' Sophie said,

'But nothing princess,' grandmother snapped. She quickly put back on a large smile and brought the focus back to the special day. 'Come on, it's your birthday and it's time for breakfast.' The laughter at an end, Sophie got to her feet and helped her grandmother up. Sophie grabbed her bright yellow dressing gown, threw it on and followed her grandmother, who was already heading out of her bedroom.

The window over the first landing of the stairway, seemed brighter than it ever had. The stained glass appeared to want to tell a new story, on this birthday of all birthdays. As Sophie took her first step on to the cold wooden staircase, the sound of skidding, slipping, franticness could be heard below. Not a moment later, she was nearly thrown on her back, for a second time that morning. Anchor, her grandmothers huge and extremely dopey German Shepherd dog, wanted to wish Sophie a happy birthday in his own special way. Bounding right at her, his ears forward, his tongue out, whimpering away, the bundle of loveable fur was very excited. It took five minutes to get to the kitchen. Anchor played his part well. He held Sophie up long enough to give grandmother time to get the birthday cake candles lit. Eventually arriving at the kitchen, she flung the door open. Sophie knew what was coming, she thoroughly looked forward to the birthday cake breakfast every year. Stepping into the room, once more a chorus rang out,

'Happy birthday to you, happy birthday to you.' This time grandmother was able to finish the song. Sophie, imagining how good the cake was going to taste, took a deep breath and blew out the sixteen candles. The candles out and taking a good look at the cake, Sophie wasn't disappointed. It was yet another of grandmother's masterpieces. Her birthday cakes were always four stories high, no more, no less. Each layer was totally squint. The icing was so runny that the layers would slip apart, only just held together with hidden, wooden, kebab sticks. More icing lay on the side of the plate, over the edge of the plate and on the table than on the cake. It was imperfectly perfect and tasted so good, especially at eight o'clock in the morning. 'Looky, looky, what do I have here?' grandmother said. Anchor had his paws on the old, very well used wooden kitchen table. Sophie, looking on with her huge, green eyes, as wide open as she could get them, sat back on to one of the wonky kitchen chairs. Her focus had been on the cake. She hadn't, goodness knows how, even noticed the box that was sitting on, and just about covering the entire table - it was gigantic. Grandmother was nowhere to be seen - she had disappeared round the back of the huge present, to put the cake out of Anchors reach.

'What have you gone and got me?' Sophie asked in a very excited voice.

'Well, you just have to open it to see,' grandmother replied, her head appearing from round its side. 'Don't keep me waiting.' Grandmother was as excited, if not more than Sophie was. Anchor's head was tilted, looking beyond the present, his eyes wide for a completely different reason - the out of reach cake!

Sophie was not going to be able to reach, to unwrap the biggest present she had ever seen in her life sitting down, so she stood up. The paper was all shades of yellow with sixteens everywhere - Sophie loved to have everything yellow. She frantically tried to find an edge to pull. Running round the table, searching every part of the wrapping, she couldn't find a loose enough piece to pull. Grandmother was not the tidiest of cake makers but she could wrap a present.

'Come on, what is taking you so long?' Grandmother was getting inpatient. 'Tear it, come on.' Just as she said it, Sophie gave up trying to be tidy about it. With one of her short, but sharp nails, she stabbed the centre of the wrapping. Having created a small hole, she pushed her finger in and the full on wrapping paper ripping commenced.

Grandmother was not a wealthy woman by any means. She made do, she got by, pretty much just about hung on to the house. She had to - it was a promise made by every generation when inheriting it.

A promise that had gone on since records of its existence began. In today's world, this promise was written into a legal document. The house was always to remain in the family and always to remain debt free. That was not the easiest of things to do with such a large old house. It was especially hard in a time where making a living was hard to do, let alone at the age of eighty. However what grandmother did better than anyone was make things. Particularly wooden toys, particularly dolls houses. Her talent was discovered by accident by one very lucky toy shop owner. Many years ago, long before Sophie had arrived to live with her, grandmother had put lots of her toys in her garden with a sign - 'free to good home' written on them. She had run out of space in her attic. Her hobby had taken over and she needed to clear space for her hobby to continue. A happy coincidence saw the toy shop owner visit a friend, who lived in the square, on that very day. He took the lot. He was a lovely man, but also a good businessman. He saw an opportunity, so left some money in an envelope. Since that day many years ago, although they never met, every two months he would return to find a garden full of toys. He would leave an envelope and take everything. It gave grandmother enough money to be able to afford the big old house, to survive, and once Sophie had arrived, to keep her fed and happy.

As Sophie pulled the last piece of paper away, the three sets of expectant eyes watched as the box appeared to open in slow motion. The masterpiece gradually revealed itself. Finally the present could fully be seen - it was a dolls house. It was, however, not just any dolls house. This one stood four foot high and was an exact replica of the house they were both standing in.

'Oh, grandmother that is the most beautiful thing I have ever seen,' Sophie said. The house they both lived in had seen far better days. The roof leaked, the windows let in the wind, the front door got stuck and the garden was overgrown. But the dolls house was perfect in every way.

Sophie was not your usual teenager. Her early life had shaped her into the young woman she had become. A person who enjoyed being alone and living life in her books. She hid in plain sight. People just did not notice her, a fact that she was happy about, if it had ever crossed her mind to notice. If you asked anyone if they knew Sophie, their response would be, 'who?' So the dolls house, which would be seen as a child's gift or an adult's collection, was quite simply the most perfect birthday present for Sophie. Grandmother knew her so well. Sophie loved it. It was a visual representation of the eight years of love and memories Sophie had experienced in the worn, but homely home, with her loving grandmother on this day, her 16th birthday.

Grandmother had been working on her masterpiece for two years. To see it in all its glory was bringing all kinds of emotions to the surface. Hidden away at the very back of the attic, the space she used for her toy making was small. This was the first time she had properly seen it. She hadn't even seen it properly the night before. After she had staggered down the stairs with it, helped by Anchor, who was generous enough to offer his back as a living, breathing trolley, all they had time to do was frantically wrap it. They couldn't dilly dally, just incase they were caught in the wrapping act.

It was magically magnificent. Every wonderfully

crooked window glowed, inviting those viewing to come in. The bright red front door - it made the house look as though it was smiling back at everyone. The wonderfully perfect, wobbly cobbly red footpath leading up to the front door. The small red garden gate pushed slightly open, waiting for the house's visitors, all seemed so real. Sophie reached forward to open the front door to see what was inside. As she did grandmother took her hand,

'Oh my princess, that can wait for later,' grandmother said.

'Later! Grandmother but,' Sophie was not happy at being stopped.

'But nothing my princess, school is calling. It has got late and the bus will be gone. So run upstairs my one year older beauty, we shall investigate Dragon...' Grandmother stopped herself before finishing her sentence, ushering Sophie out the kitchen door and back towards the cold wooden staircase. Anchor, the only one left in the kitchen, was now alone with the cake!

Head down, as always her eyes avoiding contact with anyone she came across, Sophie went through her uneventful school day of invisibility. It was Friday, the last day of the week and its end could not come quick enough for Sophie. When it did and only then, once in her seat on the bus that was to take her home, did she allow herself to once more get excited, about the wonderful dolls house she was shortly going to be able to properly investigate. The bus as always was full. The noise of laughing, joking, shouting, screaming and gossiping, all blended into one great big loud rumble. Being cramped in such close proximity to people and the unknown they brought, Sophie's heart usually raced for the full ten

minutes, every morning and every evening during the
short bus ride. She was normally always alert and
ready for when her stop appeared. Today however she
wasn't. Sophie had been lost in her head, excitedly
thinking about what the evening was going to bring.
Thankfully for Sophie, an odd silence fell over the
bus, which brought her out of her imagination. It only
took her a second to realise it was her stop, 'that was
a close one!' she thought to herself. Standing up, she
was aware of a male standing in the aisle. She began
to panic. It was her stop. She wanted to get off, but
she couldn't ask the boy blocking her path to move,
that would be far too much interaction. There was an
empty seat right next to him, she hoped that he would
sit down on it as she got closer. She couldn't
understand why he wasn't. Her head bent forward,
her eyes on the floor, she reached up and pressed the
bell to signal the driver to stop. Using her peripheral
vision she made her way forward, avoiding any
obstruction - feet, bags, boxes, jackets, the boy! He
was still standing motionless as she came right up
behind him. The bus was fully stopped, what was she
going to do?

Just as she was about to go back to her seat and
continue past her stop, Sophie's prayers were
answered. He started walking forward and off the bus.
'Hooray' she said in her head. In her excitement she
took eyes from the floor, she looked up to watch
him leave. That was a mistake. The person who was
sitting next to the standing boy who had now left,
looked up and they made eye contact. She was
completely uncomfortably distracted. In that split
second, the unpleasant boy had just enough time to
kick his bag into her path. It all happened so fast.
Sophie caught her foot in the strap of the bag and it

caused her to lose her footing. She fell hard to the floor. On her way down, Sophie's hand got caught between a bar and a seat - it tore skin. The secondary effect of her hand being caught, was that she had no way of stopping the inevitable impact of her head. She managed to turn her head slightly, hoping that her full head of red curls would soften the blow. It really didn't. As her head made contact, the loudest of solid bangs rang out through the bus, making everyone who heard it take a sudden intake of breath. It was horrible.

Then, the silence broke, the bus filled with laughter. Sophie's head's contact with the floor left her feeling dizzy. Her knees were sore, her skirt wet. Her hair was covered in dirt and grit from the wet and dirty floor. Her hand, that she managed to pull free, was bleeding heavily. She wanted to stand but she couldn't get her balance, so Sophie crawled down the bus towards the driver and the exit.

'Get off the floor you stupid girl, you will be getting reported for your antics, playing around on my bus. What's your name?' The horrible adult was supposed to be there as a protector to the innocent, on the daily horror of the bus journey. Sophie reached up with her hand that wasn't bleeding and took hold of a rail. She managed to pull herself to her feet. Once up, she took a moment to steady herself, adjusted her bag on her shoulder and then at surprising speed she made her escape. Jumping off the bus, she lost her balance and bounced off the stone wall opposite the bus stop, her head was spinning. The sympathetic students left on the bus could still be heard laughing. Sophie looked up and saw the bus windows filled with faces watching her. She was no longer in her invisible daily life. She leant on the wall and stood up straight, trying

to look as confident as she could. Getting her balance,
her eyes still spinning in her head, she was not aware
enough to notice the ground was icy. Her first
confident step was met with a slip. She grabbed the
wall again. Having managed to stay upright and after
a short pause, she tried again. Taking a deep breath
and holding it, without looking, she ran in front of the
bus, across the road, past the boy she had watched
leave. On automatic pilot, her vision blurry, somehow
not being hit by any of the keen to get home, early
Friday afternoon commuters, she made it to the
square.

Arriving at the familiar, old, rusted iron gate, with
its few patches of red paint that clung on to where
they had once been lovingly placed, Sophie reached
forward, with blood dripping from her hand to turn
the handle. It was frozen! Angry at its refusal to open,
out of breath, sobbing uncontrollably, her body full of
adrenalin, she threw her bag over the gate and
climbed her way over. Having landing heavily but on
her feet, she made her way up the short snow-covered
path, into the darkest part of the front garden. As the
house came into sight, Sophie stopped. She didn't
want her grandmother to see her in such a state. She
stood sobbing, her head throbbing from its impact on
the bus floor, her vision going in and out of focus. A
day that was to be a happy one - her sixteenth
birthday, her grandmother, her cake, her dolls house,
Anchor, why had the universe decided that a happy
day was to be so painful, embarrassing and sad.

Standing looking up at the red front door, tears
running down her cheeks, Sophie staggered. Through
her blurred vision, she saw and managed to grab on to
one of the ivy covered trees beside her. Nervous she
would fall, she slowly lowered herself onto a small

moss covered rock. Dropping her head into her hands, the blood from her open wound finding its way inside her jacket, running its warmth down her forearm, the world spinning out of control, Sophie didn't know what to do. She wanted to get back up and walk into her home like nothing happened. Sitting up straight, she lifted her head and reached back to the tree that had helped her down to the rock, hoping it would help her back up. With the last bit of strength she had left, holding tight to the damp tree, she went to stand. As she did, her mind went blank and her eyes rolled back into her head. She fell to the side, into the coarse overgrown flower bed, unconscious.

CHAPTER 3

It was that time of day again, when Anchor could always be found in one particular place. Perched on an old chair, looking out through the worn, crooked, living room window. The house's heating having not come on yet, Anchor's breath was steaming up the cold glass every time a bark left his always smiling face. It was unusual for him to be barking. Normally all that could be heard was an impatient, excited whimper. Grandmother had come to investigate what all the noise was about, so had made her way from the kitchen to join him. In her high pitched voice, she playfully asked,

'What is all the noise about?' Anchor's response was to jump off the chair, run to the front door and start barking again. She was more curious than ever now. She turned, her short legs a blur, and joined him at the front door. Having arrived, grandmother stepped in front of her furry companion. Anchor clearly did not appreciate such a move. His ears popped up as high as they could, his wide eyes looked up at her and with a whimper, he let grandmother know that he was not amused. In his opinion, she should step aside and let him be the one to greet Sophie, as he did every day, first! His nudging and gradually increasing in volume whimpers, were totally ignored by grandmother, as she turned the big handle.

The old door always put up a fight. Her well practised technique of pulling hard, leaning back and using all her tiny weight to defeat the stubborn hinges, who would much rather have stayed closed, meant it was always a short fight. With every victory, came the loud squeak of the defiant, rusty hinges losing their grip. The door open, grandmother was hit with a cold blast of fresh air as she peeked through the small gap. The gap was big enough for her to see, and small enough that Anchor could just get his nose out to sniff for his best friend.

'Sophie, hellooooooo,' grandmother said in a cheery voice. Looking down the wobbly cobbly path, with its covering of snow, towards where the trees created a darkness she could not see through, she waited for a response. There was nothing - no voice, no footsteps, no crunching of the icy snow. Having waited for a moment she called out again, this time a little louder. Still nothing.

Alex, who was still standing outside the gate, heard grandmother's second shout. It pulled his attention, from the dark spot of blood he had been transfixed by whilst waiting to see if the sobbing sound he thought he heard, could be heard once again. Looking up from the ground and beyond the gate, towards where the shout had come from, Alex could see that the dark, damp, patch of blood at his feet was not the only one. Similar smaller patches were heading up the snow-covered footpath, to where the dark canopy of trees started. As Alex tried to see anything, in the darkness, he began to feel something he had become accustomed to in his dream state. Something he had only had once in his waking life. A heat was spreading from his chest, radiating through his body. The red mist he experienced standing in front of the canteen's audience, three years earlier, was quickly making its return into his reality. As hard as Alex tried to keep control he could not. The red

mist developed into the same pure rage he had felt
that day and in his dreams since. As the rage took full
control of him, as before, he was hit with a second
wave of heat. The second wave had previously caused
the tray he held at that time to melt, crack, shatter into
pieces and spray those nearby with its contents. There
was however a difference that evening. Unlike in the
canteen, where he experienced the emotions, pain,
memories, images and visions from all that sat around
him, this time they weren't coming from anyone -
they appeared to have no point of origin.

Through the rage, the pain and emotions, Alex
somehow managed to hang on to the voice he had
heard calling out. To stay focused on the vision of
blood at his feet. The trail of blood that made its way
up the garden path. To the reason for him being there
in the first place, the sound of sobbing. He had to get
in. Without any preparation or run up, with one
powerful explosion of energy, Alex dropped his
shoulder and hit the gate purposely. It flew open. The
heat, the rage and all he was experiencing suddenly
left him. The gate open, Alex calmly stepped inside.
His breathing and his racing heart slowed with every
step he took closer to the dark, overgrown garden.

Having reached the edge of where the darkness
began, Alex paused to give his eyes a chance to adapt
to the dark before stepping off the frozen snow, onto
the visible wobbly cobbles. He could smell the
dampness from the surrounding ivy covered trees,
which hadn't had the joy of fresh, unrestricted air for
some time. The path curved, which took him out of
sight of the gate he had brushed aside. His eyes, now
comfortable in the reduced light, could see, a few
steps ahead of him, a curled up bundle of clothing on
one of the dead looking flower beds. As he got closer

he was able to make out, resting on the curled up bundle of clothing, was a mass of curly, fiery red hair. The same red hair that had adorned the vision that had barged past him, on his victorious walk home.

'Hey, you ok?' Alex quietly asked, arriving at the side of the bundle. There was no response. Squatting down, he poked at, what he had calculated, where the shoulder would be. There was no reaction at all. Worried for whoever this girl was, Alex decided to go and get help. As he stood up, having heard noises the out of sight grandmother shouted,

'Sophieeeeeee, princess are you out there?' Alex bent back down and in one quick movement, scooped grandmother's princess up, grabbing her bag as he did. With her motionless head on his shoulder, he made his way towards the voice. Moving out of the darkness, the wobbly cobbly path disappearing back under the snow, Alex was greeted with the deepest and most frightening bark. He stopped instantly, as though the snow had frozen around his feet, freezing him to the spot.

'Anchor, shut up you dopey dog!' Grandmother had got as much of a fright as Alex did. As scary as Anchor's bark was, the pureness coming from the voice of grandmother took away any fear that Alex had felt. He continued towards the very old looking, very large red door, which grandmother still had slightly ajar. Looking at the gap, Alex could see a small hand holding the door open, above which was an eye peeking out at him. Not much lower than the hand he could also see the wet, black, glistening nose of Anchor. Alex realised the height of the nose and that clearly, it belonged to a rather large dog.

'Oh, oh, oh Sophie! What's happened?' grandmother said, trying to get the door open. Once open wide enough, Anchor shoved his head out. Taking one look at the stranger approaching, with an explosion of power, his huge shoulders flung the old door and its stubborn hinges wide open and he headed straight for Alex. Alex was surprisingly calm. He assumed he was carrying someone of great importance to the furry bounding monster, so quickly calculated that he would be fine. The speed in which Anchor left the house was impressive. Unfortunately, the speed in which he left the house meant on the frozen snow, he was equally impressive in his ability to be unable to stop. Alex, who by this time had stopped walking towards the house just incase he was wrong in his calculation, had nothing to worry about. Anchor's legs went everywhere but where they needed to. His paws skidded all over the place, taking him right past Alex into a berry covered holly bush, which as quick as it engulfed him, bounced him back out, throwing him flat on his back in the freezing snow.

'Don't mind him love, quickly, quickly come in,' grandmother said. Alex didn't have to be told twice. He made his way quickly to the front door. Anchor was left scrambling and wiggling, trying to get himself back on all fours. Whimpering away, he was showing the true patheticness of his lovable character as he did. As Alex climbed the couple of steps to the front door, grandmother stepped back. The only light was coming from the hallway. Until then it had meant grandmother had appeared as a silhouette to Alex. Having stepped back, the hallway light lighting up her face, Alex could see a very concerned expression on her well worn and friendly face.

'Don't dilly dally love, hurry, hurry,' grandmother said.

Anchor had at last got to his paws. Having learnt his lesson, he was walking very slowly back toward the house. This gave Alex some comfort, as if there were any issues with the big dog as he stepped into the house, the door could be shut behind him. Taking his last step to safety, the unconscious redhead in his arms, he came towards the light of the dimly lit hallway.

'Purple!' An awkward pause followed grandmother's exclamation. She had seen something in Alex's eyes that unnerved her.

'Sorry what?' Alex said, breaking the awkward silence. He received no response. Not really sure what he heard and with his arms beginning to get tired, he continued with his last step into the old house. Finally in. However as he stepped over the threshold something hit his right hand. Taking his breath away, he was struck by a lightening bolt of electricity. At that very same moment, Sophie's eyes popped wide open.

'What? Who? Hey, put me down!' a frightened Sophie said with a hint of anger. The words came from her 'angry' lips as grandmother would call them, visibly skinnier than her usual full lips. Doing as he was told, Alex's reaction was to instantly drop her to the hard, rug-covered, wooden floor.

'Crap, I am so sorry!' Alex said. He quickly went to help her back up, offering her his hand. Sophie pushed it away. Still in a daze, she had forgotten what had happened before and tried to sit herself up. Her blood covered hand caused her to slip as she pushed on it. It also sent a shooting pain up her arm, the shock of which caused her eyes to pop wide open again.

'Princess, are you ok, what's happened?'

grandmother said. His help not wanted Alex had stepped back, which made room for grandmother. She bent down to offer her help. As she did, she saw the blood that had found its way up Sophie's arm and soaked her clothes, 'Oh love, I feel light-headed.'

Alex was standing just inside the door, a few steps back from the scene of his not so gentlemanly act. Everything happened so quickly. Taking a moment to settle himself, he looked down at his hand. It was throbbing from the sharp pain he had received as his welcome into Sophie's home. Turning it over, he could see the small, dark dot in the crease of his right hand, between his thumb and forefinger, the one that he had always thought was a mole, and it was bleeding.

He went to take a closer look. As he did, there was a loud bang from behind him, followed by a blast of cold air. The big old door had been thrown open by a charging Anchor. It hit Alex, which knocked him off balance and had him falling towards Sophie, who had not yet got to her feet. The only thing Alex could do, was put his arms out in the hope that he could stop himself from landing on her. His actions partly worked. He managed to stop his whole body landing on her, but his hand, his bleeding hand, landed on Sophie's injured, blood covered hand. As soon as he made contact, he once again received the same lightening bolt of electric shock!

'Aaaaaaaaaaaa!' Sophie let out an ear-piercing scream. On this occasion, not only was Alex subject to the pain, it appeared that when he touched Sophie, it caused her to share the experience. Her automatic reaction was to pull her hand out from under Alex's. She grabbed hold of it with her other pain-free hand, and threw a stare at Alex that Medusa would have been proud of. She stood up. Her eyes were full of tears, ready to burst free at any moment. She turned to grandmother,

'What is happening?' she asked.

'Well my dear, I am not entirely sure!' was grandmother's response. Alex had also got to his feet. He was standing motionless with the big, furry, not so friendly looking Anchor standing with his teeth showing, just inches from him. Grandmother took Sophie's non blood covered hand and pulled her towards the kitchen,

'Son, follow along now, I will sort you out as well!' grandmother instructed Alex. He wasn't sure whether it was safe to move. In a nervous voice he replied,

'Well, I would!' Grandmother turned back to see what the problem was, she let out a little chuckle and said,

'Anchor you dopey dog, come on.' Anchor did as he was instructed, as his teeth returned into his usually smiling face, to the relief of Alex.

Alex watched as the three made their way through a door at the end of the hall, situated off to the side of the staircase. He took a moment to look around. Through the dim light he could see a very worn, but homely home. A large Turkish rug beneath his feet, which almost covered the entire hallway, was showing the signs of its years of wear. At points where it was closer to the wall, what must have been the original, brighter shades of red could be seen. Beyond the rug's edges and leading to the four doors that left the hallway and staircase, were floorboards. They were also well used, worn away, where years of footsteps had been taken. The walls were stained, a dark line at hand height ran down the right side. They

were a beige colour, apart from on the left wall before
the staircase, where there was a huge mural of a tree.

The tree's branches made their way over the
doorway that was closest to the front door, up towards
the high ceiling and then ran up the staircase. The tree
itself had no leaves, no colour, other than the brown,
thick trunk and branches. Alex had a feeling of
sadness come over him as he followed its reaching
branches out of sight, into the darkness, up the stairs.
He wondered why anyone would paint a dead tree in
their home? The dim light in the hallway was
provided by two, very ornate wall lights. Their
detailed design was hidden by their lack of light.
They appeared to be only just hanging on. Their
fixings drooped forward, clinging on at the point just
before letting go. Despite all the worn, not so
uplifting decoration and the coldness of the
atmosphere, there was still a homely and familiar feel
to the strange place he found himself in. A muffled
voice interrupted Alex's visual inspection,

'Young man, where are you?' grandmother called
out. There was an authority to her voice that Alex
couldn't ignore. Without responding, he made his
way towards the door the three had gone through
moments earlier. Having opened the door, Alex's
eyes were forced to adjust, as unlike the hallway, he
was greeted with a very bright light. He was also hit
by a wall of heat which surprised him. Having
adjusted, Alex looked around a room covered in
cupboards. They were everywhere. On the floor, on
the walls, and strangely one hanging from the ceiling.
Each one of the cupboards had a different colour,
shape and design. Alex confirmed, by the sight of an
old range style cooker, he was in a kitchen. Half the
room was hidden, as on the kitchen table which sat in

the middle of the room, was a huge house - Sophie's unexplored birthday present. Unable to see anyone, Alex quietly announced his arrival,

'Hello.' From one side of the huge dolls house at ground floor level, a head appeared. Out popped the smiling face of grandmother,

'Come, come my dear, let's have a look at you.' Alex made his way round the side of the table and its house. Once clear of the obstruction, he saw Sophie bent over a very old and rather stained porcelain sink, wedged between two of the fun, bright, quirky looking cupboards. It sat a lot lower than Alex would have expected. It was clearly positioned perfectly for grandmother's height convenience. Sophie was holding her hand, the cut was worse than Alex first thought. A big flap of skin was visible, hanging off the side.

'Oh, jeez, what the heck happened to you?' Alex said. Sophie didn't raise her head or respond. She was too busy focusing on holding back the tears.

'Princess, hold this on tight while I have a look at this young mans injury,' grandmother instructed.

'Oh, no I am fine, honestly, it's just a little cut or something,' Alex said. Not taking no for an answer, Sophie's cloth in place, grandmother walked over to the rather startled looking Alex. 'Seriously, I am fine.' She wasn't paying any attention to him. She grabbed hold of his wrist, turned his hand over and had a good look.

'Oh!' What she saw caused her to exclaim. She stepped away from Alex, pulled her shoulders back and stood upright, as though she had seen something horrific. She tried to hide whatever shock she was experiencing, for whatever reason, with a smile. Her, trying to be reassuring vacant smile, did not work,

'What? What is it?' Alex asked. As far as he was concerned, there was just a slight bleeding from what was on old imperfection. Her reaction seemed more appropriate to something far worse, worse even than Sophie's gaping wound.

'It's fine my dear, nothing to worry about, as you say you are fine,' grandmother responded. It was clear grandmother knew something - the placing of the wound, the pain she had witnessed him feel as he entered through the old, red front door. It was also clear, she did not want to talk about whatever she was thinking, to Alex. Turning back to Sophie, grandmother nearly fell over Anchor, who, being the slobbery guardian of the household, was sitting right behind her, watching on.

'Oh you stupid mutt, what are you doing?' grandmother snapped. Thankfully, with the plethora of cupboards close by and her not so tall height, she managed to catch herself. Anchor did not like being told off. He turned towards Alex with every intention of giving him a bark, or at the very least a growl, to make himself feel better. Instead, having made eye contact with Alex, he found himself coming over all soft. He fell to the floor, quickly spinning onto his back into his, 'I want attention' ballet pose. This consisted of his back legs stretched out to one side, one front leg stretched out as far is it would go, the other front leg bent at its knee and his head fully stretched back, showing off a very teeth-filled, upside down smile. Alex wasn't really sure what to make of it. Was he being sucked in for a covert attack, or was he a 'stupid mutt' and he should go in for the fluffy stroke?

After a couple of moments of watching a motionless, perfectly posed fluffy monster, Alex, who was not feeling as welcome as he did earlier when he received his invitation from grandmother to enter the house, decided to take the safer option and reverse himself out of the unknown zone. He made his way the long way round the house-covered table, to join the two ladies still positioned at the sink. Having taken another look, Sophie's hand appeared to be worse than he thought the first time he saw it,

'That actually looks really bad. Should she go to the hospital?' Alex asked grandmother. Sophie looked up with the intention of suggesting he direct the question to her. Making eye contact with him, it was the first time she had properly looked at him,

'Do I know you?' she said.

'Erm, I don't think so, oh hang on, are you not the person who flew past me when I got off the bus earlier?' Alex replied. Still looking at him Sophie said,

'I probably was, but that's not it.'

'Ok you two, let's get this wound sorted please.' Grandmother's tone had changed again. Seriousness and dismissiveness, it was a tone Sophie was not used to. Looking back down at her hand, Sophie tried very hard to act like all was well,

'It ain't sore at all grandmother, can we just put a plaster on it?' Sophie said. The wound, that left a flap of skin hanging on her small right hand was about three inches long, running all the way down its side. Although it was now cleaned from the dirt it had gathered, from firstly the bus floor and secondly the overgrown garden, the blood was still flowing. There was clearly work still to be done,

'Yes a plaster should do,' grandmother said, there was a pause, 'Or will it?' Clearly speaking to herself and somewhat confused as to what was happening, grandmother was going through scenarios in her head. Before she could come to any conclusions Alex piped up,

'I could see if my mum is home, she is a nurse.' Alex wasn't hugely keen on the idea of leaving the house through the door that caused him pain. Equally so, he had an overwhelming urge to help the redhead he had still, not as yet, been properly introduced to.

'Son, we are fine, you can just head home,' grandmother said. As soon as she spoke the words, Anchor was on his feet. He seemed to know that the once invited guest, was now uninvited. Taking the shortest route which was under the table, crashing through the mismatched chairs to where Alex was standing, Anchor let out, not the ferocious, get out of here bark Alex expected. Instead, quite a friendly little woof came from his happy looking face. Alex wasn't really sure what to make of the situation he found himself in. He had an overwhelming urge to help, but he didn't want to be disrespectful either. Not concerned about Anchor any more, he took a confident step past him and placed a hand on Sophie's shoulder,

'Are you really ok, I will go it's fine, but are you ok?' Alex asked. Sophie, who was looking down at her hand, felt a warmth filling her inside. A familiar feeling of safety washed over her. The tears that she had been able to hold back with a fabulous strength, were suddenly let loose.

'Right young man, that is really enough!' grandmother said. If Anchor was not going to do his job, she would. The tiny elderly lady had more strength in her than expected. She spun Alex round. Pushing him from behind, she guided him back towards the kitchen door.

'Woe, woe, woe!' Alex exclaimed.

'No, your help is no longer required, it is time for you to leave!' Grandmother was beginning to get quite cross. Sophie was experiencing all kinds of new tones from grandmother, on this day, her 16th birthday and anger - this was a tone she had never heard, not once. Alex got the hint. Not wanting to cause any more of a scene he headed out of the crazy, multicoloured, cupboard-filled kitchen, out to the main hall. He wasn't followed by the little grey haired whirlwind, he was however followed by Anchor.

'Well that was interesting my friend. Can I assume we are friends?' Alex squatted down in front of Anchor keeping his hands at his side, just incase they weren't. 'This is some place you live in.' Anchor's ears twitched and adjusted themselves forward, to take in all that was being said. 'I guess I should really get myself out of here then.' Anchor tilted his head and took a step closer to Alex. 'Oh you want me to stay?' Alex reached forward with the back of his hand. It resulted in an instant lick coming from nowhere, almost ninja like in its surprise, speed and precision. Alex had never lived with an animal of any kind, so was not used to the relationship that could be had. Although, he had always had an affinity with any animal he came across. He would always talk to them as if they were human, always respected their space. So with the invite of a friendly, slobbery lick, Alex took his cue and went in for the furry fluffle.

'So we are friends then, cool.' Alex sat back on to the floor. As he did, the huge, scary monster of a German Shepherd fell to the floor as well. He got himself comfortable between Alex's legs, not quite into his full on ballet pose, but enough to show Alex that he wanted some more love. Alex obliged as he

looked around at the dimly lit hall for a second time.
Facing the front door, he saw the branches of the
painted bare tree, reach over and onto the doorframe.
The lights suddenly flickered, Alex's heart skipped a
beat. He looked up from Anchor and saw something
move. Well, he thought he saw something move, on
the very tip of a branch, the one closest to the big,
old, red front door. With that and the fright he got
from the flickering lights, Alex was back on his feet.

'Did you see that buddy?' Alex asked Anchor,
who looked around, as though he knew exactly what
his human companion was saying. 'Ok, so I should
definitely go then!' Alex headed for the door. He
slowly reached for the handle, hoping that the pain he
experienced on his entrance would not be repeated.
Taking hold of the big, round, old handle, it did not
feel like he would have expected - it was warm.
Thankfully and more importantly, there was no pain.
Turning the handle, he looked back at Anchor and
said, 'Well my friend, hopefully I will see you again
soon,' then pulled the door open to leave, the hinges
squeaking as they always did, in protest at being used.
Not only was the handle strangely warm, but so was
the air outside. With the door fully open, Alex was hit
with warmth, not the cold blast that he had expected.
Then for a moment, out of the corner of his eye, he
thought he saw bright daylight. As quickly as the
warmth and daylight were there, they were gone.
'Buddy I am losing my mind in here!' Alex stepped
out, turned and gave Anchor a smile and then closed
the big, creaky door behind him. The handle had
returned to normal, as cold as he would have expected
on the frosty winter's evening. He made his way
down the steps and along the uneven path to the dark,
overgrown, grim looking section of the garden. As he

walked into the canopy of darkness, Alex was aware that it wasn't actually as dark as he recalled on his first visit. He had the unnerving feeling that there were eyes watching him. His pace hastened as fear started to take hold. The corridor of dead trees and ivy that on his earlier visit had seemed quite short, now seemed a lot longer. Alex moved from his hastened pace into a run. As he did, even though there was no snow or ice in the covered corridor, one of his feet went from under him. Catching himself before falling, he stopped and looked down to see what had caused his slip. By his foot, growing between the dark, dirty, red coloured cobbles, was the tiniest of yellow roses. The rose wasn't the only thing new - the path itself had changed. When Alex had entered earlier, following the sobbing and drops of blood, the path he walked on was covered in slippery, old, black coloured moss.

The fear was not subsiding. His ability to question what he was seeing with clarity was not possible in his fight or flight state. So Alex ran, he ran as fast as he could, bursting free of the not so dark canopy, back into the snow-covered part of the front garden. He didn't even try the stuck fast gate, he cleared it in one jump. The resulting landing was as ungraceful as Anchor's attempt of travelling at speed on the snow and ice, on their first meeting. Having slipped on his landing, yet again Alex was on the floor. He found himself sitting on the cold, wet, snowy, icy footpath. Looking up at the old, red, rusty gate, where the evening's strange collection of events had begun, Alex couldn't help but wonder if what had happened, had actually happened!

CHAPTER 4

It had been a long and hard day for Melissa. However she was happy having made it to the end of her first week of her new job, without any problems. She loved her job, well, she loved the looking after people part of it. She didn't like the politics and management quite so much. To avoid issues, she had a tendency to make friends with her patients rather than the staff she worked with.

'Miss Rice, hold up!' Melissa thought she had managed to avoid the conversation that was about to come. She knew the voice - it was the hospital's human resources manager. He was a tall, skinny man with a screwed-up face, who thought he was the ruler of all. She kept walking. The noise of the slightly heightened breeze whistling round the outbuildings of the old hospital, could give her the excuse of not hearing him. She hadn't handed in the documents required by her new employers, she couldn't, she didn't have them. She really didn't want to speak to him.

'Miss Rice!' The man called out again, louder and in a much more curt tone. Melissa hesitated in her pace, a mistake, as she knew fine well he would now know she had heard him. She gave in to the inevitable, turning to greet him with a smile and a wave.

'Evening Mr Sullivan, are you finished for the day?' Melissa put on her sweetest and most innocent voice.

'Sadly no Miss Rice. As always, I find myself

chasing people for items that should have been submitted, timeously, but seem not to have been,' he said. Melissa knew exactly what he was talking about and that she was indeed the target for his not so hidden accusations.

'Oh dear Mr Sullivan, I do hope you manage to get that all sorted quickly,' Melissa said acting innocently, trying very hard to keep her sarcastic tone as hidden as she could. She didn't do a very good job!

'Miss Rice, I do not appreciate the attitude. You know fine well what I am talking about. Ultimately if you do not provide me with your national insurance number, copies of your qualifications and proof of address, not only will you not be getting paid, you will also not be returning to work next week!'

He left her with no question as to the terms of the situation.

With every move to a new town or village, Melissa had to find new everything. In some places it was easy, but this town was proving a challenge to find the person who would help her out. She couldn't go back to the previous people who had helped her, as she couldn't return to the places she had lived and worked before. The risk of bumping into someone who would recognise her was too high. For years, she had managed to stay ahead of the questions. She wasn't about to let this place be the place that finally caught her. If there was a person that could catch her out, she felt that Mr Sullivan could be the one. She realised that she had to be more careful than she had ever been.

'I apologise Mr Sullivan. I meant no disrespect at all. I have been on earlies all week. Getting up at 4am, I'm just not awake enough and keep forgetting. I'm on lates next week, so I promise I will have all

you need then. In fact if I'm passing over the
weekend, I could drop the papers off if you want?'
With a spin and flick of his boney head he left,
ominously muttering as he did,

'You better!'

Melissa stood for a moment, shaking her head at
the stupidness of the man. As she stood watching Mr
Sullivan go out of sight, snow began to fall. One very
large snowflake made her laugh as it landed on her
nose and tickled.

'Mother Nature, I can always rely on you,' she
said lovingly, looking up. She watched as the snow's
intensity grew. A slight flutter, turning into a sky full
of thick, silent, playful flakes of snow. Her peaceful
moment of enjoyment was short lived. An ambulance
came racing round the corner, its lights flashing and
siren echoing, bouncing off the old hospital walls.

Putting the stress of her conversation behind her,
she headed across the car park to find her car. It
wasn't an easy task. On arriving in the early hours of
the morning, the huge car park was almost empty.
There were no visitors, no Dr's for their day patients,
no cleaning staff, no office staff, just the cars of the
people who were the real heart of the hospital - the
nurses. At the time her shift finished, it was leaving
time for the visitors. To give herself at least half a
chance of getting home without too much delay,
Melissa parked as close to the exit of the car park as
she could. Even then, with the size of the place, she
struggled to find her car.

By the time she won her game of hide and seek
with her beaten up, very unserviced little red car, the
snowfall had come to an end. Thankfully, as
unserviced as it was, it was as loyal to her as she was
to keeping her little metal friend. After a couple of

laboured turns of the engine, it came to life. The snow that had just fallen and settled on the windscreen was brushed aside by the windscreen wipers. Unfortunately, the energetic little blades were no match for the ice that had formed during the long and cold day.

'Oh damn it!' Melissa said out loud, realising she had no de-icer or scraper in the car. With no other option available to her, she cranked up the heat as high as it would go and sat waiting for the ice, as cold and as hard as Mr Sullivan, to melt.

Sitting waiting, Melissa couldn't get out of her head that the idea of coming to this place was a mistake. She'd had to leave the last place she lived very quickly and hadn't made proper plans. It was a cycle that had gone on for many years. She tried to live in places that were busy - large towns and cites, where she could get lost in the crowds. The last place was such a place. The hospital she worked in was like a town in itself. She rarely saw the same face twice. Staff moved around the departments so much, it was easy to hide. While she was there, she had managed to work enough to keep her and her son clothed and fed, just. She had also managed to replenish her emergency escape fund. In the past she hadn't had to use much of it. This time had been different. Being very happy where she was having been there for over a year, Melissa had let her guard down. That was a big mistake. Someone recognised her. In a panic, she left her work without a word, pulled her son out of school, packed up her car and left. Having made no plans, she sold the month on the road to her son as a fun holiday. Even though they stayed in cheap accommodation, they went through the emergency fund quickly.

Just as the money was about to run out, an opportunity popped up. Owners of an old house who lived abroad, wanted someone to stay in it over the winter. Basically they wanted to make sure that the house didn't freeze, the pipes didn't burst and that it wouldn't get burgled. It wasn't perfect, as it was very close to an area she had worked before which was risky. As quickly as they had moved in she found the job, which was also not perfect. Melissa couldn't shake the feeling that this Mr Sullivan was going to be an issue. In the places she lived and worked before, she chose her places of employment very carefully. Usually hospitals that didn't ask too many questions. Most hospitals were just happy to get a nurse to fill their many vacancies. As long as she provided some qualifications, showed that she worked hard, showed she knew what she was doing, she was good. But this Mr Sullivan, after only a week, she was worried.

Having a big heavy coat, scarf and hat on, the heat that at last was filling the car, was getting Melissa uncomfortably warm. So, snapping herself out of her stare into the void of problems she faced, she decided to step out and see if the ice had melted on the windscreen at all, even just enough that she could scrape it away with her glasses case. Pulling at the handle, pushing the door slightly, a blast of cold wind came out of nowhere and took the door right out of her hand. The loss of grip gave her a fright, but not as much as the bang which was followed by,

'Woof, woof, woof!'

With the door fully open and the wind having done its job, Melissa peered over the door to see what had caused the bang. What she saw was a girl sitting on the wet, slushy, car park floor. Standing next to her was the giver of the barks. A friendly faced Labrador, which was looking right up at Melissa, whilst barking.

'Oh, my goodness, I am so sorry, the wind just! You know what it doesn't matter, are you ok?' Melissa didn't get a response. Having decided the dog was not scary, she closed the car door and walked round to face the young lady. The car park lighting wasn't great, but as she bent down to give the girl a hand, a colourful hearing aid caught her eye. Looking back at the dog, who was not moving from the side of his friend, Melissa said,

'Oh, that makes sense.'

'I can hear you, you know!' The quietest of voices came from the girl sitting in the cold and wet. Melissa felt so stupid. She should have known better. She had been a nurse for over twenty years. With her brain and dedication she could easily have been a doctor, but that just wasn't for her.

'I am so sorry. Come on let's get you up!' Melissa said reaching out a hand. The interested and trusting companion watched silently, as Melissa got the girl to her feet. Once she was up, he stepped back to her side. Instinctively the girl reached down and took hold of his harness. She began to walk away.

'Hey, are you ok?' There was no response. Although the girl said she could hear, Melissa thought maybe as she had walked away, the distance between them now meant she couldn't. Trying not to give her another fright, Melissa walked past the girl who was wrapped up in a red coat, big thick scarf and woolly hat. Her blonde hair looked cute poking out the sides of the hat. Once she had passed her, Melissa turned and asked again,

'Are you ok? You are soaking wet you poor thing.

Can I help?' The wind's victim who was looking down, noticed Melissa's legs. They were covered in what she recognised as a pair of nurses trousers, so she stopped.

'Thank you for stopping. Now do you mind me asking, can you hear me now and see me?' The girl looked up at her. In a very quiet voice she said,

'Yes to both. I am impaired, not fully blind. My hearing aid gives me some hearing and I lip read the rest.' Melissa switched into helping mode. She put her arm round the young girl's shoulder, who asked,

'Do you work here?'

'Yes. I am a nurse in the geriatrics ward. My name is Melissa and you are?' There was a pause, as the young girl took a moment to decide whether she should be sharing her name with this stranger.

'Vicky!' She decided yes she should.

'Ok Vicky, are you hurt at all?' Melissa asked.

'No I am fine, just a bit wet. Can you tell me what that bus is over there? The one about to leave.' Melissa was hoping it wasn't the one she was heading for, she felt bad enough already. After squinting to see, Melissa made out the number and told Vicky,

'It's number 38.' The instant look of disappointment on Vicky's face told Melissa that it was indeed the bus she was hoping to get. 'Look, this was my fault, can I call someone for you?' Melissa asked.

'No, not really. I live with my parents, but they will both still be at work,' Vicky responded. The attentive puppy had picked up on the lack of forward movement and sat himself down. His tail wagged as he did, sweeping aside lumps of slush.

'Look, I'm sure it's not what you would normally do, but I could give you a lift to catch up with the bus if you like.' Melissa's kind offer went against the basic rule of never get in a car with a stranger. With all the challenges Vicky had faced during her life, along with her incredible strength and positivity, she was an incredibly good judge of character. Her furry companion had the same trait and the fact he was sitting happily, wagging his tail, gave Vicky extra confidence in her decision to accept the offer.

'That would actually be really kind of you, if you don't mind. I was going to go into town on the 38 for some shopping. I then usually get the 36 out to where I live. So maybe you could just drop me in town and I will get the bus home, I feel a bit too wet for shopping,' Vicky confidently suggested. Melissa had only been living at her new home for a couple of weeks, but she knew that the number 36 bus went past the square she now called home.

'I can do better than that. I live in St Georges Square. So if your home is anywhere near that, I can drop you off there. You can text your family and tell them who I am, my number, where I live and my car registration if you want, incase you are worried.' Melissa couldn't believe what she was saying. She was always so careful not to be open with people, to let people into her world. So to tell a stranger where she lived and to suggest giving out all her details, that was very out of character.

'St Georges Square, are you kidding me,' Vicky said.

'No not at all,' Melissa responded.

'That's where I live!' Vicky said. Melissa, without hesitation took hold of Vicky's arm and said,

'Sorted. We shall get you home.'

'Thank you, oh this is Bart by the way.' Vicky gestured towards the smiling furry face. Opening the passenger's door, Bart jumped into the footwell. Vicky followed and in what was a well practised manoeuvre, placed her legs round him. As she closed the door for Vicky, Melissa realised she had forgotten, for a few moments, about her situation. As much as she would never have wanted Vicky to be knocked over, she was glad to have the company for the drive home. She then made her way round the old red car and climbed into the driver's seat. The car was still running, which as she sat down, reminded her of the reason she was initially getting out.

'Oh the ice.' So she got back out again. As she did, she caught the windscreen wipers switch. Activated, the struggling blades happily threw a big lump of soggy ice in her face.

'Ha ha ha ha ha.... oh that's just funny.' Wiping her face, Melissa looked back to see Vicky full on belly laughing,

'Why thank you,' Melissa said. However the windscreen was now clear, so she got back into the car. 'Yes ok, that was kind of funny. Was certainly instant karma eh?' Melissa conceded. With the windscreen now clear of the snow and ice and the condensation dried up, at last they could both be on their way. On their way that is to the huge queue that was not moving, at the exit of the car park.

'So Vicky, what were you in for today?' Melissa asked.

'Just a check up on my eyes. They haven't got any worse over the last two months, so that's good,' Vicky replied. Melissa looked over at the short blonde haired, beautiful young girl sitting next to her,

'What can you see?' she asked. Vicky didn't respond as quick as Melissa would have liked. She didn't want to overstep the mark, ask too many questions, so she said, 'It's ok, you don't need to tell me, it's fine.'

Vicky replied quite happily,

'No it's fine, I was just looking to see what I can see.' Vicky giggled to herself. She had quite a comically literal brain. She had learnt over the years that her unwittingly funny personality made people laugh. Rather than feeling embarrassed and awkward, she made a conscious decision to go with it. So when asked a question like Melissas, her instinct was to respond with 'the car in front.' And she did.

They both laughed.

'Vicky, you are quite the character aren't you!' Melissa said.

'I guess so. Although, I think the answer you were hoping for was a little more clinical. Basically, my sight is sort of tunnel vision. My dad says I am like a race horse, blinkered and focused, ready to go.' Melissa raised her eyebrows and smiled, whilst letting out a slight chuckle at this very impressive young woman. Eventually the traffic moved and they were on their way. The drive that took Melissa about fifteen minutes in the early hours of the morning, at this time, on a Friday afternoon, with schools finishing for the day and people leaving work early, was going to take a good forty minutes.

The time on the journey was well spent. As they got to know each other better, particularly talking about living in the square, the barriers came down.

'How old are you Vicky?' Melissa asked.

'I am seventeen now. Mum doesn't like me going out by myself, but I have to. Life is for living right?' Vicky responded. Impressed at the confidence and maturity of this young woman, Melissa got a little choked up.

'Wow, I would have put you in your twenties... oh, not that you look that old,' Melissa said. Vicky laughed,

'I know, my mum and dad say I have an old soul,' Vicky said.

At last, the drive that ended up taking fifty minutes was coming to an end. Melissa turned the car into the icy road which wrapped around the snow-covered green,

'Alex! What..?!' She could see Alex, her son, sitting on the pavement looking up at an old gate, which was not where they lived.

'What is it with you young people today, is the floor the latest place to be?' Melissa said jokingly. Vicky hadn't seen what Melissa had, so she tried to focus on where Melissa was looking,

'Oh that's the new boy. I have seen him about, he's quite cute,' Vicky said.

'That new boy is my son,' Melissa replied. Vicky, without thinking, in her innocence, which was not beyond her years, blurted out,

'But he's white. I mean very white! I mean you're black... oh goodness.' Melissa was very used to that reaction and was ready with all kinds of funny comebacks, but with Vicky she didn't feel the need. Vicky was right - Melissa was a tall, physically domineering, beautiful black woman.

'You are correct of course, on both counts. It's a long story, but that's my boy.' Stopping the car Melissa rolled down the window. In a very loud voice which made Bart drop down in the footwell, she shouted,

'Alex are you ok?' Alex raised his arm and waved. He didn't turn round, he knew it was his mum. He knew it before she spoke, having heard the familiar rattling exhaust as it drove into the square. Alex continued staring at the place he had been ejected from moments earlier,

'So you are good then?' Melissa asked, looking for a little extra confirmation as to his well-being. Alex waved his response again.

'I am going to take that as a yes. Let's get you home Vicky. Is it ok if I just pull into our drive? I can help you across the road if you like?' Melissa asked.

Her face red, blushing from her embarrassing remarks, truth be known mostly for the 'cute' comment, Vicky responded quietly,

'That's fine. I can make my own way home.'

Coming to a stop after a small slide on the icy driveway, Melissa jumped out the car. She then made her way round to the passenger's door to offer help. It wasn't needed, as by the time she got there the door was already open, Bart was out and Vicky was half out.

Their movement caused the sensor light over the front door of the house to come on. Its light shone on Alex's school bag which was sitting on the bottom step. Melissa's motherly instincts kicked in - she was getting concerned. Alex was always so careful with his few possessions. Abandoning his bag on a wet step with no one watching over it, that was totally out of character.

Meanwhile, Vicky, now out of the car, was concerned about other things. Was she in any shape to potentially meet Melissa's son after her earlier fall in the wet, slushy snow of the carpark. She reached round to her back. Her coat and trousers were still a bit wet. She wanted to be introduced to the cute boy, but wanted to put on her best show. Soggy trousers were not her best show, so she decided to quickly head home and hope to meet him another time. Unfortunately, circumstances were to go against her, as a concerned Melissa had already disappeared, off down the very slippery drive towards a slow moving figure. The figure was walking along the pathway outside the garden.

'Hey mum.' Alex greeted his concerned mum with a hug. They had arrived at the entrance to the drive at the same time. There was no escape for Vicky. Melissa looked him up and down to see if all was in tact. His face was as cute as ever, all arms and legs present. Her eyes that never missed a thing, except for people walking past her car door apparently, stopped at an odd looking stain. Just below the cuff of his school blazer, the cuff of his white shirt could be seen. On it was a spot of blood. Melissa was a woman who had been through a lot in her life. She knew what the spot was, but did not react. She was very good at hiding her thoughts and emotions until she got the full story, whether the story told was true or false.

'What's been going on?' Melissa asked. Alex paused before answering,

'You know what mum, I genuinely have no idea,' was Alex's response. The security light on the house had gone out. The tall holly tree at the entrance hid the street light from the driveway. With no Christmas decorations lighting up the front of their new, no doubt temporary home, Alex got a bit of a fright when out of nowhere Vicky appeared,

'Hi.'

'Oh, sorry, I was going to take you home wasn't I,' Melissa said to Vicky, who smiled and said,

'No, again really it's fine, I will see my way across the road.' Alex didn't say a word. He had done more socialising than he usually did outside of school hours already. But then he noticed a second smiling furry face of the evening,

'Who's this?' Alex asked. Melissa realised she had not been her usual polite self. With her concern for Alex, she hadn't provided any introduction between the two damp teenagers.

'Vicky this is Alex, my son. Alex this is Vicky, I knocked her over at work.' Alex snapped his head round from talking to Bart,

'You what?' Alex asked.

'It's fine. It's not as bad as it sounds. I slipped as much as she knocked me over. And this is Bart.' Very kindly, Vicky made Melissa's accident seem not quite so bad. Bart was taking a great interest in Alex. Well, more the scent Alex was carrying of Anchor, but Alex was enjoying the attention,

'Hey buddy.' Alex went to bend down and say hello properly. As he did, the shadow he had been casting over Bart moved and he noticed the fluorescent harness, so he stood back up.

'It's ok, you can say hello, he won't bite.' Vicky's sense of humour relaxed the moment as everyone laughed.

'Do you have to get home, or do you want to come in for a hot drink?' Melissa asked Vicky.

'Well mum and dad still won't be home. Although I could do with changing, seeing as I am still a bit wet,' she replied.

'Don't worry about that, look at me,' Alex said. Turning round, he showed Vicky how wet he was. He was wet from the top of his head to his feet, his curly hair even more curly from the dampness.

'You win,' Vicky said.

'Honestly, it's a competition I would be happy not to win. I am freezing!' Alex said. As if he knew what was happening, Bart had already turned and was pulling Vicky in the direction of the house in darkness. Melissa put her arm round Alex and said,

'By the looks of it, the decision is made.'

As Vicky stepped forward and away from them, Melissa whispered into Alex's ear, 'What's wrong?' She knew her boy very well, better than many know their children. He and his safety were her life. Outside of work and school, they were pretty much together one hundred percent of the time. She knew that he would not normally have spoken to Vicky as much as he did. She also knew that him being over friendly meant he was hiding something. Alex didn't say a word.

Arriving at the bottom of the steps, Vicky politely stopped, bent down and picked up Alex's bag,

'Here you go, I assume it's yours.' Vicky held out the bag for Alex to take. Alex was a gentleman, always had been. From the four year old boy, who used to struggle with the big heavy security door at his nursery class as he tried to hold it open, not only for his fellow classmates, but also for the nursery staff, to the sixteen year old who jumped a gate to help a young girl. He was also extremely self sufficient. So it was a new experience for him to see that chivalry can also come from the fairer sex.

'Thanks,' Alex said, taking the bag from her. Melissa had passed them and made her way up the steps to unlock the big old door. For being big and old it opened with no hesitation, squeak or grind. Stepping in, she switched on the hallway lights and realised she could see her breath as much as she could outside. She turned to Vicky and said,

'The house hasn't got any central heating I'm afraid. But we will get the fire going in the kitchen downstairs, you'll soon warm up.' Then turning to Alex, Melissa asked 'Alex can you take her down while I go and get changed.' The irony of the one person who was not wet going and getting changed hit her, at the same moment it did Alex and Vicky,

'Ha ha ha, yeh ok, let's all go and get the fire on,' Melissa said, changing her plans.

Opposite the front door was a door to the side of the big staircase and that's where Melissa led them. After heading down the very small, curved wooden staircase they appeared in a room, which by its entrance, Vicky expected to be dark, dingy and quite spooky. In fact it was the opposite - new and homely. To one side was a very ornate fireplace. On the opposite wall, a collection of very understated kitchen units. At the far end of the room was a kitchen table and a door, which lead out to the back garden.

'Alex, can you nip and get some coal?' Melissa asked. Alex's hand was still quite sore from whatever had happened earlier. He had hidden the wound, which was still bleeding, by keeping his hand in his pocket. Melissa had seen the blood on his cuff and that he had been trying to keep his hand hidden. She was well aware that something wasn't quite right, but thought she would go along with Alex's, not usual with her, lack of openness to see what would happen.

'Erm, ok, yeh, I can do that,' Alex replied, grabbing the coal bucket. He forgot himself for a moment. He took his injured hand out of his pocket, picked up the coal bucket and went to throw the remnants of coal that were left in the bottom, onto the fire grate. His left hand gripped the handle, his right wounded hand grabbed the base. As he began his throwing action, he caught the spot that was still bleeding. Catching it caused him to let go of the bucket all together. It was sent flying into the fireplace with a very loud bang which echoed around the big, open, cold kitchen. Alex grabbed his hand and ran to the sink.

'What have you done to yourself?' Melissa very calmly asked. She knew nothing was life threatening.

'I cut it somehow going into the house down the road. The one you can't actually see because of the overgrown garden, you know the first gate,' Alex said. His words sparked Vicky's interest.

'You went into that place?' she asked. Melissa looked over at her,

'Why, should he not? Should I be worried about that?' Melissa asked.

'Well, there are all kinds of rumours about that place. You never see the owner. There is a young girl, you see her sometimes, but no one actually knows who owns the place. We all assume there is an adult in there, but then some say it's just full of ghosts and the girl isn't even real. They say the house was falling down before the really spooky garden got overgrown. I have never seen the house and I have lived here all my life.. and you went in there?'

Alex, his hand under the very cold water of the tap, did not respond. Melissa wanted to ask more, but she didn't know this new acquaintance that well yet, so responded with,

'I am sure that's all just silly nonsense, ghosts, ha ha ha.' Turning back to Alex she had a look at his hand. The water was running clear and she could see the smallest of puncture wounds, 'Looks like you stabbed it on something. Is that not where your mole thing was?' Alex wasn't sure whether to respond or not with the unknown guest present, so didn't. Melissa opened up a drawer to the side of the sink and produced a first aid box. After a quick search, she found and took out the smallest plaster.

'Smallest plaster ever, for the smallest cut ever,' she said with a jovial voice. 'I am sure you can manage to get some coal now that we have that gaping wound sorted!' she said with a laugh. Alex didn't say a word and went back to get the bucket. At the same time, Vicky stood up from the seat at the kitchen table that she had placed herself on. She was going to leave. She felt embarrassed for sharing stupid rumours. She wrongly assumed, the 'cute' Alex would be one of the cool kids, one who would be all about the gossip. Vicky wished the tile covered kitchen floor would have opened up and swallowed her.

'I really should head home. My mum will be getting in about now and will worry,' Vicky said, even though deep down she wanted to stay. Alex just smiled and headed out the back door, out into the dark and cold to collect the coal. Melissa was more curious than ever to find out what he was doing in the spooky house. Hoping he would speak freely with Vicky gone, she was not going to stop her from leaving,

'Ok, well you know where we are, you have my number if you fancy a hot chocolate any time. Are you good to see yourself out?' Melissa asked. Before Melissa had finished her sentence, Vicky was halfway up the tiny staircase and heading out of sight.

'Thanks for bringing me home. Hope your son is ok, bye,' Vicky shouted back. With that and the sounds of Bart's claws slipping on the wooden stairs having disappeared, followed by a bang of the big front door as the two of them left, Melissa stood, waiting for Alex to return. Finally the old glass back door opened. Having a quick look around Alex saw that the guests had left. Looking over at his mum, he said, 'There is something not right with that house!'

CHAPTER 5

'Grandmother, what was that all about?' Sophie said through her tears. Her hand was still in all kinds of pain. She wasn't sure if it was from the cut she received on her exit from the bus, or from the contact made by her and her male visitor. Or maybe it was both.

'Oh nothing my princess, nothing at all. Don't you go worrying about anything. Come on let's get this hand of yours sorted.' Sophie could hear in grandmother's voice that something wasn't quite right. Choosing to ignore the tone, she decided not to question any further. The cloth that was supposed to be sorting her hand, was now soaked through. As Sophie removed the cloth, the wound opened. Not having ever seen anything like it before, Sophie got a fright. Her hand was not the only thing that looked a mess. Her eyes were bloodshot, her face was pale, paler than her usual redhead complexion and her clothes were dirty and wet.

'Maybe I should go to the hospital,' Sophie said, with a vulnerability that woke grandmother from her blinkered vision of the situation to its reality.

'Well princess, that is probably a good idea. I would like to see you get fixed, but you know how I am, so erm-'

'It's fine, I know,' Sophie interrupted. As long as Sophie could remember, grandmother had never left the house. It was something that was never talked about, it was just the way it was. But on this occasion Sophie knew she needed help and although she didn't admit it, she was scared. Her loner life in the outside world, meant Sophie was very good at looking after herself. However, the evening's events had unsettled her and she really would have liked some company, if she was to go to the hospital.

'Let's get that covered up again before you go. When you get back we can get on with your special birthday day,' grandmother said. She left Sophie with no doubt that if she left, she would be going alone. Grandmother found a bandage, from one of the many full with 'stuff' drawers and covered up the wound.

Bandage in place, Sophie headed for the kitchen door. The coolness of the hallway was a relief from the heat of the kitchen. She was still in her thick winter coat, on top of her school uniform. Along with the fresh air, Sophie was greeted by a bounding Anchor. Having seen Alex out, he was trapped in the hallway.

'No, no you leave her alone just now,' grandmother said to Anchor. Sophie walked straight past him giving him no attention whatsoever, straight for the front door. It was very unlike her.

'Bye,' is all Sophie could manage, as she stepped out into the still night. Not a breath of a breeze. The overgrown garden muffled the sounds of the outside world. There was an eeriness that did not go unnoticed by her.

Vicky having left, Melissa was able to ask the questions she wanted to without the concern of a stranger being present.

'What do you mean, not right?'

'Mum, the house was weird. Well actually the house was quite cool but weird. The people in it were,' he paused, struggling to find the words to best describe them. His pause didn't give him any words that would have given Melissa real insight. All he came up with was 'they were weird.' Alex had put the bucket of coal down in front of the fire and made his way over to the sink, where he went to wash his hands.

'Well firstly, what were you doing in that house in the first place?' Melissa asked. Alex explained what had gone on. The sobs he heard, the blood outside the gate, the girl, the grandmother, the dog and the rush to get him out of the house. He did however, miss out the part about the pain he received on his hand when entering the house. The fact he received the same pain when he touched the girl. Seeing something move on the hallways tree when he left the house and finally, the out of season rose on the footpath as he left the garden.

'I did suggest that I come and get you. Her hand was bleeding really badly and the cut looked deep, from what I could see.' Melissa went into nurse mode instantly. Forgetting about the rumours that Vicky had talked about and the description of the house by Alex as being 'not right.'

'Do you think she would have gone to hospital?' Melissa asked. Alex looked at her and raised an eyebrow. She knew fine well that meant no, 'Should I go round?'

Having had a moment away from what had gone before, Alex's curiosity about the house and its occupants was growing. This was a perfect opportunity to go back to find out more, this time with back up.

'I think that would be a good idea,' Alex replied, his eyebrow returning to its natural state. 'Could you give me a minute to get changed first? I am soaking.'

He hadn't even finished his sentence before he had
disappeared out of sight, up to the tall ceilinged
entrance hall, then up the three flights of old carpeted
stairs, to his bedroom. Alex didn't feel the cold from
the old dark house as he quickly changed. He was
strangely excited about returning to the house he had
been evicted from. His wet clothes were flung on the
floor. His usual jeans, fleece jumper and trainers on.
As he arrived on the second floor landing, Melissa
appeared from her own bedroom having taken the
opportunity to get changed herself. Both in a hurry,
they collided and the first aid box Melissa was
holding went flying. Being so crammed full, the
fastenings keeping it closed stood no chance as the
box hit the floor. Its contents exploded in every
direction.

'Blast, quickly Alex, come on, help me out here.'
On their knees, they scrambled about, collecting and
squashing everything back into the box. Due to the
disorganised fashion of shoving the items in, the box
did not close, so Melissa held the slightly open box
tight under her arm, hoping that she wouldn't drop
anything. 'Lead the way young man,' Melissa said as
she closed the front door behind them. They made
their way back down the slippery driveway. Stepping
out on to the slippery footpath of the square, Melissa
noticed Vicky across the road. They must have been
quick in getting changed, either that or Vicky was a
slow walker, as she was just going into her house.

'So, haunted. Vicky said haunted,' Melissa said in
a questioning tone. She wondered if Alex had
experienced anything while he was there, or had any
thoughts on Vicky's description.

'Yes, but you also said that's silly nonsense,' was
Alex's response. Melissa had experienced a lot in her

life. She had never seen anything she would describe as a ghost, but was also not naive enough to think they didn't exist,

'Well, I know, but gossip,'

'Is the evil of all evils!' Alex interrupted his mum. He had heard the sentence on many an occasion. As sarcastically as he said it, he did however agree with her. Gossip, rumour spreading, whatever you want to call it, was something he had been most unlucky enough to experience, far too often in his life.

As they made their way down the footpath, a figure appeared from the gate to which they were heading. The figure glanced in their direction and then turned and walked away from them, towards the main road. Alex had a good idea who it was, so he shot off like he had heard the starting pistol of one of the many races he had run. His footing was surprisingly good considering how slippery the path was. His arrival at the side of the figure was quite impressive. He came to a stop with what looked like a perfectly judged skid. It wasn't, it was luck. He was correct in his assumption, it was Sophie.

'Hey!' was Alex's out of breath single word greeting. Sophie didn't get the fright that you would have imagined, with having had someone race up behind her. Not saying a word, holding on to her injured hand and wearing the same wet clothes, she looked up at Alex. They looked at each other without saying a word. Sophie was getting the same feeling she did when she looked into his eyes in her home a little earlier, a feeling of comfort.

'Alex, is this the young lady?' Alex was snapped out of his awkward trance, as Melissa arrived at the scene.

'Yes,' Alex replied. Melissa switched into nurse

mode.

'So, I hear you have a bit of an injury on that hand of yours.' Sophie looked over to who was causing the huge shadow to be cast over her. As always with strangers, Sophie felt uncomfortable. Having quickly realised she was probably the mother, who was a nurse, she lifted her hand up. She showed off the hand wrapped in a bandage, which was already showing signs of blood.

'I think I need to have a proper look at that,' Melissa said. Alex could see that Sophie was nervous. Having managed to get his breath back and his awkwardness under control, he said,

'It's ok, this is my mum, the one who I said was a nurse.' Sophie noticed the first aid box under the arm of the maker of the shadow. It gave her some comfort. She didn't really want to go to the hospital. If this was a way of stopping that inevitability then great. So she offered up her hand again.

'We might be better doing it inside, if that's ok with you? You know, better light, water and stuff.' Melissa saw the reservation in Sophies eyes, but continued, 'You can come to ours if you want?' Sophie shook her head assertively. 'Ok, can we come into yours?' Melissa asked. Sophie wasn't really sure what to do at that point. She didn't want to go off into a stranger's house, even though the son of the stranger had helped her earlier. But then grandmother had chased him out the house and didn't answer the question, 'what was that all about?' So something was not quite right there either. Looking down at the floor in silence, Sophie weighed up the options and the facts. Finally she said,

'We can go into mine.'

As they turned and headed back to the open gate,

Melissa put a comforting arm around Sophie. Alex, following close behind, couldn't help but wonder how she had opened the gate, the gate he had decided to jump, seeing as it put up so much resistance to him. She didn't look like she had that much strength in her. Once inside the garden, Sophie turned to Alex and asked him, with an attitude-filled tone,

'Can you close the gate you left open earlier?'

'No,' Alex replied, 'I mean, no I didn't leave it open, it wouldn't open.'

Sophie was confused. She knew she hadn't opened it when she left, it was already open. It had crossed her mind to close it, but she didn't. She had decided, with it being so heavy and rusted and with the frozen water adding that extra glue to its hinges, there was no way she would have been able to close it. With no real conclusion as to why the gate's position was open, Alex did as he was told. With a preemptive build up of strength, he pulled as hard as he could. The gate, to his surprise, provided no resistance whatsoever. With the force Alex had put into it the weight of the free moving gate was torn from his hands, rapidly returning to its closed position. With his eyes wide open, Alex watched as the gate spent only a spilt second in the closed position and then bounced right back at him.

'Woe!' Alex exclaimed. Incredibly he managed to catch the fast moving gate, avoiding yet another injury his mum would have to deal with. Gate back in hand and this time with a gentle guiding touch, Alex slowly closed the gate. On hearing the click of the latch and the gate now secure, he let go.

By this time, Sophie and Melissa had disappeared off into the overgrown garden. They were completely unaware of Alex's gate closing misadventure.

However, two sets of eyes from beyond the gate had seen everything.

'Having fun?' Vicky and Bart were standing watching.

'Not really,' was Alex's response. Just before closing her front door having got home, Vicky had been alerted to something happening in the square by Bart. She had watched the distant blurry figure of who she assumed was Alex, run down the street, followed by Melissa, to a third, out of focus figure. Her nosiness was always going to get the better of her. She made her way back down her garden to the gate to get a better view. Watching sneakily, she could just make out the three figures heading back towards the haunted house. Vicky was not the type of person to let her disabilities stop her from experiencing life, quite the opposite. They gave her an insight into how fragile, short and too complicated life can be. Much to the admiration of all that knew her, she got more confident and life-living every time her disease progressed. There was no way she wasn't going to go and find out what was going on. She made it just in time for Alex's near miss to come into focus. 'What are you doing in there again?' Vicky asked.

'The girl has a cut. Mum is going to have a look at it,' was Alex's honest reply.

'In there!' Vicky was genuinely scared of the place. However, her curiosity was overcoming her fear and her, up for any adventure self, was kicking in, 'Can I come in?'

Alex was surprised at the relative stranger's bold request. Not usually the best at thinking on the spot for responses, he surprised himself when, without a pause, he did,

'Not really my place to say,' knowing fine well the girl he was rescuing was out of sight, so he could not ask for permission.

'Ok, bye then.' Vicky was embarrassed. She couldn't hide it, her cheeks winter pale skin glowed a bright pink. Alex saw the flushed face and wanted to say the right thing, but his focus was catching up with his mum. Not saying a word, he turned and started to walk away. Bart took his cue and did the same, pulling Vicky away with him. Not even two steps away from the gate, a loud metal sounding bang came from behind them. Vicky and Alex spun back to face each other - the gate had unlatched itself and swung open.

'No!' Vicky exclaimed. In her mind, the haunted house rumours had just been confirmed. She ran back across the road to the safety of her garden. There she could watch from a distance, safely. Alex on the other hand reacted very differently. He calmly walked back to the gate, took hold of it and closed it. He watched Vicky's dash back across the square and was going to shout after her, but he wasn't one hundred percent sure what she could or could not hear, so he didn't.

'Alex!' Melissa's voice echoed from within the canopy of ivy she had wandered into with her patient, 'are you coming?' Not running, walking quickly, Alex finally left the gate and made his way towards where his mum's voice was coming from. As he entered into the darkness, he looked down to see if the yellow flower, not in keeping with the time of year, that had caused him to slip on his dramatic exit from the same place not that long ago, was still there. He was momentarily distracted from his search by the cobbles. They seemed brighter than they did before. Looking around, everything seemed brighter, newer somehow. Returning to his flower search, he was beginning to wonder whether he had indeed imagined it. Finally, there it was. Squashed, but the tiny yellow rose was there. Content he wasn't losing his mind, Alex left the tunnel of the not so dead looking trees with their fresh green buds. He was just in time to see Melissa and the, to him, still unnamed girl, stepping off the snow covered footpath, on to the steps which were strangely clear of snow and ice and up to the big red door.

'Can you hold on here a minute?' Sophie said to Melissa, as she turned the handle with her uninjured hand.

'Of course, yes,' Melissa responded in her caring voice. Sophie disappeared in through the door, as Alex arrived at Melissa's side and asked,

'You not going in mum?'

'Not yet, she asked me to hold on here. She will be back in a minute I'm sure,' Melissa responded. Sophie hadn't closed the door properly and not long into their wait, a nose appeared at Anchor height. That was followed by a paw, which with a little help from his nose, prised the big old door open. Melissa took a step back as his huge head appeared, followed by his strong thick neck and massive shoulders.

'It's ok mum, he's fine,' Alex said. Stepping forward he bent down and put out his hand to greet his new friend. 'Hey buddy, did you miss me?' A whimper and a lick and they were fully acquainted once more.

Being right at the open door, Alex could hear a debate going on in the hallway. 'I don't want that boy back in tonight.' Alex recognised the voice of the old lady, who had pretty much chased him out earlier. As sweet as her tone was, the words were certainly not so sweet, or welcoming. Alex looked into the hallway over Anchor. Something was different. Like the dark tunnel, it looked brighter. His eyes followed the floor to the base of the painted dead tree he had seen earlier. It didn't look so dead any more! The branches were showing signs of budding leaves. Leaves that, if he hadn't seen them with his own eyes, he would not have believed were actually growing. The painted tree was growing!

'Grandmother, please, I don't want to go to hospital and they may be able to help. Remember he said his mum was a nurse!' At the same time as they were having their discussions, Anchor's half in, half out situation got grandmother's attention. There was some strong wagging of the tail going on and no barking. Sophie saw grandmother looking and quickly took advantage of the moment,

'Look, Anchor is fine with them, please.' She was met with silence, so she quickly tried to come up with another reason to let them in, 'plus the cloth is already leaking.' Alex, hearing how much Sophie wanted his mum's help, looked away from the hall and up at her and said,

'Mum I think you should just go in.'

'And I think we should wait until we are invited,' Melissa said. She had also heard the conversation going on behind the door, but didn't want to be disrespectful. 'Mum, I know the old lady is saying she just doesn't want me in for some reason, but the girl needs some help, clearly. Just go in mum.' The relationship the two of them had was such that she didn't need to be told a second time. The concern in Alex's voice was real.

'Ok, can you get hold of the dog?' Alex did exactly that, he grabbed his neck and confidently hugged him,

'On you go mum.'

Reaching over the huge shoulders of Anchor, she pushed the door open. Alex was waiting for the loud squeaking of old hinges but there was no sound. The door swung open freely. Sophie and her grandmother were standing on the rug in the hallway and came into sight.

'Good evening, I do hope you don't mind me coming in. I just wanted to get on and sort this young girl's hand, if that's ok?' Melissa said, before grandmother had a chance to say anything. She wanted to break the ice and hopefully give the impression that there was never any question that she would not be helping Sophie.

'Oh, yes of course, please come in.' After grandmother appeared to be so adamant that they weren't getting in, the words surprised Sophie and Alex, they sounded so genuine. Aware of what Alex had said about the old lady not wanting him to be in the house, Melissa turned back to Alex and said,

'If you want to head home and get the fire started, I can handle this from here.'

'Yes, yes my dear, you head on home. We girls have this all under control.' Grandmother jumped on the opportunity of getting this young man away from them. Sophie was so confused by her grandmother's reaction to the boy, who after all had only been nothing but nice, other than falling on her hand and causing inexplicable pain of course.

'Grandmother, really, what's your problem?' she asked. Confrontation between them was something very new, Sophie didn't like it. She felt uncomfortable saying what she did, but she had such a strong and inexplicable connection with the now twice evicted boy.

'It's ok,' Alex said, whilst standing up from his crouched position. He stepped back, showing his intention to leave. Bending forward to give Anchor a final pat on the head, Alex leant on the doorframe. As soon as he made contact with it, the shooting pain he received on his first visit to the house returned, with massive force. Unable to breathe, let alone let out a scream, he removed his hand. In the very same moment the lights in the hall went out. No one moved.

'Enough!' came a very loud shout from the stern voice of grandmother. Alex looked back at the doorway just in time to see the face of grandmother appear from the darkness, grab hold of Anchor and pull him back into the house. As soon as Anchor was clear of the door and Alex took a step backwards off the step, the lights flashed back on. Grandmother slammed the door shut.

Standing on the footpath facing the house, Alex held his arm tight, in an effort to stop the shooting pain from traveling any further than his hand. His eyes closed, concentrating hard on calming himself, he started breathing again. His breath was fast and shallow. The cold fresh night's air felt sharp on the back of his throat. Slowly opening his eyes, everything was out of focus. As his breathing slowed and the pain subsided, his vision began to clear. As it did, he could see that the very spot he was standing on was clear of all signs of snow or ice. At his feet and around them, Alex could see the brightest of new looking red cobbles.

Looking closer at their colour and fabulous individual detail, he realised that the snow and ice that was remaining around him, was also clearing down the path and into the garden. Clearing from where he stood. His feet were acting like a single rain drop, that when it lands in a puddle, creates a perfect circular wave, spreading ever outwards in a perfect circle.

Alex was torn. He stood looking up at the bright red front door, that was being washed by the thawing snow and ice that had covered the house's roof, windowsills and walls. The clear water running down every part of it, caused the moon's reflection to dazzle him as he stared into it. Alex didn't know what to do. Should he stay in this place with its strange attraction, but that was also the cause of incredible pain, or should he just leave? He wasn't welcome inside, so he assumed that also meant he wasn't welcome outside the house itself. But he couldn't leave his mum, Melissa either. His back and forth decision process was always going to end up in the place it did. As though he was speaking to the house, Alex resolutely said,

'I am staying!'

CHAPTER 6

The, not so bright hall lights back on, Melissa was still not completely sure what was happening, as she recalled the one word of Alex's impression of the house and its occupants - 'weird!' She looked down at Sophies hand. What she saw sprung her into action. Putting on her nothing to worry about voice, she said,

'Right ok, let's get you to the bathroom.'

'Kitchen is fine.' The words came from a fast moving grandmother, who shot past them to open the kitchen door. Sophie followed, throwing a glance and a very slight smile at Melissa as she did.

'Oh, that's beautiful,' Melissa said as she entered the kitchen. She gestured towards the birthday present dolls house, that still hadn't got the full attention and investigation that it deserved. Having followed her grandmother, Sophie had made her way to the kitchen sink. The red drops of blood were still visible from her first visit. Having not received a response to her comment on the dolls house, Melissa re-focused on what she was there for - 'now then, let's have a look.'

Melissa peeled back the cloth. It was no longer a fresh, bright, white colour. It had been replaced with a dark, foreboding red. Sophie began to silently cry, as Melissa's removal of the cloth made the wound visible. Her tears dripped into the sink and mixed with the dried, red drops from earlier, which hadn't been washed away. She wasn't really in any pain, her hand felt numb, so Sophie didn't really know why she was crying. She was happy that she didn't have to go to the hospital, she was happy her grandmother was, as always, by her side. But she couldn't stop the tears from falling.

'Let me dry those tears princess.' Grandmothers tone had returned to the sweet one Sophie was more accustomed to. Looking up from her hand and into the eyes of her grandmother, Sophie saw that she was not the only one who was emotional.

'Looks like you need help drying your tears as well grandmother,' Sophie softly said. The moment of vulnerability broke what had become quite a cold atmosphere. The release of tension evolved into the two of them laughing. Meanwhile, Melissa had the wound fully visible and was cleaning the blood away to get a proper look at what she was dealing with.

'So little miss, you probably should get some stitches, that really is quite the cut you have there,' Melissa said.

'Can you do that?' asked grandmother.

'I am afraid not. I don't have those supplies in my first aid box, sorry,' Melissa replied. Along with reading every story book she could get hold of, Sophie always enjoyed learning new things, so she had completed a first aid course. Having glanced at the contents of the first aid box she said,

'Is that butterfly stitches?'

Melissa replied quickly, 'Yes they are, but they won't work. They aren't the best thing for this cut I am afraid.' Sophie was not about to accept that answer. She saw an opportunity. She didn't want to have to head to hospital, for a second time. With her knowledge of biology, along with her first aid training she had an inkling that they may just work. Plus Melissa had said, 'they aren't the best thing.'

'So they won't work at all then?' Sophie asked, knowing the answer, but wanting to give Melissa her place.

'Well, if we put enough on and bandage your hand, that may do it,' was Melissa's response.

'Let's do that then,' grandmother piped up, very happy with the option of Sophie staying at home.

'Would you hold the cut closed for me please,' Melissa asked grandmother. Pinching the wound together made Sophie flinch. With one quick final dab to make sure the area was dry, Melissa started sticking the butterfly stitches in place. Thankfully the first aid box had plenty, the cut needed them.

Having finished with her nursing duties, Sophie all bandaged up and calm having been restored to the loving home, Melissa couldn't help but feel her welcome had come to an end. Looking around she caught sight of the birthday cake. 'Perfect,' she thought. It gave her an opportunity to make small talk. Her protective personality wasn't going to be happy leaving straight away, she needed to know that the young girl was going to be safe.

'So someone has had a birthday. The cake looks lovely,' Melissa said. She looked between grandmother and Sophie waiting for an answer. There wasn't one. She thought that maybe the words had been more of a statement than a question, so she tried again, 'does it taste as good as it looks?' It worked, as Sophie replied,

'Grandmother's cakes are the best.' Sophie was not usually the first to speak. She was surprised at her grandmother being so quiet. They didn't have many people visit, but when they did, grandmother was always the best host, full of conversation. The house also played its part - the plentiful, crazy coloured kitchen cupboards, magically providing food and drink for every persons likes and even the quirkiest of tastes. But today Sophie saw none of those qualities from grandmother or the house.

'So whose birthday is it and can I have a piece?' Melissa was stepping out and pushing her own boundaries by being so pushy. Sophie was pleased when grandmother at last began to speak. She was quickly disappointed though, as it was only to encourage Melissa to leave,

'Oh no, it's really not that good. It's probably best for us to get back to our birthday celebrations ourselves. I have lots of plans.'

Melissa figured she wasn't going to get anywhere, so said,

'Ok, that's fine. Well, we live two doors up from you, so if you need any further help please just come over. Any time.'

With Anchor taking the lead, she picked up her first aid box and headed out of the kitchen, back into the hall. Something moving caught her eye as she approached the front door, just as it did with Alex earlier. A movement on the tip of the now very leafy covered painted branch, made her pause. She focused hard on the spot she thought she saw something, but there was nothing. So she went to leave. As she reached out for the front door handle, a faint high pitched sound and a tiny breeze passed her right side, causing her curly shoulder length hair to move as it did. Sophie, not being far behind Melissa, had exactly the same experience. Both looked to see what it was, both again saw nothing. Whatever it was must have also made its way past Anchor, who let out a bark, turned and disappeared up the stairs in a blur of bouncing fur.

Melissa was unsurprisingly quite keen to leave at that point. She took hold of the door handle and at the same time, being her usual polite self, said, 'Well, was nice to meet you, hey! I don't even know your name.' The door open, not waiting for a response, she said, 'I am Melissa and my son who you met earlier, that's Alex.' Melissa was out and on the top step. Grandmother had passed Sophie and taken hold of the door handle, ready to close the door. Before she could, Sophie replied,

'I am Sophie and this is my grandmother. Oh, Anchor was the one who disappeared upstairs. Thank you again for my hand,' Sophie was going to go on but was interrupted by grandmother, who was suddenly interested in her not so welcome guests,

'How are you related to Alex?'

'I found him.'

Melissa instantly realised the magnitude of what she had just admitted. She left without another word. In all the years they had been together, she had never given anything away about her or Alex. Not only that, what she had said out loud was something she had never said to anyone, not even to Alex. Shaking her head to herself, she stepped off the steps and into the garden that had lost all signs of winter.

Alex, after his decision to stay, was standing patiently on the path out of sight, hidden by the shadows created from the canopy of trees and ivy. He was in a place that although he couldn't be seen, he could see and hear anything that may happen. As the front door opened he didn't know what to think, as he watched his mum leave the house and then say what she did, in answer to grandmother's question.

The slow moving Melissa, wrapped up in her own head, was completely unaware of Alex, who stepped into the light as she got closer. He was pleased that her stay inside hadn't been too long. He was pleased that he could ask her about what had happened inside the house, but he really didn't know what to say to her regarding her words, 'I found him'. Alex had stepped out of the shadows and should have easily been seen. Melissa was right in front of him. 'Hi, is she ok?' Alex said. He got no response! 'Mum, hello?' Still nothing.

Her shaking head, which had been looking at the ground, was now looking up. She was looking right at him, but still she did not respond.

Melissa was still walking at him showing no signs of stopping, when Alex put his hands up to stop the now inevitable collision. With a raised voice he said 'Mum!' Again there was no response, no reaction. Alex had no time to move so he aimed his hands towards her shoulders to prevent the full impact. Inches from him, Melissa still clearly had no intention of stopping. Four inches, three inches, two inches, one inch. Alex waited for the impact. Nothing, he felt nothing. Not even the slightest of pressures. Melissa had past him and was heading into the shadows. Alex was left standing completely confused. His mum had just walked right through him!

Not turning round and staring at the closed front door, Sophie, for the second time that night, said 'Grandmother, what was that all about?' She wanted to know what and why she had been the way she was, to both Alex and Melissa.

'Let's get some of that birthday cake before Anchor's impatience gets the better of him,' was grandmother's response, in a very happy and smiling voice. 'So glad you don't have to go to hospital.'

Sophie shook her head, then, very unlike her, she went against her loving guardian, ignoring the suggestion of retiring to the kitchen for birthday cake. She opened the free moving, big, old, red front door with every intention of calling Melissa back.

'Sophie, what are you doing?' Grandmother stepped past her and slammed the door closed. 'Come on princess, let's get that cake.' Sophie was left in no doubt as to whether she had a choice in the matter. Grandmother took it a step further. Rather than allowing Sophie to follow in her own time, grandmother took hold of her arm and led her back to the kitchen.

Entering the kitchen, Anchor appeared at Sophie's side. He was back from his unsuccessful chase of whatever had buzzed past him in the hallway. Letting go of Sophie's arm, grandmother headed round the table to the cake. Sophie was left standing, giving Anchor the attention his nuzzling nose had insisted on. She followed as Anchor dropped to the floor looking for more, ending up sitting next to him, her back resting on the closed kitchen door.

'Grandmother, please tell me why you have been like you have with them,' Sophie's voice, soft and thoughtful. Her tone made it even harder for grandmother not to tell her the reasons.

'Should I be cutting this cake, or should the birthday girl?' Sophie gave up pressing for any further information and got herself up from the squeaking Anchor. As she did, she noticed something hanging from under the table. On all fours she crawled her way over to take a closer look. What she saw made no sense,

'Grandmother, the table has grown roots!' She was right. Directly under where the birthday gift sat, small hanging tree roots were coming through the table.

'What are you saying?' grandmother asked.

'Tree roots, look, there are tree roots under here.' Sophie stood up and took hold of the dolls house to get a look underneath. As much as she pushed, pulled, shook and lifted, it didn't budge. 'Grandmother, the house is stuck to the table!' Grandmother turned away from the work surface, where the fabulous cake sat waiting to be enjoyed and looked towards her creation. She was ready to have some fun with Sophie. To tease her for her lack of strength and explain away whatever was under the table. But as she looked at the dolls house, she saw something that took her by surprise. Tree branches were growing out of the roof of the house. Miniature tree branches growing, budding and leafing as she watched.

Knock, knock, knock. Three loud bangs coming from the front door took Sophie's attention from the table and its rooted property. Hoping it was her previously evicted guests returning, she dashed out the kitchen door, shutting it behind her. She wanted to make sure she had time to get to the door and invite the guests in, before grandmother got there and had a chance to do the opposite.

She needn't have worried, as grandmother was more interested in what was happening on her kitchen table, than in who was at the front door. She walked round its entirety, coming to a stop at the front of it. There was a light coming from inside the house's crooked windows. Bending down, not that she needed much bending to get to the height of the front door, she looked inside. Peering in the windows, the rooms seemed to be as they should. The only place not seen through the windows, was the hallway. It was hidden behind the tiny red door she had lovingly made.

Having opened the tiny, incredibly inviting red door and just as she looked inside to see if anything had changed, she was dazzled by the brightest flash of light. At the very same time, she heard a shout come from the hallway - 'Alex!'

CHAPTER 7

Melissa hadn't registered that the path was completely clear as she left the house and walked unknowingly through Alex. She was too wrapped up in her head, thinking about what she had said - 'I found him.' As she stepped out of the free-moving gate back out into the wintery square, her front foot slipped on the frozen ground. Having kept her balance and been pulled back into reality, she looked back at the unseasonably spring like garden. 'What on earth?' Melissa said out loud. Wondering if it was some sort of optical illusion, she went to step back in through the gate to take a closer look. Lifting her firmly placed foot from the snow covered outside path, she moved forward. Before she could get any further, with a loud bang, the new looking iron gate slammed shut. Melissa's heart was in its fight or flight state, beating fast in her chest as she stepped up to the gate. Her hands rested on the top of it as she peered over, looking to find some sort of plausible explanation for it closing.

The place outside the gate was well worn from the visitors going back and forth that evening, each one of them having had their own unexpected experiences. Melissa's garden viewing came to an end, as again her mind went back to her answer to grandmother's question. Talking to the universe, out loud she said 'What have I done?'

'I don't know, what have you done?'

Melissa got such a fright she jumped, again. It was Vicky. She had left the safety of her garden having seen movement from across the square. With her limited tunnel vision, she could just make out that someone was leaving the haunted house's garden. She was desperate to know what the inside of the spooky, never seen house was like. Vicky and her cheery, somewhat excited voice had really taken Melissa by surprise.

'Vicky... I didn't see you there,' she said.

'Well that's twice this evening then.' Vicky laughed as she said it, 'So is it haunted? Are there real people in there?' said Vicky, bombarding Melissa with questions. Melissa had other things on her mind, she wasn't in the mood for talking.

'Sorry but I have to get home,' walking away from Vicky as she said it.

Vicky and Bart were both left standing looking towards the hidden, old house's garden, hoping to get some sort of hint as to what had gone on. Finding some extra courage, she walked up to the gate to take a closer look.

'Well Bart, that's different.' The coming alive, tidy looking garden was not what she expected, let alone the lack of winter in it. She was used to seeing an overgrown garden, a rusty old looking iron gate and no signs of life. But now the gate was no longer rusty. The footpath up to the shadowed tunnel was showing off bright cobbles, brightening with every moment that passed. She watched as each cobble moved as it brightened. A perfectly curved, wonderfully wobbly cobbly path was coming to life. Nature was joining in - the trees were showing signs of life, the ivy was not looking as dark, dull or dead as she was used to. Vicky looked to see where Melissa had got to. She was just walking into her driveway. Once out of sight, she took hold of the

handle of the gate which was not as cold as she
expected. Vicky's adventurous side had fully got the
better of her. All fear was replaced with curiosity. She
so wanted to get inside for a look at what was out of
sight. She had come to the conclusion that she would
be fine. Both Melissa and Alex had been in and made
it out, twice, after all. Although she hadn't actually
seen Alex leave the second time, she figured she must
have just missed him.

'What?' Vicky said in a confused voice. As hard
as she tried, she couldn't push the gate open. It would
not budge, not even a millimetre. Although visually it
did not look like it, it felt like it had returned to its
rusty and frozen solid state. Far from the free-
swinging gate she had witnessed a little earlier.

Trying with no success once again, she noticed
movement on the floor. It was a slow moving Alex.
'Oh are you ok?' There was no response. Knowing
Melissa would not have had time to make it up her
drive and into her house, Vicky shouted 'Melissa,
HELP!' Her words echoed down the street, easily
finding their way to Melissa. Despite her distracted,
full of questions confused mind, Melissa was quick to
react, as she returned once more.

'Alex is on the floor, I can't get the gate open!'
Vicky said in a panicked voice, as Melissa appeared
at her side. Stepping forward to look where Vicky
was pointing, the out of breath Melissa saw nothing.

'Seriously Vicky!' Melissa said in an unimpressed
voice. 'There's nothing there.' Vicky pushed Melissa
out the way,

'Look. He is there, behind the gate on the floor,'
Vicky said, whilst reaching through the bars of the
gate and prodding Alex who let out a moan. 'Try the
gate! Please try the gate.' Melissa, shaking her head,

did as she was asked. The handle turned with ease. The latch was now free of its secured place as Melissa pushed the gate, but it did not budge. Not sure why it was being so stubborn, Melissa looked again. There was still nothing there - no Alex, no reason the gate should not swing open. Melissa, not about to be defeated, gave the gate an extra hard shove. It moved slightly, but bounced back closed.

Having heard his mum say that she had 'found him' and then having been walked through by her like a ghost, Alex had chased after his mum in panic. In his haste, he lost his footing and fell into the gate, slamming it shut with his head. He was the reason the gate slammed unexpectedly behind Melissa when she left. Time having passed and partly because of Vicky's prod, Alex had come around from the small concussion. 'What the heck mum?'

Using the gate for assistance, Alex pulled himself up to his feet.

Still holding on to the gate, Melissa felt the movement through her hands. It caused her to let go. She stepped back and watched as the handle she had just let go of turned and, the gate started to open. As far as Melissa was concerned, it was opening by itself.

'See, it's Alex,' Vicky piped up from behind her. Melissa's wide open, unblinking eyes, watched, as the gate reached its fully open position.

'There is no Alex!' she said in a very stern voice. Frightened, she backed away from the open gate. 'There is no Alex. Vicky, I don't know what you are playing at, it's not funny!'

'Vicky, can you see me?' Alex asked,

'Yes, obviously. I think they did something to your mum in there, she doesn't seem right?' Vicky said.

'Who are you talking to? Stop this, seriously stop this NOW!' Melissa had taken hold of Vicky's shoulders and was looking right into her eyes as she shouted her instruction.

'Alex is there, he is there. Why can't you see him, he is there,' Vicky said. When Melissa took hold of Vicky, Bart started barking. He could sense the tension rising, tension which was being directed unacceptably at his charge. Alex reached out to touch his mum's shoulder in an effort to calm her down. Vicky let out a scream, as instead of resting on her shoulder, she watched Alex's hand pass right through his mum. Alex stumbled. His weight transferred as he expected to rest on his mum's shoulder and it took him off balance. He looked down at his hands, they looked fine to him. He touched them together, they felt firm. As far as he was concerned they were definitely there. Was Vicky correct, had something happened to his mum whilst she was in the house? Was his mum a ghost?

'Mum, something is wrong, mum, please answer me, I am here, mum, why can't you see me?' Alex was panicking as much as Vicky was petrified. Melissa was a mixture of angry and still frightened. Bart, the clever dog he was, realised what was going on. He stopped barking, left Vicky's side, walked past Melissa and right up to Alex. In one quick move he jumped up and rested his paws on Alex's chest.

'Look, see he is there.' Melissa turned to look. She saw Bart on his back legs, leaning on an invisible object.

Alex was pleased that two out of the three living things could see him, but he needed to know what the situation was with his mum. 'Vicky, you can see me and mum?' Alex asked.

'Yes, you are both as clear as each other.' As she said it she reached out and touched Melissa's arm, 'and apparently I can touch her.' Melissa was paying no attention to Vicky, she was watching Bart. He was still resting on and licking an invisible object. Then she saw his fur move. Its movement was in keeping with it being ruffled by a hand.

Vicky had made her way over to Alex. She was curious as to whether she could touch him, as she did Melissa. Holding her breath she reached out, she was too slow. Alex, who was thinking the same thing, had reached out to take hold of her shoulder. His hand went right through her. The strange reality of what had happened did not stop Vicky, she continued her reach towards Alex. Her hand, rather than being placed on his chest, went right through it. There was no friction, contact, restriction, it was as though he wasn't there.

'Oh crap,' she said as she stepped back into Melissa, who was definitely solid. No ghostly passing through one another, the two of them were real. All life left Alex's face as he realised, he was the anomaly. He looked over at his petrified mum. Could the day get any stranger? Calmly, Vicky had been analysing the sequence of events in her head. She broke her silence as she realised, 'Bart touched him!' She was right. Bart had touched him, leant on him, had his fur ruffled by him. Her realisation seemed to help in calming both Alex and Melissa,

'So you can see him Vicky?' Melissa asked,

'Yes quite clearly. He is standing right there,' was Vicky's response. Melissa was coming back to a place of mature assessment of the situation.

'So I can't see or hear him. He can see and hear me and we can't touch. You can see him but can't touch him and Bart seems to be able to see and touch him,' Melissa said. As she was talking, Alex had stepped outside the gate, on to the frozen footpath. Melissa, who was looking at the floor as she clarified the situation, noticed the snow and ice was melting. It was melting in the shape of footprints, Alex sized footprints,

'Alex?' Melissa said with a questioning tone. 'Is that you?'

'Yes, mum can you see me?' Knowing fine well she couldn't, he asked anyway. There was no response,

'Alex has stepped out of the gate Melissa, he's right in front of you,' Vicky said.

'I don't see him, but look, the snow is melting,' pointing at the floor, right at where Alex's feet were planted. Alex lifted his foot and saw what his mum was seeing, a defrosting footprint. He stepped to the side of his mum and placed his foot down again, waited a moment and lifted it. The same result. He was melting snow!

'Vicky, are you seeing this?' Vicky and her tunnel vision had indeed seen the footprints. She also saw that Alex was disappearing. His voice was getting fainter with every step he took away from the gate. He was vanishing before her eyes.

'Alex stop, go back into the garden.' Vicky's instruction seemed odd, but he did as he was told.

'Why?' he asked Vicky, looking back at her as he walked back in,

'That is why. You were disappearing as you came towards me. Now you are as clear as your mum is to me. It's this place. I told you there was something creepy about it.' Vicky's courageous curiosity was back. She was very happy the gate was open as she followed Alex and stepped through it.

'Can you still see me Melissa?' Vicky asked.

'Of course I can. Not sure if you should be going in there though!' Melissa didn't want another disappearing person to deal with.

'I disagree, I think this is exactly where we should be. We need to figure out what has happened to Alex.'

Alex agreed, 'Well it appears I can't leave the garden, so the best thing to do is go back I guess,' he said.

'Yep, let's do that,' said Vicky.

'Do what?' was Melissa's response, still unable to hear or see Alex.

'Alex said we should go back to the house.' Bart had joined Vicky. Having taken hold of his harness, he was pulling her past Alex and towards the dark canopy of foliage. Nothing was said as Alex turned to follow. Melissa, left standing outside the gate, watched as the two she could see, disappeared out of sight.

Talking to herself, Melissa said 'well I guess I should be going in as well.' Not knowing what was going to happen, she bit her lip and took a big step through the open gate. Her entrance was quite uneventful. Standing on the clear wobbly cobbly pathway, she stopped to make sure she could still see herself, she could.

By the time Melissa had made her way back through the darkness, Vicky was standing on the top step, looking up at the bright red front door. Melissa couldn't believe what she was seeing, aware for the first time of what she had missed as she left, angry with herself for letting her secret out. The house looked so different. The cobbles were a bright red, not as red as the door but new looking. The snow was gone and the house itself looked as though it was smiling at her. The windows' crookedness, creating the most welcoming of smiles.

Knock, knock, knock. Full of curious confidence, Vicky banged on the door. Waiting for an answer, Vicky reached out to Alex again. She wondered if being closer to the house meant that his lack of solid state had changed.

'I wish you would stop doing that,' Alex said, as again Vicky's hand went through him.

'Oh, yeh sorry, does it feel odd?' Vicky asked,

'No, not really, it's just kind of strange having a hand go through me.' Before Vicky could say anything the door opened.

'Sophie,' Alex shouted out hoping to get a response.

'Hello,' Sophie said looking at Vicky,

'Hi, erm sorry to bother you but can you see Alex?' said Vicky, not beating around the bush.

'Sorry?' Sophie said, a little confused by the question to say the least. Vicky went to speak, but was interrupted by Melissa who had arrived at the bottom of the steps. In a eerily calm voice, she said,

'Hi, just wondering, can you see my son? Apparently he is standing right next to this young lady with her dog, and I can't.' There was an awkward silence as Vicky and Melissa waited for a response. Sophie was trying to figure out whether she had a couple of mad people on her doorstep.

Alex wanted answers and knew this group of people were not the ones to give them to him. The old lady. The grandmother who had not wanted him in the house. He was convinced she knew something and that is who he wanted to speak to. Stepping to the side of Vicky and round Bart, Alex walked up to the open door. Due to the doorway being full of Sophie, Alex's path to finding grandmother was being unwittingly blocked. He quickly figured that if she couldn't see him, she probably would also not be able to touch him. Alex went to walk through her. This time as he stepped over the house's threshold, there was no pain coming from his hand, no overheating of his body, no fear. What happened next, happened so quickly, Sophie had no time to react. Alex was real once again. Unaware his state had changed, Alex continued walking to where he wanted to go and collided with Sophie. The contact came with such force it knocked her back off her feet. She was heading for the hard floor once again until Alex, in an incredibly swift movement, managed to catch her and pull her in to him. Just inches apart, they stood staring into each others eyes. Together they felt unexplainably happy. The moment and silence was broken, by a loud and relieved shout from the garden,

'Alex!'

CHAPTER 8

It was clear, grandmother knew more than she was letting on that evening. Sophie and Alex found themselves standing together, inside the transformed, friendly, perfectly formed, incredibly inviting, bright red front door. Melissa was confused and relieved that her son had appeared from nowhere. She was stood looking up at him on the gorgeously red, wobbly cobbly footpath. Vicky and her companion, standing on the top step, were transfixed by the painted tree on the wall of the dully lit hallway, which seemed to be moving. All had no idea what had happened and what was to come. All, in that moment, felt a welcoming warmth from this unexpectedly wonderfully perfect of homes. A calmness had washed over them all, taking away the fear, the shock, the panic that each of them had felt on some level over the evening.

'Come in, please all of you come in.' It was grandmother. Her voice echoed through the hall from the kitchen doorway. It was friendly and inviting. 'Come on princess, bring your friends in for some cake.' Sophie stepped back from Alex and looked over her shoulder towards grandmother. Grandmother could see the confusion on her face, so she continued, 'maybe we should get to know our new neighbours after all.'

Melissa was fully aware she had given away a secret that she should not have. She was also fully aware that grandmother had taken great interest in what she said - 'I found him.' However that reality did not stop her from happily walking back into the house, she was as keen as everyone else was to find out what had happened to her son. Vicky and Bart didn't seem so quick to accept the invite. That was because they were both still taking in what they could, of the hallway. Sophie had instinctively taken hold of Alex's hand and was leading him towards the kitchen. Their hands were clasped naturally tight together, as though they had been acquainted for a period of time much longer than they had. Alex liked the feeling. It felt right. He felt at home and he felt a warmth in his heart that he had not felt before in anyone else's company, different to the usual safe warmth he felt with his mum.

Anchor had managed to squeeze his way past grandmother. He was gingerly making his way over to his guests. One particular guest was of great interest to him - Bart. Like grandmother, he had not left the safety of their house and garden for many, many years. To have had new human visitors was exciting enough, but to see a furry companion, well, Anchor's excitement was always going to get the better of him. His initial gingerly progress became a full on bound as he passed Sophie and Alex. Bart didn't know what to make of this huge ball of fur and teeth heading towards him, so in a smooth and quick move, he hid behind Vicky. The moved surprised her, he had never been anything but protective of her. On this occasion she had been left in the line of fire. The shaking Bart peered round from Vicky's short legs,

'Anchor, come here!' grandmother shouted, seeing the poor, defenceless, smaller than average Labrador cowering. Anchor of course paid no attention whatsoever and continued his bounding. He overshot Vicky, but stopped just in time to be face to face with the dog that was going to be his new friend. Woof, woof, woof, woof. Bart found his voice, giving Anchor the message that the friendship may be one sided. Anchor's eyes popped wide open and he stayed focused on the vicious beast, who maybe wasn't going to be his friend after all. He slowly backed away.

'Anchor you silly mutt, come here.' This time Anchor's selective hearing chose to hear grandmother. He gladly did as he was told and dashed back to the safety of the kitchen.

All were now in the house. The front door closed, Melissa brought up the rear of the group as they all entered the kitchen. Its cupboards looked even more colourful and splendid than they had earlier that evening. Still sitting on the table was the ever-changing birthday present. The replica dolls house was showing as much life as the actual house it imitated.

'So who would like some cake?' Grandmother seemed to have only one thing on her mind. 'Cake, you must all have some cake. No, no, wait one moment, all wait where you are.' Out of sight, hidden by the dolls house, grandmother could be heard opening and then rifling through a drawer. 'Ah, here we go, don't you move.' Her guests did as they were told, staying silent as they waited. From beyond the dolls house a collection of noises and exclamations came from grandmother, and then finally,

'Happy birthday to you, happy birthday to you...' grandmother began singing. A flickering light could be seen reflecting off the cupboard doors, as grandmother with her high pitched, somewhat out of tune voice, made her way to the waiting audience. It was quite an awkward moment, but with the domino effect of Melissa, followed by Vicky and finally Alex all joining in with the singing, the moment passed. Arriving at Sophie and the song complete, the very tasty, slightly squint, slightly sloppy looking cake had its candles blown out. 'Lets get this cake cut up. I think we all deserve a piece,' grandmother announced.

Melissa was unusually quiet for such an occasion and situation. Having entered the house, the questions she had wanted to ask seemed to have gone. As had her motivation to try and remember the questions. She was just content to go along with the ride and see what happened next.

'And who is this young lady and friend?' grandmother said looking at Vicky. Her view had been blocked when shouting from the kitchen door, so she was completely unaware that her invitation to enter the house had included two extra guests.

'I'm Vicky, and this is Bart. He is my dual purpose dog,' Vicky said with confidence.

'Oh lovely. So many of our furry friends in this world are not given the place and respect they deserve.' Looking directly at Bart, she said 'it's lovely to meet you and welcome. I shall look forward to getting to know you better.' Bart seemed to understand everything that was being said to him. He sat back and let out a gentle woof of acknowledgement.

'Where are my manners? Vicky, this is my granddaughter Sophie and this is our own special friend, Anchor. He is slightly dopey but always fun, and Bart, he is harmless.' Having finished with the introductions, grandmother looked over at Sophie and smiled.

'So I guess you would like some explanations?'

grandmother said. As she did, she noticed that Sophie and Alex were holding hands.

'So you two seem to have become friends.' Sophie, being embarrassed by the focus on the hand holding, dropped Alex's hand and walked over to the cake.

'Would anyone like a drink?' grandmother asked,

'I would like something stronger than a soft drink to be honest!' was the very quick response from Melissa, 'but a cup of coffee will do.' Grandmother walked to the corner of the room where she collected a small set of ladders, which she took over to a brown coloured cupboard. Like every cupboard door in the fabulously colourful kitchen, its door was as crooked as the windows on the front of the house. Having climbed up the steps, she opened the cupboard door and the kitchen was instantly filled with the smell of fresh coffee,

'Oh, I always love that smell,' grandmother said, whilst reaching in and producing what looked like a home made mug, the size of two normal mugs. There was not a part of it that was uniform in any way. The huge handle, which reached from the top to its bottom, was as squint as the rest of the sparkling brown mug. The whole thing looked as melted as the birthday cake. With a 'Here you go dear,' grandmother passed her guest the mug from the top step of the ladders.

'Thank you,' Melissa said taking hold of the mug, not sure what she was receiving. Was she to pretend that she had been given a cup of coffee, was she supposed to be making it herself?

'Oh be careful, you will spill it!' grandmother said. With the full weight of the mug in her hand, Melissa realised that she was holding more than just a mug.

Slowly lowering it to eye level, she peered in. As she did, the breeze created by grandmother closing the cupboard door caused Melissa to blink, as the steam from the hot coffee was blown into her face. 'Try it, I am sure it will be good,' grandmother said. Everyone in the room, including Sophie, was transfixed. Having lived there for so many years, Sophie's experience of the kitchen was that the cupboards were always full. She just assumed it was delivered when she wasn't there. She was questioning that thought completely. Melissa cautiously took a sip.

'My goodness, that is perfect,' Melissa said. And it was. It was the perfect temperature, the perfect strength and to top it off, it had something 'stronger than a soft drink,' that she had requested.

'Anyone else while I am up here?' grandmother said, looking down on everyone from her step ladder.

'I am fine thank you,' Alex politely replied. Sophie didn't answer, she went over to the kitchen sink to help herself to some water from the kitchen tap. Vicky on the other hand,

'I would like a strawberry milkshake, with real strawberries, cream and a sprinkle of chocolate flakes.' She thought she was being very clever. Grandmother climbed down the steps, leaving them where they were. She then made her way over to the other side of the kitchen, to a purple coloured door. It was at ground level, no ladders required. As quick as the door was open, grandmother produced a tall, spirally, twisted glass, filled with the order. Exactly as requested. 'Wow,' Vicky took the glass, nearly dropping it as she tried to take a hold of its twisted shape. Having tasted its contents, she continued with her critique, 'double wow!' Then she downed the contents of the glass, quicker than her stomach would have liked.

Grandmother had not been given a lot of choice in the matter, but she had decided to embrace the changing house and its visitors, for the moment anyway. The changes had brought back many happy memories of what once was. Closing the cupboard door, she said,

'Do you all know how wonderful it is for me to be able to do this once again? There have been far too many, less than magical yesterdays.' She knew that what had happened, could not be forgotten by her guests. She had spent too long guarding what she had to. For the first time, in far too many years, grandmother was letting her guard down. Arriving at the table, grandmother pulled out a chair to sit down. It was the chair she always sat on when in the kitchen. Crooked legs and a back that looked like a tall oak tree, its branches spreading out to support her as she sat down. No one was talking, they were waiting to see what grandmother was going to say, or do, next.

'I know you will all have questions. Firstly I have to say before you ask them all, please consider that there will be consequences to the knowledge that I would share with you.' Grandmother stopped mid sentence and looked over at Sophie, she was back at the side of Alex. 'What has happened today and this evening princess, from you seeing something move in your bedroom this morning, to you two coming together, in pain and now clearly in a connection that you probably don't understand. It is something that I have both dreamt of and dreaded. If we carry on down this road, there will be no return.' It was at this point Alex spoke up.

'So what has happened to me is permanent, I can't leave here?'

Grandmother looked confused,

'What do you mean, you can't leave?' she asked,

'Mum couldn't see me. I could see and hear her, but couldn't touch her. When I came back into the house she saw me again.' Grandmother's face dropped. The enormity of what Alex had said was only clear to her. The house coming to life was exciting, but what Alex had just said was frightening. Grandmother's heart was beating faster than usual. Questions dashed round her mind. How was it possible? What was going to happen? Who was this boy? How had his appearance done what no one thought could ever be done? The happiness of reliving the unexplainable wonderfulness that could be experienced in her home was leaving. A glazed look came over her. Staring through everyone in the room, stories of times and a legend forgot were being brought out of the places in her mind where she had hidden them. Each one arrived with a spark, like little explosions.

'Grandmother are you ok?' Sophie said. Leaving Alex's side, she knelt on the floor next to grandmother and put her arm round her. The barriers to where the memories had been hidden now broken down, grandmother's conscious mind was full. She blinked and looked into Sophie's concerned eyes,

'So we have gone beyond the place of no return. What has happened here today, there is no going back. Only forward. You have all joined this story many thousands of years from its beginning. I do not know how today has come about and why, however one fact is very clear to me. A chapter that has lasted more than three hundred years of yesterdays, has finally come to its end.'

'So if Alex can't leave, seeing as we have also

been in this house, does that mean we can't either?'
Vicky asked in a sarcastic tone. Holding up her empty
glass she then said, 'I don't mind really if all your
cupboards can produce milkshakes like this on
demand.' She was hoping to break the ominous
tension and make everyone laugh. No one did. Sophie
stood up and pulled out the chair next to her
grandmother and sat down. Alex stepped forward
behind her and rested his hands familiarly on her
shoulders. Bang!

'What was that?' Melissa exclaimed. She had been
resting on the kitchen door and felt strong vibrations
from it, as the loud noise was heard from outside the
kitchen.

'I'll go.' Alex's confidence was growing from his
day that saw him take a stance on the bus, to entering
a strangers scary looking garden. Melissa stepped out
of the way as Alex opened the kitchen door and
confidently stepped out,

'The front door is open isn't it?' grandmother
asked. She nudged Sophie to get her attention and
then pointed towards the dolls house.

'Yes,' Alex replied,

'It's fine, just close it,' grandmother said. Alex
walked into the hallway and straight up to the door.
He took hold of it for the briefest of moments and
slammed it shut. Sophie and her grandmother
watched, as at the very same time, the dolls house
front door slammed shut. As Alex began his walk
back to the kitchen, he was stopped by the loud, high
pitched buzz of an insect. He tried to see where it was
coming from, but could see nothing. He did however
feel something. His right shoulder was knocked.
Whatever had been buzzing towards him and had hit
him was gone. The hallway fell silent. Not sure what

had just happened, he ran back to the kitchen.

'Did you see that grandmother?' Sophie asked. The answer was yes, but she wanted to know what Sophie thought she saw,

'No,' was her less than truthful response,

'Really, the door, the front door...' she stopped mid sentence not wanting to sound crazy.

'The front door what?' said grandmother,

'Well, you saw it shut, but there was something else, there, erm,' Sophie said,

'Yes,' grandmother needed her to say it, 'tell me, what did you see?' By this time Alex had returned to the kitchen, slightly out of breath and holding his shoulder.

'I think something flew out the door, or through the door, I don't know,' Sophie said. She was going to go on but before she could, Alex interrupted,

'I think whatever it was flew through me.'

Grandmother turned her attention to Alex,

'You felt it?' she said,

'Felt what? I certainly got hit by something,' Alex said. Grandmother stood up and tottered quickly out of the kitchen. Sophie, still sitting, reached forward and tried to open the dolls house front door. Pushing with her forefinger it did not move. She pinched the tiny door handle and gave it a turn. Although it did turn, it released nothing. The door remained firmly shut. Like all dolls houses, to gain access to the inside of the property there was a big hinge to the side so the whole front could be opened. Melissa, knowing that, had joined Sophie and without saying a word, flipped the latch on the side which kept the front in place and tried to swing it open.

'It's stuck.' The first words Melissa had spoken since receiving her perfectly made coffee with a kick.

She had no more luck than Sophie had just had trying to open the front door. Just as Vicky stepped forward to have a go, grandmother returned.

'No more playing games. Alex I need to ask you questions and I need answers. Anyone who is not of this house should not have felt what you felt.' Grandmother kept making assumptions about the evening's events. Each one, as it turned out, were far off the mark. Grandmother had at last been awoken to the truth. What was happening could be the end of anything good. What was happening could be the end of any hope that the happiness that once was, what had been forgotten, could be returned.

'Before I ask you any more questions, I need you to come with me,' grandmother said. Standing holding the kitchen door open, she gestured towards Alex. He looked over at his mum, Melissa, who pulled an unknowing face and shrugged her shoulders. Anchor provided some encouragement. He had come up behind Alex and was nudging him forward. To Vicky's surprise, Bart left her side and joined Anchor. Alex looked back at the two of them, a little annoyed at the contact that was getting firmer with every nudge. He got the not so subtle hint and said,

'Ok, ok.'

Alex, Melissa, Sophie and Vicky left the kitchen, followed by the two dogs, their tales wagging, happy that they had successfully done their job. As soon as Alex was close enough, grandmother grabbed his forearm and pulled him towards the front door. On arriving at the closed door, grandmother said,

'I need you to do something for me. I want you to rest your hand on the doorframe.'

'Why?' asked Alex.

'I need to see something,' was grandmothers response.

'Sorry, but until you tell me what is happening here, I think I would prefer not to,' Alex resolutely replied. Grandmother still had hold of Alex's forearm. Catching him by surprise and giving Alex no choice, she lifted it up and pushed his hand onto the doorframe. As quickly as it was placed, Alex was thrown back as though had received a massive electric shock.

'Alex!' Melissa shouted as she ran over to Alex. 'Get back you horrible old woman!'

Having shouted the hurtful words towards grandmother, she felt bad as quickly as she had said them, but her focus was Alex.

'I'm ok mum, it's fine.' He wasn't. The point on his hand that for years he thought was just a mole, that had bled earlier, was sending shooting pains up his arm, into his chest and up into his head. Holding his breath and closing his eyes, Alex tried to get control of the pain. Achieving partial success, he slowly opened his eyes and looked towards the door. As his eyes began to focus, he was completely distracted from the remaining pain he felt by what he saw,

'Can you guys see that?'

Melissa, Sophie and Vicky were kneeling round Alex, each with a comforting hand on his arm. They weren't looking at the door. 'Look.' Alex pointed to the door. Following the line of his finger to where it was pointing, they all turned to look.

'What are we supposed to be looking at?' Melissa asked,

'That, the doorframe!' Alex replied,

'I'm not seeing anything,' Vicky piped up,

followed by, 'but that doesn't mean anything,' she
said with a giggle. Alex was completely confused.
Why couldn't they see what he was seeing. Sitting
himself up and pushing his comforters aside, he got to
his feet and made his way over to take a closer look.

'You all really can't see this?' Alex asked again.

'What are you seeing boy?' grandmother asked.
Like the others, she could only see the old door and
its frame, newer than it had been, but there was
nothing special about it.

'It's beautiful,' Alex said. It wasn't a word he
could remember ever saying, but it was the only word
that could describe what only he could see.

'I think the bang on your head on the garden gate
has effected you Alex,' Vicky said in her joking
voice.

'Let alone what just happened,' Melissa said with
a far more serious tone. She was getting very
concerned for her son and had lost all patience with
this old woman, whose mood and focus seemed to
change as quick as every breath that came from her
mouth. 'I want to get you checked out, we can't see
anything and...' Melissa stopped herself before going
further. As concerned as she was, she didn't want to
panic Alex.

'Let the boy speak,' grandmother said. She was
not about to let him leave as she stepped in between
Alex and the front door. She knew there was more at
stake than anyone there could know. As physically
strong as Melissa was, her motherly protective
instincts were even stronger. It didn't take much to
push grandmother to one side with one arm and to
protectively pull Alex in to her with the other.

'Alex, don't let your mother keep you from what
has begun. If you are seeing what I think you are,

what you have is no concussion!' Grandmother's words were no match for the arm of Alex's mother, who guided him from the house and away from an angry looking grandmother. They left behind a confused looking Sophie and Vicky and two dogs, who were sitting next to each other, like they had known each other for the longest of times. As Alex stepped through the doorway on to the top step he said,

'Mum, the doorframe, it was lit up. I couldn't make out what they were, but things were moving!' Melissa did not respond. She had not heard him. Her arm that had been wrapped round him fell to her side, empty. Alex was gone.

CHAPTER 9

Alex felt a tickling sensation as his mum's arm passed through him. It was a totally different experience to the ones he'd had earlier, when his mum had walked through him and Vicky's hand went through him. Looking down to where the tickling sensation was coming from, Alex watched his mum's arm. As it moved through him, tiny sparkles of crackling light fired in every direction.

'Where did he go?' Sophie said in a surprised voice. She closed her eyes, holding them shut for a few moments. On opening them slowly, she hoped to see that Alex had re-appeared.

'Old woman you better start giving me some answers. Stuff your questions, where is Alex?' Melissa had pushed her way back into the house. She looked around to see if somehow he had slipped past her, back inside.

'What are you talking about? He is right there.' Vicky pointed to where she could see Alex standing just outside the front door.

'You can see him?' grandmother asked in a curious voice. It was a fact she had somehow missed when the group had entered the house and described a similar experience earlier. 'Interesting. Go and get him for me.' Vicky was slightly confused at the request, as far as she was concerned Alex was standing within a couple of feet of grandmother,

'Oh, hang on, ok, right, so he has gone again!' Vicky said. She had missed Melissa's arm falling through him, she was too busy looking at the ever growing painted tree. 'You know that I won't be able to touch him either, yes? Remember the same thing happened earlier,' she said looking at Melissa.

Having realised he was not there, but was there, again, Alex had turned back to look at the house. His focus was on the doorframe. It had begun showing the same details lit up outside as he had seen inside. Lines, patterns, shapes, so bright it was difficult to make out what the details were actually supposed to be. Although Vicky had a good idea that her getting him in was not going to work, she reached out of the doorway to take hold of his arm.

'Nope, see I can't get him!' Vicky said. 'The sparkles were pretty though!'

'Sparkles, what… it doesn't matter, but you can see him?' asked Melissa. Vicky's attempt to take hold of him had taken Alex's attention from the doorframe. As he looked over at the group, only Vicky was making eye contact with him,

'Can you hear me?' Alex asked,

'Yes, I mean yes Melissa I can see him and yes Alex I can hear you,' Vicky replied.

'Vicky, what you are able to do, it makes all the sense in the world. Well not in this world, but it does in the world that Alex is in,' grandmother said. Her words quietened the noise of heavy breathing, muttering and dog whimpering. 'Let me explain. Your illness is a symptom of the world in which we live. It is a symptom that does not actually have to be. Everything that is happening right here, right now, has more importance than any of you could perceive.' She looked over towards Melissa, 'I am sorry if I have appeared to be strange this evening. My purpose here is to protect this place. To protect the other place. To protect all that are both here and there.'

Before she could continue, the tree moved. All inside the house saw it. The movement didn't come from the fast growing leaves, it had come from something sitting on the tip of a branch end situated on the wall, above the doorframe, 'Old friend, it is good to see you. But why are you being seen?' grandmother asked.

'Woof, woof,' Anchor added to the conversation,

'Yes I know, but he touched the frame and nothing,' grandmother responded. Anchor and grandmother, oddly to the onlookers, seemed to understand exactly what each other were saying. Anchor walked up to the doorframe and jumped up at it. He rested his paws on a particular point, began sniffing at it and then let out another knowing bark in the direction of grandmother.

'Alex,' Sophie exclaimed. He had stepped back in through the doorway to see what Anchor was barking at. His return inside made him visible to all once again.

'That bit, it doesn't have any light coming from its shapes,' Alex said, having taken a closer look at Anchor's focus of attention. Anchor, happy his job was done, popped back down onto all fours.

'Oh,' grandmother said with a knowing excitement. She disappeared off to the kitchen, moments later returning with two small splinters of wood. One was no bigger than a centimetre and the other about three. When she built the fabulous dolls house birthday present, she had wanted to make it as real as possible. She had decided the best way to do that, was to add a few parts which she took from the unexpectedly, wonderfully, perfect of homes itself. The two small splinters she was carrying, had come from the skirting board at the base of the tree and from the doorframe. She had built them into the dolls house, exactly at the point she had taken them from the house she was imitating. Anchor's keen eye and indication to the dull patch on the doorframe had jolted her memory. In that moment, she also understood why the dolls house was imitating everything that was happening - the roots growing through and under the table, the front door opening and closing, the light coming from inside.

Firstly, grandmother bent down and replaced the splinter at the base of the painted tree. As soon as she did, they all felt and heard quiet rumbles under their feet. Small undulations could be seen pushing up and out from the wooden floor at the base of the tree, visible at the edge of the red rug. As they grew and spread, making their way under the rug, they cast shadows, adding extra patterns to the beautiful rug, now full of new life.

'Roots, they look like roots.' Sophie's observation received nods of agreement from the group of onlookers. Bart and Anchor both let out a bark as the growing, spreading roots, passed under their paws. The roots had seemingly grown as much as they were going to and the tree itself began to creak. The flat painted tree, was not so flat anymore. The trunk could clearly be seen, its aged bark tracks pushing out. The branches began moving as though they were in a gale force wind, the leaves creating so much noise that the dogs barks were muffled. Everyone in the hallway was getting buffeted around as the noise and wind got louder and stronger. Sophie and Melissa grabbed each other in an effort to stay in the place they stood. Vicky took hold of the still open front door and grandmother grabbed the half tree trunk that had appeared. The growing, movement, vibrations and wind coming to an end, grandmother, with her balance restored, made her way over to the doorframe.

'This is the reason why Anchor,' answering his barked question, as to why there was no light coming from the part of the doorframe he had indicated at. She placed the tiny one centimetre splinter into the part of the doorframe she had taken it from. It was barely visible, certainly unnoticeable if a person didn't know where to look. As soon as she did, Alex, who was still standing in the doorway let out a yell. An ear piercing yell that stopped the dogs from barking instantly. The doorframe that had been lighting up and moving in an unnatural way had engulfed him. The open doorway was filled with a light as bright as the sun and Alex was trapped in the middle of it. The cool winter air that had been coming in through the open door, was replaced with a heat that had caused Vicky, Melissa and Sophie to back away. The door of the living room flew open as the house offered them an escape and they accepted it gladly. Grandmother however had stepped forward as the rest stepped back. She was stood right in front of Alex. Seemingly unaffected by the bright light and its heat, she reached her hands up to him.

'Alex, it's ok. You will be ok, don't fight it,' grandmother said. Alex had gone quiet. She could see in his face he was in pain and wanted to calm him. She had a good idea of what was happening to him and knew that fighting it would cause him more pain than he could bear.

Alex was feeling everything. Every person's pain, every animal's pain, every part of Mother Nature that was in pain. Alex didn't hear grandmother's calming words, he couldn't. What he was and where he was, had not been for thousands of years. As wise, knowledgable and experienced as grandmother was, what Alex was experiencing was beyond her understanding.

'Alex, stay with me,' grandmother said, hoping that she was getting through to him. Alex, having fallen silent for a few moments, began to scream.

'Grandmother, come over here. Please!' Sophie shouted from the safety of the calm, quiet, comfortable living room.

'No, I have to help him,' was grandmother's response. She felt he could take no more. Her hands gripped Alex's arms, the heat somehow not affecting her as she tried as hard as she could, to pull him free from the trap of light. With all her strength, she could not move him a millimetre, it was as though he was set in stone. Letting go of his arms and raising up on her tiptoes, grandmother reached up to take his face in her hands, hoping that somehow that would bring his focus to her. As the tips of her fingers softly touched his cheeks, a burst of light exploded out of Alex. It threw her across the hallway, her flight coming to a painful stop on the bottom step of the staircase.

'Grandmother!' Sophie exclaimed, leaving the safety of the living room and running over to where her grandmother sat.

'I am fine. Go to him, go and help him,' grandmother said. Sophie was glad to see her grandmother was fine, but with the heat from the light burning the skin on the back of her neck as she crouched in front of her grandmother, ten feet away from Alex, as much as she wanted to, how could she possibly get close to help him. Her eyes squinted from the brightness and the heat, as she looked to see if there was a route that would keep her out of the light. There wasn't.

'I can't grandmother, I can't,' Sophie said, whipping her head so that her hair fell, covering her neck from the burning heat. Melissa felt helpless as she looked at Alex. It went against every bone in her body to just stand and watch, to do nothing.

'Do something. This is your house, this is your doing, help my boy,' Melissa shouted over to grandmother. Vicky put her arm round her. Bart and Anchor stepped in front of her and nuzzled at her hands, all trying to comfort her in their own way.

'Help me up princess, we have to do something,' grandmother said. Taking hold of Sophie's hand she got to her feet. Looking over to Alex, who could only be seen as a silhouette in the centre of the light, grandmother said, 'Come with me. Stay behind me you will be fine.' The pair started to make their way back over towards him. Sophie did as grandmother had suggested and took cover behind her. As they edged slowly closer across the uneven floor, Melissa shouted out to them,

'Wait. Look.' Alex had fallen silent. The solid black silhouette, which was all they could see of him, was being punctured by two faint purple lights. The lights came from the place his eyes would be. The hint of purple in Alex's eyes, that could on occasion be seen by those who looked closely enough, was visible to all, in a most unusual way.

'It's him,' Sophie said under her breath. The feeling of safety she felt within her dreams whenever her shadowed saviour arrived, was exactly what she was feeling in that moment.

Alex was not the only one who had gone quiet. The sound of the growing tree and its leaves, the dogs barking, all had stopped. Alex was motionless, he looked as though he had been placed in a state of cryostasis. The bright light around Alex had dulled, the purple lights looked brighter now in contrast. As the group looked at him, something else could be seen that could not be explained. Light could be seen beneath Alex's feet. He was floating.

Sophie had stepped out from behind her grandmother. The air having cooled, the radiated heat she had been hiding from gone, the hallway's temperature returning to what it should be, she walked right up to Alex. Her heart pounding in her chest, nervous as to what may happen to her, she placed her hand on his arm. There was no reaction, she felt nothing. Looking up into the purple light of his eyes, Sophie thought she heard a whisper. She was sure it was Alex's voice. Staring into his eyes, her hand slowly moved down his arm towards his hand. As soon as their hands touched, a warm pulse of energy passed between them. The pulse left as quickly as it arrived, as the light holding Alex vanished. Trying to catch him, Sophie's small self had no chance of holding up his dead weight. They both fell to the floor. The fall was like a starting pistol to grandmother and Melissa. They both arrived at the location at the same time, crashing into each other as they did. Vicky didn't leave the safety of the living room. She was happy not to get involved but just to watch with Bart and Anchor, who were also happy to be out of the unpredictable hallway.

'I'm fine, really I'm fine,' Sophie said. She had got herself to her knees, looking at Alex who was face down on the floor. She reached over and tried to turn him over. Again, her size and weight relative to his, meant that as hard as she tried, she could not budge him. Melissa joined Sophie on the floor and without any communication, they performed a perfectly synchronised pull, rolling Alex over. On his back, lower half in and upper half out of the house, he made no movement.

'Why isn't he moving?' Sophie looked back to her grandmother and asked.

'I don't know.' was her reply.

Having checked him over physically, Melissa was happy that nothing was broken. She got to her feet and stepped out of the house so that she could take hold of his shoulders,

'Can you guys please help me lift him somewhere more comfortable,' she asked. Vicky was happy to help and made her way out of the safe place, taking hold of his left leg. Sophie got hold of his right,

'One, two... three,' Melissa counted down to the lift. As she arrived at number three and put all her energy into lifting him, his upper body, the part of him outside the house, started to fade. Her hands were no longer touching him, 'No, no, not again, pull him inside girls, NOW!' she shouted at Sophie and Vicky. They reacted instantly. With one hard pull, surprisingly, they managed to get Alex fully inside the house, just before his upper torso was completely gone. He was now completely visible and touchable.

'One, two... three.' Melissa counted down again. This time she had full contact with Alex's shoulders and together they managed to lift him up and off the floor. On their feet, taking his full weight, grandmother appeared and helped by supporting him at the waist.

'We can take him into the living room. There is a nice big sofa in there we can put him on,' grandmother said. Having shuffled their way in, they deposited Alex as gently as they could onto the overly sized, worn, brown leather sofa covered in pillows.

Melissa began a more thorough medical assessment of her son. He was breathing, his pulse was normal, his temperature seemed to be fine. Everything seemed to be fine, but he was completely non responsive.

'My instincts are telling me to call for an ambulance. Can you give me any reason why I shouldn't?' Melissa asked, directing the question at grandmother, figuring, hoping, there was a chance grandmother knew what was happening to her son. There was clearly more going on than her medical training had prepared her for. Melissa was holding out for a reason not to have to take Alex to hospital, where she would inevitably have to answer a lot of uncomfortable questions.

'Can you give me a moment?' was grandmother's response as she left the room, closing the door behind her.

'Where is she going now?' Vicky's question was ignored by everyone as Melissa said,

'You look as confused as I am Sophie. You live here, is this normal?' Sophie, who had been leant over Alex, resting on his leg, sat back on her heels.

'I have lived here since I was eight and it's always been an odd, but fun place to live. Honestly, until Alex's visit earlier, nothing like this has ever happened.' Pausing as she reflected back over the day, she realised maybe that statement wasn't entirely true. 'Although, you know what? I thought I saw something in my room this morning and that was before Alex had been here, before I had even met him.'

'What was it?' Vicky asked,

'It was the doorframe, I think it was like a butterfly

or something. It was gone as quick as I saw it, but there was definitely something there,' Sophie replied. She then recalled how when she pointed it out to grandmother, she seemed to get annoyed and then quickly changed the subject. Without saying another word, Sophie stood up and left the room in a hurry, slamming the door behind her as she did. Melissa and Vicky were left behind, wondering what they should do.

'I am up for an adventure or two…' Vicky, standing behind the sofa looking down on Alex, was interrupted before she could finish her sentence,

'I am not!' Melissa interrupted. Having made her decision, she took her mobile phone from her pocket and began to dial. As the phone rang, she had time to reflect on what to say when they answered and began their questions. She had still not managed to get hold of official, fake, documentation to say who they were. Miss and Master Rice were still Miss and Master Herd. But Miss and Master Herd had been on the verge of being discovered as not really being Miss and Master Herd. That's why they left where they had lived previously, in a hurry.

'999 what is your emergency?' Melissa closed her eyes, took in a deep breath and then hung up the phone.

'Vicky can you stay here with Alex please. Just shout if anything changes.' Melissa stood up and left the room, in search of the house's full time occupants. Anchor had been sitting at the door, unlike the two that had already left, he decided not to follow. Having seen Vicky move from the back of the sofa round to the front to sit next to Alex, followed by Bart, Anchor decided that it seemed like a good idea to do the same. Having made his way over, he sat down next to the motionless Alex and placed his chin on his chest.

Standing in the hallway, Melissa listened for any sound that would have given her a hint as to the location of Sophie and her grandmother. Waiting, she took a moment to look around. The floor was still uneven from the roots of the tree, the wall still cracked from where the tree had pushed itself out from it. The staircase was in darkness, apart from small hints of colour given off by the limited moonlight shining through the stained glass window. Turning round, Melissa looked at the door where the awful image of her son in pain had been. His screams coming back to her, sent shivers down her spine. A silent river of tears began falling from her eyes. Staring at the door through the blur of tears, Melissa saw a pulse of light shoot around its frame, creating a hypnotic, beautiful wave of patterns. She wiped her eyes and looked again. The pulse of light seemed to bounce as it reached the bottom of the door frame, returning in the opposite direction, repeating the same sequence as it reached the other side. Like a heartbeat, it danced its way back and forth from one side to the other. Transfixed by the light, Melissa didn't even notice when Sophie appeared next to her.

'What is that?'

Melissa jumped as Sophie spoke. Not having any answer and remembering her purpose in leaving Alex, Melissa asked,

'Where is she?'

Sophie didn't say anything, she just pointed towards a closed door on the other side of the hallway. 'Ok,' Melissa said, leaving Sophie to stare at the light show by herself.

Without knocking, Melissa turned the handle,

pushed open the big, heavy, dark wood door and
stepped into the room filled with books. If there were
shelves, they couldn't be seen for the wobbly stacks
of books piled from the floor, almost to the ceiling.
Some looked ancient, some looked new and they
formed a corridor which Melissa was funnelled
through. The floorboards squeaked with every step
she took and every step she took, caused movement in
the particular stack of books she was passing.

'Hello,' Melissa said quietly. She was nervous to
make too much noise, just in case she caused an
avalanche of books. There was no answer. As she
made her way round a bend in the claustrophobic
corridor of books, it widened. Again, she said 'Hello,'
this time slightly louder. The feeling of oppression
she had been feeling, caused by the thousands of
books bearing down on her, eased, as she stepped out
and away from the last two piles.

The surprisingly large room she found herself in,
was being dimly lit by one huge chandelier. The light
from each of the lightbulbs was being restricted by
small, moth eaten, red, tassel edged lampshades. The
bulbs light was further dulled by a thick covering of
dust, which Melissa could smell being burnt off as the
bulbs warmed. At the far end of the room, Melissa
could see a huge desk. On it was a single reading
lamp, which was lighting up scattered scraps of paper
and grandmother's face. She hadn't noticed Melissa,
she was too busy intently reading whatever the scraps
were telling her. The desk's thick, uneven edged top
was slanted off to one side, held up by four bark
covered tree trunks. Apart from the scraps of paper,
the desks surface was the only tidy looking expanse
in the room.

As Melissa tried to make her way over to where

grandmother sat, she slipped. Looking down at what had caused it, she saw that the dark floor was completely covered in discarded books. Shuffling her feet along the ground, under the books, like a snow plough making its way through thick snow, she pushed her way through. Finally at the desk, she rested her hands on it. Using the cold wood as support, she looked across at grandmother and asked, 'Can you hear me?' Still she got no response.

Shaking her head, Melissa made her way round the desk through the slope of books falling from it, books that had no further use or interest to their reader. So as not to slip or fall, she held the edges of the desk tightly. Up close, beyond the scraps of paper, Melissa could see that the top of the slanted desk was as natural as the legs that held it up. It was a cross section of what must have been an incredible, huge tree. Its uneven edges stretched eight feet in one direction and six feet in the other. On its surface were intricate carvings, which Melissa thought should be investigated at a later date. Round its edges, hidden in the shadows, were crooked drawers, some closed, some fully open, some ajar. Each one added to the challenge of making it round the desk without falling.

Seemingly completely oblivious to Melissa's safe arrival at her side, grandmother intensely stared at the scraps of paper. On them were sketches of rooms, four of which Melissa recognised. The hallway, kitchen, living room where she had left Alex her son, and the room she was now standing in. Looking closer, Melissa could see that there were notes scribbled around parts of each sketch. The one grandmother seemed to be most interested in, was the hallway sketch. There were more notes scribbled on that scrap than on any of the other pictures Melissa could see.

The seat grandmother was perched on, looked very similar to the chair in the kitchen, but larger. The back had the same spread of branches. The seat however was not only larger, but it had what looked like a very comfortable maroon, worn, leather cushion, held in place by old brass pins. The same maroon leather covered the equally padded armrests. It looked like a fabulously comfy chair that was showing signs of its well used age.

'I can't make out the handwritten scribbles. What do they say?' Melissa asked, not expecting a response.

'They don't tell me what I want to know. That is what they say!' grandmother said, frustrated, her focus and interest in the very old looking scraps of paper not giving her what she was looking for. 'I was hoping they would give me answers to what has been happening to your...' sitting back in the chair she looked up at Melissa, 'I was going to say, "your son," but he is not, is he?'

Melissa stepped back and angrily responded,

'I am his mother. I have always been his mother. I have sacrificed more than you could ever know for MY son!'

In moments of confrontation or stress, Melissa had an incredible ability to act, think and speak with such calmness and clarity. 'I spoke out of turn this evening. I said something to you that I should not have. But I can confirm to you, I have and always will be the best person in Alex's life. Yes I found him, he had been abandoned. Not a single day has passed that I haven't tried in some way to find his family. I have stayed true to the note that was left with him.' Melissa couldn't help herself, 'From what

I have seen here tonight, I have been a more loving and protective mother to Alex than you have been to that poor young girl, who was making her own way to hospital tonight. And you question me and my place as Alex's mother!'

Melissa's speech took grandmother by surprise. She completely ignored the challenge to her suitability as a caring grandmother, she was only interested in one thing,

'Where is the note?'

'The note?' Melissa asked,

'Yes the note. Where is the note left with Alex when you found him?'

Grandmother's interest in the note annoyed Melissa. Her son was lying unconscious in the living room and rather than giving her answers to help him, she was focused on a letter written sixteen years ago. Grandmother stood up and took hold of Melissa's hand,

'Come my dear, you need to get me the note,' she said excitedly grabbing Melissa by the arm. The strength of the little old lady surprised Melissa, as she got pulled back towards the minefield of books.

'I don't need to go and find the letter. It's with me at all times,' Melissa said, struggling to stay on her feet. They stopped in the middle of the room, directly under the chandelier,

'Let me see it,' grandmother said. Melissa had always been nervous of the letter being lost, or being found by the wrong person. So ten years earlier, she had the contents of the note perfectly duplicated in the handwriting it was written in, tattooed on her body. There was two parts to the note. One part was tattooed across her left upper back, the second was tattooed on her right side. It was a painful experience, but one she knew was worth every second of the three hours of self- inflicted torture. She would never have forgiven herself if the last words left by Alex's birth mother could not be passed on to him. The most heartbreaking goodbye was tattooed on her back. The accompanying poem, or was it a spell, Melissa was never quite sure, filled her entire right side.

Melissa started to run over the tattooed words in her mind. She had memorised them all the day she first read them. A feeling of excitement was welling up inside her, as she thought she may at last have some context for them. This strange house and its two occupants, were they the two and Alex the one to make the three? Unable to hide her excitement, she was quick to pull up her top exposing her side, showing what she had hidden. The darkness of the room made it hard to read from where she stood, so grandmother slowly lowered herself to her knees. As close to the words as she could get, she began to read,

"A touch of one is not enough
A touch of two will fail
A touch of three may bring new life
A touch of three... may prevail

When two become one
When the three become two
When life is reawakened
The threes' truth will become true

'Is there more?' grandmother asked. Melissa looked down and realised that the last verse was partly covered by the top of her trousers, so she pulled them down over her hip.

Allow this legend a chance to be reborn
Allow this legend to be opened once more
Allow this legend to create anew
Allow this legend to once again become part of you"

Having finished reading all that was there, grandmother asked 'You said that there was a note, this is not so much a note, is there more?' Melissa wanted answers as much as the keenly enquiring grandmother. She let go of the top of her trousers and grabbed her top, pulling it up at the back and over her head. She kept her arms inside the sleeves of the top and her dignity at the front. The words tattooed on her back now revealed, read,

"I have watched you and I have now chosen you. You are a strong, pure and loving woman, whose dark eyes sparkle with an excitement for life rarely seen. I have chosen you to be my son's mother. I cannot tell you why I must do what I am this day, a task that my heart may not survive. However he must be safe, he must be loved, he must be kept secret from the world - this I charge you to do. Your life will never be the same, your life will never be your own, your life will be beyond hard, but you will have the love of my baby boy. At the beginning of his true beginning, your sacrifice for my son, Alex Huggins, will be rewarded with love, joy and understanding of more than you could possibly know. Now take my boy and leave this place you call home, stay safe, stay true, stay alive. I thank you with all the love I have left in my broken heart."

'I have read about a man with an unusual colour to his eyes somewhere before,' grandmother said out loud. She wasn't really directing her words at Melissa as much as just speaking to herself.

'Eyes! There is no mention of unusual eyes in what you have just read,' Melissa said. Grandmother didn't respond, instead she made her way back to the desk where the scraps of paper were still laying. Melissa, left standing in the middle of the room, pulled her top back over her head. Sitting back in her big chair, grandmother opened one of the many drawers and produced a magnifying glass, which she placed on the table,

'Where is it?' grandmother said,

'Where is what?' Melissa responded. But again grandmother was talking to herself. She frantically searched through the piles, pushing aside the scraps of paper that didn't give her what she wanted. 'Can I help you?' Melissa asked. Grandmother looked up at her and said,

'I am trying to find the drawing of the front door.'

'Was it in this pile when you looked before?' Melissa questioned,

'You know what, no I don't think it was.'

Grandmother stood up and made her way over to a shelf behind her. Stacked on it were what looked like fifty thousand sheets of paper. 'This could take a while!' Melissa thought to herself. Arriving at the shelf, grandmother looked down at the floor,

'Ah, there you are.' She bent down, picked up what she had found and returned to the desk.

'Have to admit, I was not expecting that to go so quickly,' Melissa said.

'Never assume all is so complicated, quite often the easiest reality is the right one,' grandmother replied as she picked up the magnifying glass.

'What are you looking for,' Melissa asked.

'I will know when I find it,' grandmother

responded. The only thing drawn on the scrap of paper was a doorframe. No door, no walls, just a frame. As with the other sketches there were notes written around the picture, but grandmother wasn't interested in them. She was slowly, methodically, searching the frame itself.

'Look. See I knew I had read something before.'

Melissa joined her looking into the large magnifying glass. What she saw in the sketched frame was images of all kinds of animals, trees, rivers, hills and mountains. The part that Melissa was being directed to look at by grandmother, was a section on the top of the doorframe. Mixed in with the sketches were the words,

'unnatural light from the eyes of one, chosen by the healer to become one,' below that was written a single word, 'now' and below that,

'Delivered, Received, A Gift Of Nature's Freeing Love, Yours'

Grandmother was beside herself with excitement. 'How could I not have seen that before. Look at the first letter of each word.'

'What?' Melissa asked. Grandmother replied with one word,

'DRAGONFLY.'

CHAPTER 10

'Hey, anyone! he is awake,' Vicky shouted. Anchor removed his chin from Alex's chest and barked his own alert. It had been ten minutes since Vicky, Anchor and Bart had been left alone with the unconscious Alex. Vicky had done as she was told, watching and waiting for the slightest sign of movement.

'Alex, how are you?' Vicky asked. Receiving no response, she turned away from him and shouted again,'Melissa, come here!' Looking back at Alex, something had changed. The movement she had initially seen from him was indeed slight, his eyes opening the smallest of amounts. What she saw now from his slightly open eyes was purple. Pale to begin with, but the colour got stronger and stronger, eventually replacing the blue colour of his eyes completely. Vicky had seen the purple light coming from his eyes when he was stuck in the door's light, but this was different. It wasn't a light, it was his actual eyes changing colour. Being alone with him, she was slightly uncomfortable.

'Alex?' she said in a nervous tone, 'Alex, you are freaking me out here.' Anchor was up, he had made his way over to the door and was scratching at it in an attempt to get someone's attention. Bart, at Vicky's side, was pulling at her sleeve. His interpretation of the situation was that she was in danger and he wanted to get her to safety. For his size, he was a strong little fella. Vicky, getting the hint, stood up and walking backwards, didn't look away from Alex until she bashed into the closed door. She reached back behind herself and felt for the door handle, turned it, opened it and slowly backed out of the room. Once the two dogs had made their escape as well, she closed the door.

Having gathered her thoughts, Vicky turned away from the door to go and find help. In doing so, she lost her footing on the uneven root covered floor and fell backwards into Sophie. Sophie was still watching the light that danced back and forth around the front door's doorframe. She managed to react quickly and stayed on her feet. Vicky did not. From her seated position, Vicky reached a hand up for some help, Sophie obliged,

'Seems to be a thing in here tonight,' Sophie said,

'What is?' Vicky asked, Sophie smiled as she said,

'Floor surfing!'

Anchor, completely forgetting about Alex, had wandered over to the front door. He was having great fun jumping backwards and forwards in an effort to catch the light playing on the doorframe. Bart sat down and watched, the expression on his face being one of a disapproving parent, who felt their child should be acting far more maturely. Vicky was at a point that nothing was going to surprise her, so she didn't comment on the doorframe.

'I think Alex is awake.' Vicky didn't mention the strange light coming from his eyes. Sophie quickly snapped out of her trance and dashed straight to the closed living room door. At the very same moment from the other side of the hallway, the library door flew open as grandmother, followed by Melissa, hastily appeared. Vicky repeated to them what she had just said to Sophie,

'I think Alex is awake.' Without a word they

dashed across the hallway. The dogs got left there as Vicky, the last in, closed the door behind everyone. The first person to the sofa was Sophie.

'What made you think he was awake?' Sophie asked Vicky, seeing no sign of him being awake.

'His eyes, they,' she paused,

'They what?' Melissa asked,

'They opened, they... I thought he was waking up, but they,' not able to finish her sentence, grandmother interrupted,

'They were not his eyes.'

'Yes. How did you know?' Vicky replied.

'Let's have a look at the young man,' grandmother said, whilst stepping round the low backed sofa. Melissa had taken hold of his wrist and was checking his pulse. It seemed to be faster than it should be, but nothing that she was worried about.

'Did he say anything, did he move?' grandmother asked.

'No, his eyes just opened a tiny bit. I turned, shouted on you all, then when I looked back at him his eyes looked purple!' Vicky said, standing on the other side of the room.

'So he definitely didn't move?' Melissa asked.

'No, sorry, maybe I should have stayed with him,' Vicky said.

'It's fine my dear,' grandmother comfortingly said 'nothing would have been any different.' Grandmother left the group huddled around Alex and made her way over to a comfy looking leather chair, the only single seat in the room and sat down.

'I have an idea. Not sure if it will work, but I think it's worth a try,' grandmother said to the quiet room.

'What?' Melissa asked.

'Having read what I now have, discovered what I

now have, added to what I knew before, I think that we should take Alex back to the front door. I think we should take him with you Sophie.'

'Me?' Sophie responded, turning to look at grandmother, 'Why me?'

'You, because you are part of a very important bloodline of families. Generations of which are connected to this house and others like it, in a way that is wonderful,' grandmother replied.

'We need more than that, I mean connected how?' Melissa asked. Giving Alex's cheek a gentle stroke, she stood up. She made her way over and sat down on one of the two smaller leather sofas, that were to the side of the one Alex was laying on. A loud scratching came from the closed door giving everyone a fright.

'It'll just be the dogs,' Vicky said and immediately went over to let them in. Once in, she made her way over to join Melissa on the sofa. Sophie stayed where she was. The only movement she made was changing from her kneeling position to a seated one, on the floor in front of Alex. She stayed close enough to see any changes, or to hear any words that he may whisper. She didn't know why, but she had an overwhelming desire to protect him.

Although showing signs of being well used, the living room was welcoming and comfortable. The only things that matched in the room were the seats, which were a comfy, soft, worn leather. Three tall lamps were standing around the room. Each one gave off a warm colourful light, shining through their individually designed multicoloured glass. Paintings of every genre, style and technique covered three of the walls. Each one gave an insight into the time and life of every occupant who had been lucky enough to call the house home. The wooden floor was totally covered in rugs, some colourful, some plain, some with pictures woven into them, all showing differing signs of age. On the opposite wall to the door was a fireplace. It wasn't the biggest, but like the pictures and the front doorframe, it told many stories. Protruding from the old dark wood were carvings, fascinating to whoever took time to examine them. Above the fireplace was the only part of the room that did not look cluttered. There was just one large painting - a family portrait, two adults and two children. Looking at it, Melissa thought that the mother and the two children showed a remarkable resemblance to both grandmother and Sophie.

'If you can bear with me, I shall explain how Sophie is connected, how this house and many others like it have been forgotten,' grandmother said. As she did, she stood up and walked over to the fireplace. Not being the tallest of ladies, she didn't have to reach down too far to pick up a couple of logs that had been sitting to the side of the fireplace. She placed them on to the over the top, ornately designed, empty fire grate and stood back. The two logs instantly burst into life. Their flickering flames reached high above them and out of sight as they found their way up the chimney. The supernatural flames gave off a warmth that filled the room instantly. Returning to her seat, she crossed the path of both Anchor and Bart. The flickering flames were far too inviting to look at from a distance and they seemed to have made the decision at the very same time - they were heading for the fireplace. Once there, they flopped on the floor, crashing into each other as they did. Grandmother sat back in her chair. Looking over at her expectant audience, she took a deep breath and began.

'Sophie, you and I are from a family who have lived in this house and various forms of this house, in this very place, for thousands of years. This is not the only house of its kind, but today and for too long, it is, as far as I am aware, the last one that could one day become what all once were. There is a reality, that over the last three hundred years has passed from fact to fairytale, from legend to fiction, to forgotten. Today, your sixteenth birthday Sophie, I had hoped for the first time in far too many generations, the story could once more become reality.' Grandmothers story went on as all sat in silence. Without interruption, she was so glad to be able to speak out what she had hidden inside for too long. She was tired. She had waited and kept hopeful for so many years. She had watched as new families came and went. Hundreds, thousands of days blending into one long dark day, working away at her carvings and toys, just waiting.

'I have to share with you a truth that at first you may find hard to believe. A truth that I have kept hidden for many years, over three hundred years actually. I was born three hundred and seventy years ago today. The painful truth that I have carried with me for these three hundred years is that my family are the reason for the loss of the most beautiful of realities. You, my dear princess Sophie, are my grandchild, thirteen generations removed. You come from my son and his children. My precious boy who I watched pass away two hundred and ninety years ago. You are part of this long line of family, who were part of a very different reality. We were the guardians of a gift that has long been forgotten. A gift that I learned some years ago that was given to just one man, for all of us, many thousands of years ago.'

'I don't understand. How does all this mean I can help Alex?' Sophie asked, completely ignoring the fact that grandmother had just said that she was three hundred and seventy years old.

'Having seen what has happened to you today, I believe that you, with all you are, will wake Alex up and in doing so, will wake us all up into a new beginning,' was grandmothers response. Melissa on the other hand, had not glossed over the fact that the old woman in front of her, had just given her age as an age that was completely impossible.

'How can you possibly be that old?' Melissa asked.

'I don't know. I, to this day, cannot understand how it is possible for me to outlive generations of my family. What I do know, is that it is for a reason and that somehow this house and its special guest has made it possible,' grandmother said.

'A dragonfly?' Melissa said,

'Yes, one that lives here, my home, Dragonfly Manor,' grandmother replied. Sophie and Vicky did not understand the relevance of the dragonfly and were given no time to ask for clarification. Grandmother's floodgates of memories were fully open. Going back to the beginning of her life, she explained the purpose of her and her families attachment to the most unexpectedly, splendidly, wonderfully, inviting of homes. The story began with her, three hundred and seventy years earlier, being born to a loving mother and father. She was the youngest of two children by five minutes, a twin. It was an unexplainable fact - in every generation the eldest twin was always a son. Grandmother was brought up in the knowledge that one day she, as with her mother before her and her daughter after her, would become the guardian of the place that everyone sat that evening. No one knew why or thought to question why, it just was.

One horrifying day however, generations of predictability came to an end. At the age of twenty one, grandmother's daughter gave birth to her own twins. Sadly, the son was weak and sickly and did not survive. He only lived for two short hours. The family were heartbroken. When the reality of the lost son was accepted, acceptance turned to concern. What would the future hold for their beautiful home, with the guardian of the guardian being lost. Their questions were answered two years later. Happily, grandmother's daughter gave birth to a healthy, bouncing, baby boy and all balance appeared to have been restored.

Prior to being forgotten, prior to being fiction, prior to being legend, prior to being fairytale, the power and magic of Dragonfly Manor was always trusted to the daughter, the protector, known as the 'Key Keeper'. The key itself was not a key as would have been expected. The key in fact was the special guest that resided in each Dragonfly home in every village, in every town, in every city, in every country, on every island on our wonderful planet Earth. A living, breathing, colourful, magical, gift-giving dragonfly.

As she watched her daughter's son grow, grandmother never said anything, but she sensed that something wasn't quite right in him. As well as being incredibly intelligent, from a very young age, he had an ability to think far beyond the present. It was an ability that enabled him to control and manipulate, a skill he used regularly. He wanted power. As he saw it, he did not want to be like every other weak son who sat back and watched the power of the dragonfly be passed on to the daughter. He wanted it.

At the age of eight, grandmother's grandson placed a thought in his sisters head. It was the most awful of realities and it remained with her. Not always consciously, but it was always there. His whispered manipulation was that he had overheard their own mother plotting. He told his sister that she would never become the Key Keeper. On her twenty first birthday, she was going to be killed by her own mother. It was a lie. He masterfully painted a dark picture of their mother as evil, highlighting every slight, natural, imperfection she had one hundred fold. The reason he used for their own mother's desire to murder her, was that she wanted the power of being the Key Keeper for herself, forever.

After many years of patience, many more years of whispers in his sisters ear, awake and when she slept, his sister who loved him unconditionally reached her twenty first birthday. It was time for his final push.

Grandmother's daughter and her husband had planned an elaborate birthday celebration in Dragonfly Manor, both in Earth's realm and by those who knew of its existence, in the place lovingly referred to as 'Heart'. This was the place that the Key and the Key Keeper protected. It was going to be a happy day.

The perfect opportunity for grandmother's grandson was handed to him, as all the planning was kept secret. Even better for him, on the morning of her birthday, the plan was that she was not going to be given a gift, a cake, or even wished a happy birthday by her parents.

The morning having arrived, grandmother's granddaughter awoke and made her way down to breakfast, there was nothing. The years of manipulation and lies told to her by her brother could be seen on her face. A red haired, beautiful, healthy, always happy, loving young woman, today, looked tired and sad. In that moment, despite the years of care and love she had received from her mother, her last remnants of doubt relating to the overheard conversation, told to her so many years before, were gone.

It was eleven in the morning in Heart. Grandmother's granddaughter looked out from the most unexpectedly, splendidly, wonderfully, inviting of homes to see her mother and father sitting in the garden. Rather than waiting for the inevitable, she decided to go out and confront them. As she stepped through the open front door and on to the top step, grandmother's daughter turned to look at her beautiful birthday girl. What she saw was far from a happy birthday girl. Tears were falling from her eyes, dropping on to the dry, wobbly cobbly path with every step she took. As she got closer, grandmother's granddaughter lost all of her confidence, she couldn't do it, she couldn't ask the questions she must, so she ran back to the house.

Getting up and out of her chair quickly, desperate to comfort her daughter, grandmother's daughter realised that her secret planning may not have been the kindest thing to do on such a special day. Quickly arriving at her side, she asked what was wrong. Turning to look at her mother, something snapped in grandmother's granddaughter. The only part of her mind that was hanging on to any hope, had snapped. She exploded with an anger not seen or heard in the realm of Heart since its beginning. Grandmother's granddaughter let out a scream so loud, it caused her

mother to cover her ears and step back. As she did,
she caught one of the cobbles with her heel. She fell
backwards. With her hands covering her ears, she
couldn't move her arms quick enough to stop herself
falling. Grandmother's son-in-law had turned, just in
time to see his beautiful wife begin to fall. He dashed
to her to catch her. Even with the speed in which he
moved, he was too late. The balance that Heart
brought to Earth was lost. The falling mother's head
made contact with the ground. As it did, her skull
split open and her life flowed away from her.

Grandmother witnessed the whole horrendous
moment. She had been standing at her top floor
bedroom window looking out at another beautiful day
in Heart. She couldn't move as she watched the
horror unravel in front of her. One other person was
watching from a window, her grandson. He had been
watching from the living room window. Unlike
grandmother, he was not frozen to the spot. His time
had come. He dashed from the house to the fake aid
of his sister, who was standing motionless on the top
step. Grabbing the old walking stick that lived at the
front door as he exited the house, he screamed 'This
is it!' He flew past his sister to where his father was,
sobbing, kneeling over his wife. Then with one swift
movement he brought down the heavy end of the
walking stick hard on to the back of his father's head.
As his head was knocked forward, his face was right
at his wife's and her eyes opened. She spoke her final
words,

'Save the dragonfly.' Managing somehow to get to
his feet and pick up his now motionless wife, his
vision blurred, the world spinning, he made his way
back to the house. His murderous son was
victoriously walking down the wobbly cobbly path to

survey what was soon to be his and his alone. He was totally unaware of what was happening behind him.

Having made it to the front door, the comforting sound of their long loved friend flew up to them, his colours as bright as ever. Grandmother's son-in-law lifted his wife's delicate, lifeless hand to the door handle. Placing her hand on the front door handle, with his hand on hers, he turned it anticlockwise. With his very last breath, he blew the dragonfly back inside, off the arm of his wife where it had landed and closed the door. Grandmother watched on in shock. Her beautiful daughter, lifeless, wrapped in the arms of her now also lifeless loving husband, began to fade. The act of closing the door in the way he did, shut off Heart from Earth's realm. The last memory imprinted in her mind of the realm of Heart, was that of her granddaughter, motionless, standing on the steps of the house, silently staring down at her dead parents. And in contrast, her grandson, looking up at her, screaming, in a rage that would have shifted any planets very core. Grandmother knew without the dragonfly they could not return. She watched in silence until the garden and its horrific scene faded away completely. She watched until all she could see, then and to this very day, was her Earthly reality.

Grandmother's son, her dead daughters brother, had not been in the house when the terrible events unfolded. He wasn't even in Heart. He returned later that day for the birthday celebrations to find grandmother and the house in silence, soulless.

Grandmother was torn, she wanted so much to go back to say goodbye to her lost, loved daughter. However, by doing so, she had no idea what she would have released back into Earth's realm. She didn't realise until several days later, that she could have saved herself the pain of the decision and the guilt of not going back, as the key to get back, the dragonfly, was gone. Grandmother's daughter's last words and her husband's actions, had trapped grandmother in one place and her grandchildren in the other. There are two realities in being a key and a Key Keeper - the first being that no Key Keeper could come and go from Earth to Heart through any other Dragonfly home other than their own. The second, was that only when the key was present could the door between the realms open. Those two realities were the reason for her grandson's rage - he had a Key Keeper in his sister, but he had no key.

For over three hundred years, grandmother had been torn between wanting and not wanting the key to return. She had equally looked forward to and dreaded the possibility of the day coming. She had welcomed many generations of her family, from her son's line, to the house. Not a single family member, son or daughter, changed anything within the house with their arrival, so none got to know the truth about the house and its past. Grandmother was trapped in her forgotten home, waiting. When Sophie arrived, abandoned by her parents, grandmother felt something change. An optimism returned to her, a feeling that something positive at last was to come. As soon as Sophie walked through the red door, grandmother felt as though she was looking into the eyes of her lost daughter.

Sixteen was the age that all of the young woman who would inherit a dragonfly home, were introduced to their dragonfly. A period of five years followed where they would learn all they needed to, sharing the responsibilities of being the Key Keeper with their mothers. At the age of twenty one, the responsibility became theirs solely.

When Sophie, waking up on her sixteenth birthday, saw something small move on her bedroom door's doorframe, grandmother knew with all certainty, something had begun. However, grandmother was also aware that even if the dragonfly had returned, having not had the dragonfly introduced to Sophie by her birth mother, the link with her would most likely not be. As the day had progressed, the introduction of Alex and what had happened to him, what had happened to Sophie through him and of course the notes she had read that were left for Melissa, grandmother's conflict of open the door, don't open the door, that she had felt on the day and days after her daughter's murder, returned.

'Grandmother, I don't understand. If there are other houses like this, why have they been forgotten? Surely they are still there, surely you can just go to them and go back?' The question from Sophie made grandmother smile. She smiled for two reasons. Firstly that she was wise enough to ask the question, but more importantly that her question and tone was such that she would appear to have accepted her story to be true.

'My princess, my underestimated princess, I love you more than you could know.' Proud and filled with love, grandmother continued with her story. She explained that she was correct, the dragonfly houses did and do still exist, but for over two hundred years all had fallen silent. She told of how before all the dragonfly homes fell silent, she had heard stories about the horrors her grandson inflicted on those in Heart. How being trapped in the realm of Heart, his determination to find a way back was at the cost of many. Although the ageing red front door could not return him to Earth's realm, he could however pass through his Dragonfly Manor's door, to other dragonfly homes throughout Heart. In his search for answers, it was something he did thousands of times. Each time leaving his distraught sister, locked in her room.

His understanding of the dragonfly homes and the dragonflies themselves grew and grew, as did his anger. With all he learnt he still had no success in finding a way back. One day he found himself in a small settlement in south Australia, a gold mining settlement. As soon as he saw it, the shining metal replaced his obsession of finding a way back to Earth. There was so much gold buried and he wanted it all. He enslaved and used all the people and living things he could. Mining for years and years, the poor creatures pulled out a seemingly never ending supply of gold. He would bring every tiny piece of gold that was mined, through the tiny hut that was the dragonfly home he first arrived through, back to his Dragonfly Manor.

'What do you mean, South Australia? There is a South Australia in Heart?' Melissa asked,

'In a word yes, but also no. I understand this makes no sense. Heart is a place for healing and is a mirror of where we sit right now. Well it used to be anyway. It has been so long since I have heard anything from there. I used to get news before all the dragonfly homes were gone, forgotten. Until today, I had come to believe Heart was no more,' was grandmother's response.

'But why grandmother? You still haven't answered why all the dragonfly homes have been forgotten, why you can't just go to another house and go back?' Sophie asked.

'Yes, yes, I was getting to that awful part,' grandmother replied and continued her story. She explained that with many years passing, unlike grandmother, her grandson was getting old, a reality that he thought he could not fight or change. That was until a moment's rage meant he could. Having tried on many an occasion, finally, a Key Keeper and her family from another dragonfly home a village away, who knew about the distraught locked away sister, broke her free. Even if she had wanted to, she couldn't have put up any kind of fight to being rescued, as they found her in a catatonic state, lost in her own mind.

It didn't take long before grandmother's grandson tracked down the kidnappers and his sister. When he did, as the Key Keepers husband tried to stop him from taking his sister back, with an explosion of madness, with one hand, he snapped his neck. As he fell to the floor, grandmother's grandson turned his focus to the Key Keeper, his pin prick focused eyes looking right into hers. Petrified, she ran for her front door. Her hand grabbing at the door handle, her dragonfly landed on her arm, as it always did. There was no escape for her, grandmother's grandson was at her side before she could turn the handle. He grabbed her arm at the very point the dragonfly sat and took great pleasure in squeezing both, crunching the defenceless key into its Key Keeper. Throwing the Key Keeper to the floor, without thinking, he licked his hand clean of the juices that had come from the dragonfly. As he tasted the bitterness of them, he was hit with a rush of life. The world of Heart suddenly looked brighter to him. The full strength of a younger version of himself had returned. His mind, as angry as it always was, had cleared. Grandmother's grandson had sickeningly discovered something that would keep him alive for far longer than he should be.

From that day, for generations, his focus was to find every dragonfly and consume all he needed, until he could find a way home. When the last dragonfly home went quiet, all the dragonflies gone, grandmother considered that there was a high chance that her grandson had finally aged and was no more. But she could not be certain. What she could be certain of was that the dragonfly that had reappeared that day, Sophie's sixteenth birthday, was her families key and was most likely the very last of the dragonfly in existence.

'This is where we find ourselves today. A day that if we have trust in each other and the gift that was once given to us by the most generous of protectors, could mean that we could be at the start of a new tomorrow,' said grandmother.

'But why now grandmother, why now?' Sophie asked. Grandmother, who had been sitting forward in her chair whilst she told her story, sat back to contemplate the question. Alex's arrival and all that had gone on, reminded grandmother of a moment within the thousands of hours of learning from the books and papers thrown about her library, when she came across a hidden drawer in a wall. The drawer contained papers. Written on them was a story told about a man that made it possible for the legend of the dragonfly to come into existence. It was a story that she had never heard until she read it on that day.

'The legends once told of a dragonfly that gifted us all the chance to take pain away, to bring balance to our world. What I once learnt and have never told is that the gift was given to one man. It was in a time when the world was full of pain, suffering, sadness and loss. A time that mirrors very much the time we live in now. The reality and world we live in today seems smaller to me than it once did. We live in societies that are so torn, unbalanced, unjust. Societies, individuals, that think only of themselves, governments that do not protect, but take advantage of those they govern. We, as guests on this earth, are killing every part of it and its inhabitants. We are in a time that needs kindness, understanding, compassion, the ability to understand, respect and accept others. We are in a time, I feel, that needs that gift once again. The man I read of, the recipient of the gift, he was a man who felt every pain from every rock, plant, animal, mammal, human. His name was…' before grandmother could finish her sentence, she was interrupted,

'Shuing!' The shouted name came from a bolt upright Alex.

CHAPTER 11

Waking up in the old, cold, unloved place that she had called home for more years than she cared to think about, Leilani slowly sat herself up and looked over to the window. The light from the slow rising sun dazzled her weary eyes. Its orangey red colour that filled the room, provided a warmth, a hint of comfort to the old, cold house. It was not a physical warmth, but its colourful glow gave her bedroom the impression of warmth. Looking beyond the dusty glass of the window, Leilani's eyes were trying to focus, but they could see that something was different. Beyond and above the overgrown forest of trees, she could see outside her garden's walls. The rising sun was sending out an unnatural deep red haze that filled the sky. The ominousness that she witnessed, caused her to get out from under her covers and leave the comfort they gave. It was an action that was out of the ordinary, far quicker than her usual ritual of having to work up to stepping out into the cold of another day.

Dropping down from her tall four-poster bed, her bare feet made contact with the old wooden floor and her breath was taken away by how cold it actually was. She paused for a moment to give her wrinkled feet time to acclimatise to the cold, uneven, well used floor. The moment's pause gave her time to reach out and collect her glamorously long, brown dressing gown, that had been hanging on the end of the bed. Although glamorously long, it was anything but glamorous. Old, worn, holes in the sleeves, its tie round her waist frayed at the edges. Its length to the rear as she stepped forward was stained in dirt, from all the dust collected from the house's old floors over the years of neglect. But it was hers. Not a woman who liked change, she was comfortable in its familiarity and the warmth its thinning material still seemed to give her. The years of being concerned as to how she looked were far behind her. There was no one in her life to impress anyway.

Leilani brushed past her dressing table on her way to the newly painted sky. It was covered in old dusty glass bottles, filled with perfumes that had lost their sweet odour, replaced with rotting, pungent, off-smelling scents from the years of decay they had experienced, sitting unused or replaced. Distracted by the unusual light, she ignored the tattered slippers that she had neatly placed under the dressing table chair the night before. Slippers would have given her some protection from the coldness and the splinters the old floor was happy to share. Arriving at the unpainted wooden-framed window, her view was blurred as her breath hit the cold glass, instantly steaming it up. Using the sleeve from her dressing gown, she wiped her breath away and peered through the streaks of damp that the wiping had left, to take a fuller, closer look at the sky.

What she saw was a view that she could not recall having ever seen before. The sun, not visible, seemed to be improbable as the cause of the light. It was only about eight o'clock in the morning and the sun, although throwing light, was low behind the trees and not yet visible itself on the winter morning. Leilani was confused, the light seemed to be as bright as if the sun was high in the sky. Changing as she watched, the deep red haze she had seen from her bed, now looked as though one hundred rainbows had crashed into each other creating an explosion of colour - pinks, reds and oranges, as well as blues, purples and greens, all swirling slowly from a central point. Squinting, in an attempt to hide the brightness, she tried to look into the central point. She couldn't, there was just too much light.

'Well then,' Leilani said out loud to herself. Not unused to seeing things that she could not always explain, she stood and admired the swirls of colour that were getting richer with every moment that passed. Her eyes tiring, Leilani looked down from the sky at the tall branches of the trees, that hid the world beyond the forest. They were swaying gently in a soft breeze. From the sky, to join Leilani in the audience of the spectacular show, birds were landing on the furthest reaches of the branches, filling them up. Their weight caused the branches to bend, just about reaching the point of breaking.

As the frail Leilani continued to enjoy the morning show, she got a fright. In a fraction of a second, the light vanished. The birds left their viewing point and frantically flew towards Leilani's house, blocking out the sky. It was as dark as night. Stepping back to escape the attack, she stepped on her trailing dressing gown and lost her footing. Grabbing the shabby, worn material that had once been a set of full and thick curtains, she successfully managed to catch herself before falling. The frantic moment at an end, her balance returned, she looked back out of her window. The view she saw was back to what she would normally expect to see at that time of day. A warm glow moving in, coming up from beyond the trees, as the winter sun began its rise into the day, taking the place of the cold night sky.

Nothing new to see, Leilani turned and made her way back to her bed. 'Well that was uninspiring, getting me up unnecessarily.' Again speaking loudly to herself, with a tone of annoyance to her voice. 'You are going to be cold now aren't you?' She directed the words at her bed with the blankets pulled back. 'So, one would assume at this point I am to be up!' Diverting away from the comfort of her cold bed, Leilani made her way back to her dressing table, where her searching feet managed to find the slippers she had ignored earlier. Knocking the chair in her search, a very old and grumpy looking polecat, who had been sleeping on the chair, found himself disturbed. Sleeping deeply, he was also not used to being woken at such a time of day. Not instantly recognisable in colour or size to the polecats seen scurrying around the local fields, he was big, even for the breed of steppe polecat he was. Larger, brighter white in colour with the details round his eyes, mouth and tips of his ears almost black they were such a dark brown. His large head, not in proportion to his long body, made the very few visitors to Leilani wary to approach. His continual varying levels of bad mood however, did not stop him from being a loyal protector to Leilani. Being woken up at such a time of day funnily enough did not help his mood, as he let out a high pitched barking sound in annoyance.

'Oh shut up Earl you miserable old man,' Leilani responded to his exclamation and then purposely tilted the chair, causing him to fall to the floor. 'Thank you, the chair is lovely and warm,' she said. Looking into the mirror, Leilani didn't like what she saw. An old woman, hair thinning, her drawn face's skin hanging, giving her eyes, cheeks and chin a droopy look about them. She was pale, although she

had been as a young woman, she now looked so tired
and unwell.

She reached for her powder to help cover some of
her imperfections and did what she could. Her failing
eyesight meant the smoothness of the spreading was
not to a high standard and visible to all. She pulled
her long, thin hair, back from her shoulders and
quickly whipped what hair was left into a bun on the
top of her head. The whole process took all of five
minutes. She was quickly back on her feet, her
creaking bones echoing around the silent room as her
hips and knees straightened.

'Come on Earl, let's get you something to eat.' He
didn't need to hear those words twice. In his food
excitement, he was quickly at the door. His claws
pulled at its edge, swinging it open and disappearing
into the darkness of the landing. The door shut behind
him leaving Leilani behind, who did not have
anywhere near the speed he did.

The bedroom was cold, but stepping out on to the
old landing, Leilani shivered as the air was even
colder. Grabbing at her dressing gown, she pulled it
tight up to her neck and headed for the staircase.
Making her way down the stairs, she noticed
something was not quite right. The window that
looked out to the back of the old house, had a wiggly
line running across it. The line had cleared the grime
from years of neglect, making the outside visible for
the first time in many years.

'Strange! Looks like a tiny someone has been
walking over our window Earl,' she said. Earl had
noticed the change himself, as he uncharacteristically
playfully jumped up on to the windowsill. He was
hungry and decided that enough attention had been
given to whatever it was, so he rubbed himself over

the lines in an effort to blur them, making investigation to their source pointless. 'Fine, come on then,' Leilani said. Leaving the landing, they continued their journey to the kitchen.

The day that started earlier than normal, seemed to drag on even longer than normal. Going about her business of doing as little as she could, Leilani thought the day would never end. The years of being fit, young, powerful and beautiful had gone. She had lived longer than she should have. With no hope of staying ahead of time, she had given up the fight many years earlier. Even the most beautiful show that nature had given her that very morning, gave her no joy or drive to do anything but wait for the day to come to an end, so she could once again sleep.

The only room in the house that had any order to it was the library. She spent many hours sitting in front of the fireplace, staring into the flickering flames, angrily thinking back to the life she had lived and also the life she could have lived. Her life had been filled with anger, confusion, loss, searching, finding, losing, death. She could not recall a single memory that had been positive or happy in any way. Sitting in the library, in her usual chair, today was no different. The sun outside the window that had peeked over the trees for a short time as it reached its highest point, had disappeared some hours earlier. The only light that Leilani had in the room as the afternoon came to an end, was the light given out by the fading embers in the fireplace.

Sitting in her once red, now more faded dirty brown, large velvet chair, her day of reliving her past was coming to an end. She was in that place between wake and sleep, her mind not consciously angrily reminiscing and her horror-filled dreams not having started. The one and only place her mind gave her any peace. BANG...

'What was that?' Fully awake, her heart racing, she looked at Earl, who was laid out as close to the last embers of warmth the fire was giving as he could get. Earl jumped to his feet on full alert. Not waiting for an answer, Leilani stood herself up and made her way to the library door, which, having made his way round her, was flung open by a fast moving Earl.

Stepping into the hallway, they found Leilani's front door was open. The fresh outside air, that was actually warmer than the air inside the hallway, was rushing in. Earl, a good distance ahead of Leilani, had made his way round the open door. Out of sight, he was making his high pitched alert, yelping noises. Her legs moved faster than they had for some time as she reached the door and pulled it fully open. Looking out into the garden the sky was clear and dark, the moon had not cleared the trees and the only light came from the sparkling stars, but it was enough to see that there was nothing there. Earl on the other hand, was scratching furiously at the ground just outside the front door. His yelps, with Leilani now by his side, turning to growls as he did.

'What was that light?' A familiar voice came from the bottom of the garden, coming through the trees.

'What light?' Leilani responded,

'How is it possible you did not see it? I saw it from the store the other side of the wood, it shone through the trees,' was the person's response. Making his way closer, a strong looking man appeared. There were similarities between the two, but with at least a generation between them.

'Aaaaaaaaa!' Leilani let out a scream. Having looked down to see what Earl was scratching at, she saw the ghostly apparition of the upper torso of a man, lying outside her front door on the top step. The scream turned the walk of the male approaching into a run. As he arrived, he got a glimpse of what had caused Leilani to scream, just before it vanished.

'Did you see that?' Leilani asked.

'Our wait is over. Someone has used our dragonfly!'

CHAPTER 12

'Where did you hear that name?' grandmother asked a startled looking Alex. He didn't respond at first. He was awake, but was staring into the flickering flames dancing across the surface of the logs.

'Alex, are you ok?' came the very soft voice of Sophie, who was still sitting at his side. She had placed her hand affectionately on his hand, which was pressing into the leather sofa, holding him up.

'Looks like I won't be getting a look in then?' Vicky whispered under her breath. The statement that no one was supposed to hear, was heard by Melissa. Knowing fine well what she meant, she couldn't help but chuckle.

'Where am I?' Alex said, having at last come round fully from whatever had happened to him. Looking round the room, as welcoming as it was, he felt a little lost, finding himself in a totally unfamiliar place. He shuffled and pulled his feet off the sofa, placing them on the floor whilst turning to look at Melissa his mum, 'Mum, what happened?' he asked.

'Where did you hear that name?' grandmother interrupted and asked again. 'I need to know!' Her tone was one of both urgency and excitement at the same time.

'Shuing?' Alex said, looking for confirmation that was the name she was looking for an answer to. Grandmother nodded, 'In my dream or whatever it was. Shuing, such an odd name. But I kind of feel like I know it somehow,' Alex replied.

'Who was the person, what did they look like, where did you see them?' Grandmother threw question upon question at the still slightly fuzzy Alex.

'It was me.' Alex answered just one of the many questions. Melissa had stepped round Sophie and sat herself down next to Alex on the sofa. She put her strong arm round him and pulled him lovingly into her side. Holding him tight, happy he was back, she allowed a single tear to escape from her sparkling dark eyes. It was a weakness as she saw it, that she would have never usually let Alex see. Melissa was hugging her boy so tightly, he was struggling to breathe. Along with that, his hand, head and back were sore from all that had happened to him, but he was not about to push his mum away and let her know that her loving squeeze was causing such discomfort. He was aware that, although in physical pain, some of the emotional pain and fear that he was feeling, was being squeezed away by being held by her.

'I know all that has happened tonight warrants more enquiry, but Alex, I really feel that we should get you home,' Melissa said in a firm voice. She hoped that her usual, take control of any situation personality would not be challenged. Her hopes were dashed.

'No mum, it's ok, I am ok. I think there is more I need to see tonight. Wherever I was, it was real, I know it,' Alex said. Grandmother's face lit up with excitement, but said not a word. Sophie had stood up and made her way across the room to join her grandmother. She was strangely jealous that she had been replaced as the one holding Alex. She was happy when he had said he didn't want to leave. Just as Alex did, she wanted to see more, she wanted to

know more. She also and most importantly, wanted to
know how much he may know about the silhouetted
protector in her dreams. She was joined by Anchor,
who whimpered quietly as he nuzzled at her hand,
hoping to get some attention. Sophie's mind was
elsewhere. She was looking up at the large picture
above the fireplace. All she had ever been told about
the pictures that covered the walls, was that they were
portraits of family, or places that family had happy
memories of. After grandmother's story that evening,
she couldn't help but wonder if the family portrait she
was looking at, was in fact the characters that had
played the leading roles in the saddest of endings.

'So where next?' Vicky piped up from the seat she
had stayed on with Bart by her side. The question
wasn't to anyone in particular, but the adventurous
side of her was clear to all as they looked over at her
smiling face. Bart on the other hand, appeared to be
shaking his head in disapproval, to any suggestion of
doing anything other than pretending nothing had
happened. He stood up and turned. His purposeful
action caused the harness he was happily wearing, to
bounce in Vicky's direction. As far as he was
concerned, it was time they left. Vicky of course
completely ignored his efforts.

'I think we should try the door again. Try to figure
out why you keep disappearing,' Sophie said.

'My dear I like your motivation. That is exactly
what I was hoping to do earlier. But firstly, we need
to know more about this dream Alex had,'
grandmother replied. Melissa wanted to get Alex
home. Her interest in the meaning behind her tattoos
and the words above the front door were not as strong
as it had been. With Alex being awake and seeing he
was fine, she not only wanted to get him out of the

house, she wanted to pack up their car and leave the square for good. The words 'he must be safe, he must be loved, he must be kept secret from the world' tattooed on her side were the only words at this point she was interested in. The words she had lived her and Alex's lives together by, since the day she became his mother.

'Can you stand?' Melissa asked Alex.

'Yes of course I can, I'm fine,' was Alex's response. He stood up, seeming to Melissa as though he wanted to prove his 'fine' status to her. That wasn't the case. His standing was because he wanted to join Sophie at the picture. 'I have seen these faces before. Well I think I have, but they were a lot older,' Alex said.

'In your dream?' grandmother asked,

'No somewhere different. It's kind of a blur, but I was lying on the ground looking up at them.' Alex looked down into the flames of the open fire as he searched his mind for any more information. Snapping his head up quickly, turning around to the room, he pointed, 'It was here. It was outside the front door here!' he said.

'Not in your dream?' grandmother asked.

'That would have been when you fell from the light in the doorway,' Vicky interrupted before Alex could answer. 'Remember when he fell, you guys saw him disappearing, although I could see him perfectly. Remember, he was half outside the front door.'

'Grandmother, is that possible?' Sophie asked. So much had happened that evening, grandmother needed to gather her thoughts. If what Alex was saying was true, what he saw would be of great concern to her. She wondered if it could actually be possible for them to still be living? Of course she was still living and she had no idea how, although she knew the why. But no, it simply couldn't be. It was a vision, a waking daydream, that's all it could have been, a coincidence. She needed to know more,

'Who in the picture do you think you saw?' grandmother asked.

'Well I thought it was the older couple to begin with. But actually, looking into their eyes, I am sure it's the two children. They were old though, well she was really old, he was maybe your age mum,' Alex said. Grandmother left her seat and tottered quickly towards the closed living room door,

'No, no, no, please no,' she said, as she flew the door open and disappeared out into the hall. Sophie and Anchor had left the fireplace and followed, catching the door just before it closed. They were quickly followed by everyone else. Having not actually left the safety of the living room, the crowd of faces looked out at grandmother who was running her hands over the doorframe, the light like a heartbeat still dancing from one side of the frame to the other. Her eyes were darting backwards and forwards, searching for something. 'Where are you? Please, come out.' There was panic in grandmother's voice.

'Grandmother, what's wrong?' Sophie asked, stepping into the hall.

'The dragonfly, the dragonfly. If he saw them, they would have seen him and if that actually happened… the door was opened. The dragonfly is the key. They must not get the key,' grandmother said. Not finding what she was looking for on the frame, grandmother turned her attention to the tree. She began scouring it for any sign that her colourful, winged companion, whom she had seen that day for the first time in so many years, was there.

'A dragonfly? That is what I saw in my bedroom this morning wasn't it?' Sophie asked. 'And what must have flown past me in the hallway earlier,' she continued.

'Yes princess. The key. He has been here all day. We need to find him,' grandmother said. Picking up on the urgency, Vicky, Melissa, Alex and Sophie joined in the search. The hallway had kept its temperature from the heat the doorway had given out, when Alex was trapped in its centre, but the cold winter's night was starting to make its presence known once again. The cold was creeping in from under the closed front door.

'If it was in your bedroom earlier, does that mean it could be anywhere in the house?' Vicky asked.

'Yes,' grandmother answered quickly.

'Sophie, show me your room,' Melissa said. She figured that if it was there once, it could well be there again. Plus the quicker they found it, the quicker she would have the opportunity to leave, with Alex.

'It's the first room on the right when you go up the stairs,' Sophie replied. Before Melissa could make her move, Alex was on the bottom step about to head up himself.

'What's that Alex?' Sophie asked. She had been watching Alex as he walked away towards the stairs.

'What's what?' Alex asked, stopping on the step he had climbed on to.

'There, on the side of your neck,' Sophie said, pointing as she did. Alex touched where it looked like Sophie was pointing. He felt nothing.

'There's nothing there. I don't think,' Alex replied. Sophie, convinced she saw something, walked over to take a closer look. She climbed up to the step above his, to get herself to the right height to see.

'Aaaaa!' Sophie screamed. She had got a fright from something that had disappeared under Alex's top. 'There's something on you! Grandmother there is something there.' Melissa's heart was racing as she pulled him off the step and pulled at his top. She saw nothing. Then in a flash, like a mother with her small child, she grabbed his jumper at the waist and pulled it clear over his head in a movement that was so quick, no one had time to focus on the move.

'What the heck!' Alex said. Now with no top on and nowhere to hide, he saw on his chest what looked like a tattoo. However, no tattoo moves!

'Oh my goodness, he's there!' grandmother shouted. What was there was what she had been frantically searching for. Moving freely under his outer layer of skin, visible to all who were looking at the topless Alex, was the dragonfly. 'How is that possible?' grandmother asked herself. Alex was beginning to panic. Grandmother on the other hand was calming down. She had found the dragonfly. In her calmer state, thinking more clearly, she got cross with herself for even thinking that her grandchildren could still be alive. It made no sense. Alex had described the people he saw as a generation apart. Clearly they could not have been them.

'Mum?' Alex wanted to touch it, but was scared what it might do. He had been invaded by an insect and as beautiful as it was, he wanted it out. 'Mum please, get it out of me!' he shouted. Melissa slowly went to touch the moving insect. Her fingers were millimetres away when the dragonfly reacted to her presence. Its wings became a blur as it flew over his shoulder and onto his back.

'Calm down, everyone calm down. It's fine, really

there is nothing to worry about,' grandmother said. She was so happy to see that the dragonfly had not left the sanctuary of her home. Sophie stepped down from the second step to join Alex and get a closer look. Her grandmother's calming words had taken some of the fear she was feeling away. Her presence had the opposite effect to Melissa's - the dragonfly's wings stopped. Sophie reached out. Slowly she moved her hand closer,

'Ow!' As she touched the tip of one of the wings of the dragonfly, motionless under the skin of Alex, she received a tiny electric shock.

'Yeh, ok. So whatever it is, it doesn't want to be touched then,' Vicky said. If she was being completely honest, she actually was more interested in the topless Alex than in what was happening with the dragonfly. Sophie moved away from Alex, she didn't want another electric shock so she went to join the others across the hall. The dragonfly followed her. It passed over Alex's shoulder and down his arm.

'Wait Sophie. The dragonfly, it's following you. Touch it,' grandmother said. Alex lifted his arm up in front of him to look at the dragonfly, which had stopped and was sitting on his hand. He felt no pain, he didn't even feel the movement of the dragonfly as it moved around him. It was as though he was a cinema screen, the dragonfly the movie being projected on to him.

'Sophie, I will try and touch you if that's ok?' Alex said. He reached his hand towards Sophie's. As he did, the dragonfly spun and looked right at her. Alex took hold of her hand. Nothing! They were just two people holding hands with an audience.

'Well that was an anticlimax!' Vicky said. 'The electric spark must have just been static build up from the old rug!' she said. Seeing as the experiment did not produce any exciting results, Sophie went to let go of Alex's hand. She couldn't.

'You can let go now,' Sophie said to Alex. He tried. He couldn't. Seeing that he had as much control of the hand holding as she did, without a word she lifted her arm. Stuck together, Alex had no choice but to do the same. 'Seriously, let go will you,' Sophie said.

'I can't feel my hand!' Alex said in a concerned voice. Focusing on her own hand for a moment, Sophie realised she was in the same position. She couldn't feel Alex's touch. Her hand was also completely numb. In a panic, Sophie grabbed her wrist with her free hand and with all her weight, tried to pull away from Alex. All she achieved was a hurt shoulder. Alex was still looking at the dragonfly,

'Wait, it's moving again,' Alex said. Its wings were a blur as it seemed to be building up to something.

'Alex, your eyes. They're changing,' Melissa said. She was right, his eyes were changing from the hint of purple that only those who looked closely enough saw, to being quite obviously purple. As the brightness increased in his eyes, equally so, the brightness of the doorframe on the other side of the hall also did. Not only was the light changing, but the frame's shapes, images, animals, were all beginning to move. The only part that did not move were the words at the top of the frame. The words that even after living in the house for over three hundred years, grandmother was seeing lit up for the first time ever were,

Unnatural light from the eyes of one, chosen by the healer to become one

Now

Delivered Received A Gift Of Nature's Freeing Love Yours

Everyone's attention had moved from Alex's eyes to the changing door and its frame. Except that is for Alex and Sophie. Their hands still clasped together, their focus was each other.

'Sophie, I know this feels strange but, don't you think this all also feels right?' Alex said. As he asked the question, he reached down and took hold of Sophie's free hand. Before she had a chance to answer, the dragonfly left Alex's hand and hovered between the two of them.

'Grandmother!' Sophie shouted. Grandmother, along with the others, turned to see the beautiful purple and blue metallic dragonfly spinning, growing as it did, between Alex and Sophie. Its spinning reached such a speed that its colour and form, like its wings, became a blur. Then in an explosion, a burst of supernatural light rose up between them. The light bounced off the ceiling and filled the hallway. The stream of light seemed never to end as Alex and Sophie felt a pleasant feeling of weightlessness come over them. Alex's eyes were shining a purple light as brightly as the white light between them. Sophie could just make out the purple through the white light that separated them, the familiar saving eyes from her dreams. Her heart was beating so fast and not because of the unexplained goings on, but because of what she was feeling towards Alex - a connection that was timeless, she knew him. She couldn't explain it in that moment, but she knew that for whatever reason, they were meant to meet, to come together that night.

Sophie and Alex were totally unaware of what was happening around them, Sophie transfixed by Alex's eyes and Alex focused on the white light. The numbness that both had felt in their hands was changing, it was travelling up their arms, spreading to every part of them. They were not in control of themselves any more, something else was. Alex was also experiencing something else. He was being filled with every happy, sad, joyful, painful memory that Sophie had ever had in her short life. But more than that, he was travelling through the memories and lives of Sophie's ancestors.

'Erm, guys what is happening here?' Vicky broke the silence. No one answered. Grandmother was watching in excitement. With all the years she had lived, with all the stories she had been told from generations of family in this Dragonfly Manor, she had never seen, or heard, of what was happening right in front of her. She was happy the dragonfly was still there. She was happy that the house seemed to be coming back to life. She was happy to be there, to be part of the return of hope to the crumbling world they lived in, filled with pain and anger. Grandmother at last found herself in a place where she was happy to let whatever was going to happen, happen.

Melissa knew that her son was born for a greater purpose. As much as she wanted to leave with Alex, keep him with her, keep him safe, keep him for herself, she knew that he had to be where he was. The words in her tattoo now had meaning, context,

'At the beginning of his true beginning, your sacrifice for my son Alex Hugins will be rewarded with love, joy and understanding of more than you could possibly know.'

She was sure that whatever his purpose, it was going to be an amazing one. Alex's journey through Sophie's family came to an abrupt end, as the visions found their way to the moment that Dragonfly Manor had its most horrible of happenings - the death of grandmother's daughter and son-in-law. The light began to fade, Alex and Sophie were lowered to the ground. As the last hint of the supernatural light disappeared, all feeling and control returned to both of them. Gravity once again had its power returned as their hands fell to their sides, the two's physical contact lost, but only for a moment. Filled with emotion from what he had seen, Alex stepped forward and took Sophie in his arms.

'I am so sorry,' Alex whispered in a surprised Sophie's ear, surprised but happy to be in the arms of her dreams' protector.

'The dragonfly, where is the dragonfly?' grandmother asked. Melissa had the top she had removed from Alex. As she stepped over to the embracing couple to give it back to him, she said,

'It's there.' Melissa could see the dragonfly had settled on Alex's back, its size much larger than the first time they had all seen it. Its body ran down his spine and its wings wrapped round and over his shoulders. 'Wow, that's quite impressive,' Melissa said. The discovery of the dragonfly being back on Alex made Sophie want to see, so she broke away from the comforting embrace to look. The dragonfly was motionless. Its colours looked matt on his skin. Due to its size, the veins in its delicate wings could be seen clearly. Alex couldn't help but laugh as he was tickled by the hands of Melissa, Sophie, Vicky and grandmother who cautiously and delicately touched Alex's back where the dragonfly had made its home. 'Can you feel it?' Melissa asked.

'I can feel you guys tickling me!' He laughed again. The ladies stopped their probing and stepped back. Alex took the opportunity to put his top back on.

'What happened to you two in that light?' grandmother asked.

'I don't know if anything happened. I just felt safe,' replied Sophie. She had felt no pain, there was no fear, there was just warmth, comfort and peace, as she looked across into Alex's eyes.

'The door and the frame, they're still lit up!' Alex said, changing the subject, as he didn't want to go into detail about what he had seen. It was more than a dream, he knew that. It was a view of what had once happened in the house where they all stood. Alex walked over to the door, the frame still dancing with light. Getting closer, he could see the varied selection of animals that were dancing with the light, along with scenery from the most beautiful places on earth, carved in such perfect detail. Something was different, not only was the doorframe alive, there were now tiny dulled pinpricks of light covering the door itself. Vicky, having been left at the opposite side of the hallway, had a fuller view and noticed a pattern to the pinpricks.

'That looks like a map of earth!' Vicky said. Grandmother had seen the lights before, it had been a very long time since she had, but she knew exactly what they were.

'You are correct Vicky. It's a map showing the position of every Dragonfly house around the world,' grandmother said.

'There's more weirdness than just here?' Vicky questioned,

'There is, or was, more weirdness, as you put it, than you could imagine. If you look closer, this house's light on the map is the only one that is bright,' grandmother said. Alex reached forward to touch one of the dulled lights. As soon as he made contact, every one of the dulled pinpricks became intensely bright, followed by the light on the doorframe and all its inhabitants changing. The pulsing, dancing light was becoming colourful. Accompanying the change in colour was the sound of a gentle hum, which grew with the growing intensity of the changing light. The door and its frame, unable to contain the light any longer, shot out beams of light from the doorframe and from every pinprick of light on the door itself. They bounced off every wall in the hallway, using the places they made contact as launching pads to another place. The house was filled with laser- like streaks of light going in every direction. Never breaking, the beams made their way up the stairs to the bedrooms, up to the attic work space of grandmother, into the library, living room, kitchen and out into hidden rooms at the back of the house. It was a glorious explosion of warmth and colour, a total celebration.

'This is so beautiful,' Melissa said, as one of the beams of colour passed right through her. 'Alex are you ok?' she asked. Alex was more than ok, he was being filled with joy and happiness like he had never felt. The reason she asked the question was because she could see that Alex was beginning to fade, again! Alex turned to answer and look at the light show that was happening all around him, his hand still firmly placed on the door.

'Yes mum, I'm fine. I am so fine,' Alex said. With more and more of the magical light being spewed from the door and its frame, the house began to shake, as added to all of it, was a thick wave of colourful light - the dragonfly had left Alex. Free from his back, it grew in size again, becoming the size of a giant eagle. Passing everyone, it flew up the stairs and out of sight, leaving its colours hanging in the air. With every contact the light made with the house, it changed it. The house was being renewed. It was returning to the vivid colours, freshness, newness, magical-ness that grandmother had once known. A reality that had been hinted at earlier that evening, as the kitchen cupboards showed signs of what they once were and the log in the fireplace that acted far from normal. The whole house was waking up, the whole house and its possibilities were returning.

'My princess, it's happening. We have our home again!' grandmother squealed in excitement. The dogs were running in circles around the group, Bart actually letting go of his responsible grumpy self, was bounding around like a puppy. Vicky had her arms above her head and was spinning in circles, wrapping herself up in the colours dancing around her. Melissa had moved backwards and was leaning back on to the tree that was once again growing. She had always loved trees, their presence and power gave her a feeling of comfort and safety she didn't feel anywhere else. Its branches created a canopy that covered the ceiling, its leaves a bright green, full of life. Melissa felt warm and safe.

Sophie was watching Alex. She was curious as to why he whispered the words 'I am so sorry' to her. Grandmother, with her one track mind, was contemplating whether to follow the dragonfly, she did not want to lose it again. She need not have worried, as just as she was about to head up the stairs, the dragonfly returned. It buzzed over grandmother's head, between Sophie and Vicky, went straight through Alex and into the door. As quick as it did there was a bang, which was followed by a final explosion of colourful energy. The door and its frame fell dark and silent. Everyone had been knocked to the floor by the explosion, including the bounding dogs Anchor and Bart.

'Hahahaha...' Grandmother started laughing, a contagious laugh that had Melissa and Vicky soon chortling along with her. Lying on the floor they had no idea what was so funny, as their eyes adapted to the changed, dull light.

'I have to go,' Alex announced, standing himself up.

'Go where?' Melissa asked as she also stood herself up.

'Shuing! Where it all started, that's where you need to be isn't it?' grandmother said.

'Maybe, I don't know. Yes!' Alex said looking towards Sophie. 'I saw something when we were together. Whatever it was has left me feeling that it is dangerous for me to stay here. I have got to go and Sophie I think you have to come with me!' Alex said.

'So much has happened here tonight, so much that has left me in no doubt young man of who and what you are. But if you are going to leave, before you go, I have to ask, what have you seen?' grandmother asked. Alex, as sure as he was that what he saw was real, and as much as he wanted to answer her, was still the Alex he had always been. His lack of confidence was holding him back, he didn't want to be seen as foolish. He looked over at his mum.

'It's ok Alex, say what is in your mind. Whatever it is,' Melissa comfortingly said. Alex found his voice and told the story which had already been told that evening, by grandmother. The detail in which he described the place, the people and what happened surprised grandmother. His words painted a picture that took her right back to that most horrible of days. She couldn't help but become emotional. Sophie produced a crumpled tissue from her pocket and put her arm round her.

'They were the people in the picture over the fireplace, right?' Alex asked.

'Yes!' grandmother replied.

'Grandmother told us that story already tonight. When you were unconscious,' Sophie said.

'The dragonfly that was on me, that was the dragonfly that was pushed through the door wasn't it?' Alex asked. Grandmother nodded as she dabbed at her tears and running nose. With a cough, she managed to clear her throat and compose herself.

'When the dragonfly appeared this morning, I thought it was here for Sophie. She should have been the one to become the dragonfly's keeper. Today being her sixteenth birthday would have been the start of her journey. No young lady has been able to become the key keeper since that awful day you just described. Not one has made the connection at the age of sixteen, let alone received the dragonfly's bite on their twenty first birthday. A bite in the place that you Alex, appear to already have. I thought today was the day. The dragonfly never joins physically with someone like it did you. Once the connection was made and the bite given, the daughter of the daughter along with the dragonfly would control the movement between here and there, but always as separate beings. What happened to you, from all my years of reading, has only, as far as I know, happened once. Only one has ever become one with a dragonfly - Shuing, the name you called out, the name of the man you said you saw. However, the dragonfly stayed with him, it did not you!' Grandmother paused for a moment. She looked around, the dragonfly could not be seen anywhere. 'The dragonfly leaving you, that does not concern me. However, what does concern me is that your appearance awoke the dragonfly and the house you stand in, the fact that it did not stay with you but passed through you and entered the door. If it is not here, it must be there!' She knew that the dragonfly's last connection was with Leilani, her granddaughter from three hundred years ago. Even though she did not receive the bite on her twenty first birthday, there was still a link that was made over the years from the day she had turned sixteen. It scared her that the dragonfly, awake, could have somehow been pulled back to Leilani, if she lived. Grandmother had hoped it would have skipped the generational line and the dragonfly would have connected with Sophie, but it didn't.

Grandmother began searching deep in her mind. Running over all she had seen, read, experienced and heard, she began to think that maybe her first instinct to keep Alex far away from Dragonfly Manor was the right one. As the evening had progressed, she had allowed herself to believe that Alex could have been the one who would bring life back to every Dragonfly home in every village, in every town, in every city, on every island in the world. However, searching her mind she was coming to the horrifying realisation, that his arrival could actually have the opposite result. He could have opened the door to something far from wonderful. His opening the door could be the reason the last dragonfly home could be lost to her.

Grandmother tried to stop her mind spinning out of control, by bringing her focus back to the door and its frame. It was as dark as it had been every day for the

last three hundred years. Then she noticed something!
There was one very tiny, dull pinprick of light that
had remained. Wondering if she was imagining it, she
moved in closer to look. Maybe it was a reflection,
maybe it was a hole in the door itself. As she reached
out to touch it, Alex said,

'I think that's where I was when I was
unconscious. I don't know why I think that but...' He
was stopped mid sentence, interrupted by
grandmother whose mind sparked, it had darted
through time and arrived back to the tattoos she had
read on Melissa.

'The dragonfly that lives here was never meant for
you. Its purpose here tonight was to show you the
way and what is possible. You are right. As much
hope that I hope you bring to us, if whatever is behind
that door lives and comes through and finds you, you
would be a danger to us all. You must go if you feel
you must. I know who you are Alex Hugins. No
book, no legend, no story has ever been written about
any descendant who survived or even existed after the
the one who started it all, Shuing. I believe now, that
you must be part of a family who have been kept
secret, kept hidden. I sensed a change in the house a
couple of weeks ago. I realise now, it was the very
time you and your mother became our neighbours. At
a time when Sophie turns sixteen, that is why what
has happened has happened. It all makes sense. That
is why the dragonfly has awoken and has chosen to be
seen. Alex, your true name is hidden in the rearranged
letters of your given name, you are no Hugins, you
are in fact a Shuing.'

Alex listened to all that she said. There was no
question in his mind he had to leave. He had to find
the place that he had visited, that he had been shown

in his unconscious state and that was shown to all by the door's map. The place it all began. The home of Shuing.

The afternoon and evening's events, as diverse and unusual in their happenings, had shown Alex the true strength he had inside. From the bus and the bully to the pain and the visions, he was ready to take control of his life.

'Mum, we should go home and pack some things. Sophie you should do the same. We have a long trip ahead of us, this I am sure of,' Alex said.

'What about me?' Vicky piped up. 'I could see you when the others couldn't. That seems like a good reason for me to come along, doesn't it?' She was right and Alex knew it.

'For sure, yes, grab some stuff as well,' Alex responded. Heading for the closed front door, Alex didn't even think about the fact that he had vanished from sight the last few times he had stepped out through it. He turned the handle and with the door fully open, he quickly made his way down the wobbly cobbly path, clear of snow, bright red, surrounded by green grass and flowerbeds in full bloom, towards the tunnel of fresh green trees and towards the free-swinging front gate.

'So, no problem there then?' Sophie said to her grandmother, as they watched and waited to see if what had happened before, happened again. Alex could clearly be seen leading the train of people and Bart, out of sight.

Stepping out of the gate the winter returned. The path was as they left it, slippery enough to take the most advanced Eskimo off his or her feet.

'There she is!' A voice shouted from further up the footpath. It was the weasley Mr Sullivan, the accounts manager from Melissa's new place of work. Looking up towards the voice, the group could see he was not alone. He was flanked by two male, uniformed, police officers and a female dressed smartly in a suit. 'That's her, Miss Rice, or whatever her name is!'

Melissa was right, he was trouble. Once she had left work, after having been evasive in providing documental proof of who she was, he started digging. As horrible a man as he was, he was very good at what he did and on that occasion, he discovered that someone of her description had worked and disappeared from more than a few places. He also discovered that she had a son, who appeared not to be her biological son. This led his overthinking brain to assume that maybe the boy she referred to as her son, was in fact the victim of a crime. It took him no time to convince the local constabulary that something wasn't right. Having also provided the authorities with a very good paper trail of evidence, of suspicious name changing activity, they concluded as he did, further investigation was required. The officers were not slow in arriving at Melissa, despite the slippery footpath, with Mr Sullivan grinning creepily behind them.

'Miss Rice, I am arresting you on suspicion of child abduction.'

CHAPTER 13

'Sister, how is it possible for you not to have noticed the bright light? Next you will be telling me you didn't see the unnatural sky this morning!' Lanny said, the brother of the old and frail looking Leilani. He further muttered under his breath as he turned to walk back down the footpath 'stupid, crazy old woman!' Something he regretted, as before he knew it, his head was ringing from a hit that could have come from a professional fighter.

'You forget your place, you cretinous excuse of a man.' The words from Leilani hit a second blow to the buzzing head of Lanny. Somewhere over time the roles had reversed. The twisted, manipulating, in charge character that had defined Lanny, younger brother of Leilani, the brother who had twisted Leilani's mind and taken the lives of their parents so many years earlier, was in no way in charge any more. Her frail exterior and tired mind, were far from giving up in any fight with her brother. Her brother who was the architect of the place she found herself. She had chosen her moment wisely, seeing her opportunity to take control as his mind became consumed with power and the search for more. He was too confident to see that he was being plotted against, too blind with his inflated self-worth. He never thought he would be anything but the king of all he wanted to have, to take, to steal, to kill. He missed that Leilani had been watching her twisted brother, learning from his successes and failures. She was growing stronger and he just didn't see it. With a woman's clear-minded quiet strength, at the perfect moment, she came at him. She took everything from him.

The people who were trapped with the closing of every Dragonfly home around the world, who had become slaves that Lanny had been abusing and killing when required, rose up with the false kindness that Leilani had shown them. Plotting behind his back, learning to harness what magic was left, she was able to turn the tables and masterfully manipulate his brain into a state of madness. Sadly the time had come too late to stop the death of the final dragonfly in the separated realm, lovingly given the name of Heart. Lanny had taken the life of the last dragonfly and used it for himself. This was the reason he was a young man and Leilani remained old. As sad as the loss of the last dragonfly in Heart was, it was a blessing to all on earth. If she had managed to get back through the door that had been closed to her for hundreds of years, the loss to all in Earth's realm would have been as painful and destructive as it was in Heart. Without a dragonfly, the power and the magic that she had discovered in nature within Heart, was useless in any effort she could have made to find a way back to the realm where it all started, Earth.

The skies and their changing colours that morning, the vision that Leilani and Lanny had seen on their front doorstep, all had the result of an untapped strength and energy returning to Leilani.

Leilani knew the stories, the fairytales, the legends that had been forgotten. She had spent her days researching, hoping to find fact amongst the legends. She kept her thoughts and research from her brother. As he had been searching every Dragonfly home for the dragonflies, Leilani had been searching for a way back to Earth. Although trapped in the realm of Heart, the two travelled freely through the magical Dragonfly home doors, within Heart. The map, the pinpricks of light that could be found on every Dragonfly home's front door, was their way to travel to every part of Heart. A magical and freeing gift that was given by the first, so that those who came to Heart, could see every wonderful part, meet all the most beautiful of people and animals that lived there. Lanny figured out quickly that this wonderful gift, was a wonderful way to take what he wanted. No dragonfly was needed to journey to another Dragonfly home within Heart. He and his sister could arrive without warning, take what they wanted, and they did.

Leilani's search for fact, the truth of Heart's beginning, came to an end in one particular tiny Dragonfly cottage, after being ransacked in the most violent of ways by Lanny and his scared into being loyal Sun Bears, the smallest but most vicious of the bear family. Leilani, on arrival at a new Dragonfly home, would stand motionless, seemingly unfazed, unaffected, uninterested by the devastation. She just watched on as Lanny and his bears did their worst. Once finished, Lanny and his army would leave the house to investigate the lands outside. Leilani however would remain. Once silence fell, all had left or been taken, Leilani would begin her secret search. In this particular tiny Dragonfly cottage, during her search of a room filled with books, she noticed a small protrusion high up on a wall. She dragged an old chair through the books and furniture torn up and scattered over the floor and climbed up to get a closer look. What she found, was a very cleverly concealed drawer. Having pulled it fully open, Leilani discovered torn, crumpled, brown stained papers, a huge pile of them. On the papers was written the story of a man who lived many thousands of years earlier. The story of a man named Shuing. It was a name she knew well. She had heard the stories and legends about him and where it all started and they were many and conflicting. But the papers she had found, they gave very specific detail and what she believed was undistorted fact. She had at last found what she had been looking for. Sitting down on the chair she had used as a ladder, she studied every single piece of torn, crumpled, brown stained paper.

The writings told of a lonely man who wandered the earth with no plan, no direction, no expectations. A man who spoke very few words, who was known to those who took a moment out of their lives to acknowledge him, as odd. He had a special gift, which was more like a curse! He felt all that everyone around him felt. He felt the sadness and pain of all, whether he conversed with them or whether they were just walking by. He had no control over what sadness and pain he would feel, he felt it all. He was a most unusual empath. He lived in a time of great suffering. The very few but powerful rulers took everything that they wanted, people were nothing to them but objects to be used and discarded. The balance of nature had been lost, the world was nothing more than a wasteland of despair to the majority of its inhabitants.

Leilani read with enthusiasm. Losing herself in the words, the writings told the story of an unusually tall man, who as a young man had long, curly, dirty blonde hair, with the clearest of blue eyes. As a tired old man, his hair became grey and course, his eyes dull. The weight of the pain carried in his heart and soul forced his shoulders to fall further and further forward. The very few words he spoke as a younger man became no words at all as he aged. Not a single word had left his lips for more years than he could remember.

His heart, mind and body were unable to hold any more suffering, the writings told of one particular day. He had found himself in the middle of a dark and dismal street. A roadway of mud, surrounded by broken down, dark wooden shacks, the homes of the small town's residents. Standing in the mud, he was hit by the pain of a child having found his mother murdered. The cries of the young child cut through his soul and his silence broke. He let out a scream that pierced the ears of all within a thousand miles of where he stood. Shuing could do or take no more. His tens of years of taking the pain from others as an empath were at an end. His hope of helping earth and its human race finally gone. The scream coming to an end, Shuing fell into the mud beneath his worn feet. On his back looking up, the sky began to swirl, colours he had never seen before were dancing. He tried to lift his head, he couldn't, his life's energy was leaving him. One last blink, one last effort in focusing on the renewing lights above him, the last morsel of strength left him. He closed his eyes. All went dark. His mind, for the first time, went quiet.

Some time past before Shuing awoke to the darkness of night. Sitting up, he was shocked to find himself at the top of a pile of bodies. Old, rotting, discarded without any care, loved ones. As he went to escape the unimaginable pile, he wasn't able to keep his balance. He fell down the slippery, smelly slope of death. His fall was softened by a leaf covered floor. His momentum carried him towards a cliff's edge. An old heavy tree branch that had fallen some time ago, was all that was between him and falling into a darkness that appeared to him to have no end. He was safe. His time of being lost to the world had not lessened the heaviness and pain he felt in his heart and soul. Shuing pulled himself up, got to his feet and began to walk away from the awful place. It was a walk that would take him many years to complete. In a haze, his vision a blur from that moment on, his legs did not stop until one freezing cold morning, in a place free from human life, Shuing felt nothing! The pain and despair that had filled his heart and soul, was gone.

For the first time in many years, Shuing raised his head and looked up at the sky. The very same swirl of lights and colours he had seen that day of his scream, were visible to him once again. His blurred vision began to clear. Hypnotically transfixed, he watched as the centre of the swirl began to fall to earth. There was a light mist covering the ground where he stood, it came up to the height of his knees. As he walked, his legs cut a path through the damp, cold mist, a wake undulating away from him as he did. He was heading towards the point in which the light was vanishing below the motionless sea of white. Unable to see the ground for the mist, his body did not react, his legs did not stop their purposeful forward motion when his feet took a step from land into water. Freezing cold, fresh, clean water. The water made its way up his body until he finally reached a depth where his feet no longer had contact with the ground. His legs lifted up, floating to just under the surface of the water he began to swim. Shuing was heading further and further away from land and its occupants he was happy to leave behind. The lights beginning or the end, he was not sure, was so close. His arms and legs tiring, his head and body beginning to lower in the water, Shuing wasn't sure how much further he could go. There was no sign of any land, apart from the hills and mountains far in the distance. He paused for a moment in an effort to regain some strength. As he did, his legs dropped down, to stay afloat he kicked his feet. As he treaded water, he realised he was still moving towards the lights. The water's currents were carrying him to where he wanted to be. A small amount of strength returned and Shuing went to kick his legs up to swim once again. He didn't need to, his feet felt something beneath them. Solid, slippery, moving - it was sand, gravel, stones. Shuing was walking once again. The walk in the freezing water was not a long one. He was happy as he felt the water line make its way down his freezing cold, shaking body. Looking down through the fading mist, he could see that the water was no higher than his ankles. With every step he took towards the lights, they got brighter and the warmth they emitted got stronger, thawing his frozen body. Shuing was experiencing a feeling he could not recall ever feeling, the feeling of excitement. It was short lived. As he finally stepped out of the freezing waters, the lights that had guided him to where he found himself, vanished. His cold body painfully tingling as it warmed, his muscles spent from the swim, the lights gone, his moment of excitement far too fleeting, he collapsed.

Shuing waited for the impact of a hard rocky ground. Falling, he turned to look back at where he had come from. His arms outstretched, he held his breath. The hard impact did not come! Shiung was caught by a soft, unnaturally warm ground. His landing pushed away the thinning mist revealing what had saved him any pain. Thick green grass, filled with flowers of every colour, a display of nature's lush life-filled beauty.

Shuing felt life filling him up. A youthfulness that he hadn't felt in over one hundred years was returning. Free from human, animal and nature's suffering, having spent all he had, caring for all he came across, he was being reborn. Not moving from the place he fell, he fell into a deep sleep. The quietest of sleeps.

It could have been minutes, it could have been an hour, it could have been days. Shuing did not know how long he had slept. When he awoke, it was to a warmth not only beneath him, but also from the sky above him. Not a cloud visible, the sun and its healing warmth brought him slowly from his slumber. He was waking to a place that not even his dreams could have shown him. Nature was all around him. More alive than he had ever been, the energies from the sun, the plants, the earth, the water, all of nature, had made him whole.

Shuing's days were spent exploring the small lush island he had been guided to. Over the coming months he cared for it with so much love. His love of nature and all things living around him, plant or animal, had the happy result of him becoming the island's centre, wherever he stood. Instead of the plants reaching for the sun as they grew, they would move towards him as he passed. Animals would seek him out, sit with him, follow him.

Many calm and happy months and years passed. Shuing did not count, or care to count how many. He existed and he was happy, he desired nothing more than to be part of nature's beautiful world.

A number of summers had passed and another was

with him again. As with every season, new friends would arrive. On this particular summer season, Shuing was excited to meet an insect that he had heard of in legend, but had never seen in person.

The legends that surrounded it were many and conflicting. What was known, was that this creature had been around since animals walked the earth. A part of Mother Nature's gift for over three hundred million years. The stories that were told, were of how they would show dinosaurs to water, as well as humans when they eventually walked the earth. Stories of how they would protect the weak from the strong were written in folklore. How they came in the night to close the eyes, mouths and ears of anyone that would do harm to another, so they could do it no more. Some legends told of how they would come and kill animals by biting and injecting poison into them. The actual truth being that they were saving animals' lives by removing poison, sacrificing themselves for the greater good. These beautiful insects were, from the day they arrived, there to help and protect all. The dragonfly was a true gift.

As sure as he was that the dragonfly was there, after several weeks, Shuing had still not seen it. Daily he would send a welcoming word in the direction he thought he'd heard it, often having a full conversation with what he hoped was living just out of sight. He hoped like all the other visitors, that the dragonfly would come and spend time with him.

'You can heal the earth!' The first voice Shuing had heard since arriving at his island, took him by surprise. He had been tending the flowers that were growing around where he had constructed a home for himself. He looked around. There was no one. 'You are looking with a human mind.' The voice came again. Shuing was confused. His calm and peaceful state was being replaced with a far too familiar pain returning to his head. The piercing pain in his skull took him to his knees. He closed his eyes and took his head into his hands, the pain of the world he had left had returned.

'Make it stop!' Shuing screamed out loud. As instantly as he screamed the words, he got what he asked for, it stopped. Lifting his head, he slowly opened his eyes. As they adjusted to the sunlight, he saw the shape of something large sitting on a rock, a small distance from him. Sitting on the rock was a dragonfly. It was far larger than he had imagined, but its beauty took his breath away.

Shuing did not want to scare his new friend away, so got to his feet and made his way over to where it sat very slowly. He could hear the sound of the dragonfly's wings getting louder. He feared that the volume and the increasing speed, meant that the dragonfly was building up for an escape. 'It's ok. I am not going to hurt you my friend,' Shuing said.

'I know,' a voice came from nowhere again. 'Stop looking with your human self. Not all that is, can be seen, or heard, by all.' The voice was coming from everywhere. 'You are the one who can take the pain from this twisted earth realm. You are the one who can take those suffering to a separated place. A place born many thousands of years ago. A place not polluted by hate and greed. A place where magic has been growing and where all that live and breathe, are connected in a way that could be brought into earth's reality. Having watched you over the days, months and years since your arrival, I believe you are the one, and only one, to bring it.' The voice stopped. As it did, the dragonfly left its rock and flew directly at

Shuing, who instinctively raised his arm to protect himself. The dragonfly was making no attack. It took full advantage of his outstretched arm and landed on his hand, its weight surprising Shuing as it did. The voice that was coming from everywhere, was that of the dragonfly.

'I don't understand. How can I hear you?' Shuing asked.

'You can hear because you are different. You can hear because I have chosen you. You can hear because the world needs to be saved. Without the Earth realm, the realm that was separated so long ago would not have existed,' the dragonfly responded. Shuing was caught in the dragonfly's gaze. As its wings began to move once more, reaching a blur of colour, Shuing was hit with a pain. A shooting pain that sunk deep into his hand, shot up his arm and filled his entire body.

'Aaaaaaaaaaaa!' Shuing let out a scream as loud as the day he could take no more. Shuing's arm began to drop, the weight of the dragonfly was increasing. Having grown to the size of an eagle, his arm almost at his waist, the talking dragonfly took off into the sky, leaving behind it a trail of magical colours. Shuing's body was not his own, his mind was not his own. Visions of places he had never been filled his head along with plants, animals, land, sea, full and clean, unspoilt by the human race. He was being taken on a journey back in time. Looking up in his vision, he watched as a huge rock that blocked out the sun, fell from the sky and hit exactly where he was standing. The impact shook the earth to its core, causing a ghostly shadow of itself to be pushed out. The shadow was the place Shuing was being shown, never seen and completely unspoilt by humankind.

The images and visions he was being given came to an end. The pain he had been feeling was slowly subsiding. Shuing was returning to the peace and calm he had come to know on his island. Looking up to the sky to try and find his new friend, he saw something very different. What he saw was the shadow. The separated world.

'Wait, stop,' Shuing shouted to the sky, as from it, at speed, the returning dragonfly was heading right at him. Stepping back he did not want to lose sight of the large dragonfly and its trail of colours, or be struck by it. His backwards movement was stopped by a tree. He had been moving fast, so the tree took the air from his lungs. Unable to breathe, he waited for the imminent impact.

The sound of the huge dragonfly's wings as the air was forced away from them, got louder and louder. Shuing accepted the inevitable. He rested his head back onto the tree and watched as the dragonfly flew right into him. He felt no pain! There were no broken bones, there was no tearing of skin, instead all that he felt was a revitalising energy. Going in through his chest, he felt the energy exit from his back. It disappeared, disappeared into the very tree that had halted Shuing's escape. All fell silent. Shuing stepped forward, looked down at himself. Confirming all was well, he turned and looked up at the tree. A section of bark had been removed where his back had been against it. This exposed part of the fresh, moist, newest ring of the tree. On closer inspection, he could see something had been imprinted on it - the shape of a dragonfly.

Slightly dazed from the experience, Shuing was refocused once again as he heard the voice of his new dragonfly friend, although looking around he could not see him. A couple of moments passed. As Shuing had not responded, the voice repeated his words once more. It was then that Shuing realised the words, the voice, they were coming from inside his head. His dragonfly friend had joined with him, they had become one. The gift had been given, the opportunity of a new beginning for the pain-filled realm of Earth had arrived. The dragonfly had sacrificed, gambled all that he had. Shuing could use what he had been given for the good of all, the good of himself, or indeed he could choose not to use what he had been given at all. The words Shuing had heard in his head, the words of the dragonfly, he would have to decipher them and make his choice.

'The power given is for only one, the power given is more than should be, the power given can heal or destroy, the power given is the beginning or the end. The trees, they offer you a doorway, I and my family offer you ourselves as keys. Your kind, empathic heart and soul have made the impossible possible. The possible journey of many wonders has begun.'

There were many more stories beyond that day in the papers Leilani skimmed over. Many pages that spoke of Shuing, who lived for many thousands of years travelling Earth's realm. He brought peace and love to those who deserved and needed it, not resting until the day Earth and the separated realm had balance. The spreading of the dragonfly trees to every village, to every town, to every city, to every country, to every island on our wonderful planet Earth, brought hope. Those pages and those stories were for when she had motivation and time to read them. At that moment, Leilani had found in Shuing's beginning, all she needed to know.

Leilani was fully aware that her and her brother's

actions, had brought the reality that Shuing and the dragonfly had given to Earth's realm, to an end. The dragonflies were consumed, the doors between the realms were closed, the legend was forgotten by all but her. Earth had returned in a surprisingly short time to a place of pain and suffering. Humankind's respect and understanding of one another had gone. Humankind's respect and understanding of nature had gone. Greed and selfishness caused the death of so many beautiful souls. Anger, selfishness, bitterness, violence, all returned to rule Earth's realm. Nature's beautiful animals, its lands, its seas, its skies, suffered at the hands of the humans who took what they wanted, giving no thought to the consequences.

Knowing the story and legends as well as Leilani did and now having such specific details and facts of how and where it all began, she saw an opportunity. By helping the continued demise of Earth's realm, she calculated the dragonfly would return. It had to, as with Earth's destruction would come the destruction of Heart. All she had to do was complete what she thought was an impossible task. It was all well and good to have the facts, but she had to find the place and that one human such as Shuing who could make it all possible. Many years passed. The reality that her search had to be in Earth's realm, the place she could not get to, had her getting more angry, frustrated, irrational and insane with each day that passed. Until one day, a happy accident provided her with an opportunity. Her brother's obsession with gold, was for the first time going to be of interest to her.

Lanny's gold obsession and the power he thought it would bring, had caused him to build a store, to keep it safe and close to hand. It was dug deep underground. Its true vastness was hidden by a relatively small, gold-walled building built above it - the store's entrance, hidden by the forest that surrounded their Dragonfly Manor. Inside, in the centre of its structure, amongst the many levels of gold stores, was the place he would melt and reform the gold he mined.

Lanny had hundreds of small dogs that ran about, forced to work for him in his store. On the day of Leilani's fateful visit, one of the small dogs had got in his way. His anger, always there, rumbling just beneath the surface, exploded, and the small dog's mistake of not moving out the way quick enough, ended badly. With one look to his sun bear guardians, the defenceless soul had no chance. There was an instantaneous violent attack, the bears teeth sinking deep into the flesh of their victim. Lifted from the ground, one bear shook the poor dog violently. The shaking caused blood to fly across the melting area, some of which fell into one of Lanny's vats of melting gold. Lanny's anger was increased with the impurity entering his precious gold. He yelled and pointed for Leilani to look at the cause of his increased rage. Leaning over to look, the crystal that she wore daily around her neck, somehow, possibly as simply as she had not secured it tightly enough, fell from her neck. Her surprisingly quick reactions, meant that she caught the leather from which the crystal hung. Her reactions, although quick, were not quick enough to stop the crystal from landing in the blood and gold mix. It covered the bottom half of its clear, shining pureness. Leilani's upset at her crystal being tainted was short lived. As she lifted the crystal from the gold, a picture appeared. A moving picture. The place she was being shown looked familiar. It was the very place she stood, prior to her brother's gold store being built. Well not quite the very place. It was the same place, just not in the realm of Heart. The unexpected incident had created a window to the realm of Earth!

Leilani spent some time, very successfully, working on different ways to expand the window. Having grown her collection of crystals, having caused the suffering of many an animal who had been forced to give their blood for her experiments, she created a way to see what she wanted. By altering which crystals she used, their quantities and the amount of blood, she was able to manipulate the window to see past and present and almost wherever she wanted in Earth's realm. There was more though. Leilani found a way that she could manipulate certain humans, who had certain character traits, to do as she wished. She had discovered that with the universe and all within it having an electrical current, she could tap into those currents and use them. Manipulating the universe's energies, she could whisper to those with inflated egos and greedy, nasty, self-important personalities. These were the kinds of people who would not entertain the thought that any idea that entered their heads was not their own. These people gave Leilani the puppets she needed, an actual influencing link to Earth.

It was perfect, she could bring the world down with just a gentle nudge. It really didn't need anything more than a gentle nudge. So many living in Earth's realm had strong tendencies towards selfishness and destruction. With the pain and suffering returning in huge abundance and nature being forgotten, Leilani found it was becoming easier and easier to play her games, to get what she wanted, to bring Earth's realm to a time where she hoped nature would once again intervene.

She knew that if nature did intervene, she would have to know the place and person that would be used. With all the insight she had, her control of certain people and her ability to see into Earth's realm at any moment, now and in time that had passed, Leilani could not find the one that she hoped existed. The one that nature would need. The one that would be chosen to return the power of the dragonfly to every Dragonfly home in every village, in every town, in every city, in every country, on every island, on our wonderful planet Earth.

Not finding the one, she had hoped she would at least find the place where it all started. Its location was hinted at in the notes, with reference to a very specific pinprick of light on the door's map being its location. A few years earlier, she did think she had found its location. A scientist in Earth's realm, discovered the signs of an incredible impact on earth from a meteor millions of years earlier. The scientist's findings matched the notes found by Leilani, which referred to an impact causing a 'ghostly shadow of itself to be pushed out'. The scientist's discovery was found deep in the centre of the northernmost Scottish Highlands. The impact caused a loch to be formed, a place that showed every sign that it could have been the place a small island could have existed. Using her window to Earth's realm, she searched through thousands of years in the area of the impact. Everything pointed to it being the place - strange happenings, gravity being lighter than anywhere else on Earth, creatures that should not exist still existing, but Leilani could not find the island that had been described in stolen notes from the ransacked tiny cottage.

Leilani's efforts in helping human nature to fill Earth's realm with pain and suffering, by igniting humanities self-destructive tendencies, worked. With no sign of the new Shuing or the island where it all started, she came to believe that nature, this time, would not step in. The realm of Earth and Heart would end. Their energies would be absorbed back into the universe. She had accepted that her end was close.

But today Leilani was thinking differently. Today it had all changed. The appearance of the morning's unnatural lights and the evening's appearance of the ghostly torso, had awakened her selfish hopes.

'Lanny, I need you to melt me some gold, NOW!' She spun on her heels and quickly shuffled to a dark, musky smelling room, to the back of the house. The room was filled with crystals, bottled blood and in its centre was a hollowed out tree trunk. The trunk had come from a tree she had pulled up and cut to her specifications from one of the Dragonfly homes they had ransacked. Leilani's tree trunk cauldron had some of its roots still attached. Having been ripped from the ground they had been born into, they now spread across Leilani's moss covered, cobbled floor. Having chosen a selection of different sized crystals, on this occasion six, she began carefully hanging them from the ceiling, spacing them at equal distances from each other around the edges of the tree trunk. It wasn't long before Lanny returned with two of his Sun Bears. In their teeth they held a thick bar. Hanging in the middle, between the two bears, was a huge hollowed out rock glowing red. In its centre was liquid gold.

'Pour it in then!' Leilani aggressively ordered. She

took the crystal from around her neck, still covered half way up in solid gold, and dipped it into a bottle of blood she had removed from one of the dusty, dirty shelves. The shining gold of the crystal was now covered in the crimson red liquid. She then reached forward into the centre of the liquid, gold-filled tree trunk. Lowering it towards the gold, the crystal began to spin. Closing her eyes, she visualised the question she wanted answered. 'Who was at her door?' She asked it over and over, until a picture appeared. The window to Earth's realm was open. The crystal spun so fast, it hung in the air without any help from Leilani, so she let go of the leather necklace. Standing back, she watched as the ghostly torso she had seen on her doorstep earlier appeared in the window she had opened, not ghostly this time, but in its solid form. She could not see the rest of the body or where it lay, which frustrated her greatly. As much as she had tried over the years, she could not see inside the DragonFly Manor that she knew as a child in Earth's realm. She blew on the image and the moving pictures began to reverse through time, through years and different places of the young man's life, back to the time he was a baby. Time spinning past in a blur, something caught Leilani's attention. In the blink of her eye, the black mother of the white child, had changed to a white mother. She froze the picture she was watching at that very point.

'Something is not right here,' Leilani said. Her timing from years of experience was perfect. She had paused on the very moment a heart-breaking letter was being written. Blowing again on the image, she managed to get in close to what was being written,

'Alex Hugins, oh really, how stupid do you think I am? Hugins, Shuing, Hugins it's Shuing!' Leilani was beside herself with excitement having broken the anagram code.

'Stupid? Yes I would suggest stupid, seeing as we have seen that name before,' Lanny said.

'Seen it before?' Leilani questioned, after throwing the emptied jar of blood at her brother, which smashed as it hit the floor.

'Yes. When you were looking at that place with the meteor strike, all those years ago. There was a family that lived there that you were drawn to, but you could never get to do as you willed. We never could figure out where they lived, but you were obsessed with them for a period of time. Do you not remember? ' Lanny asked. Leilani was furious with herself, but was not going to show that to her brother,

'Don't be ridiculous you imbecile. I would not have missed that name,' Leilani said. She had missed it. With a flick of her head and a stronger blow, time in the picture sped forward. She watched intently as she tried to see angles, people, places, that could help in her getting control of the people that she had been watching. The people who were connected to the life of the torso, that she now realised could well be a descendant of Shuing.

'Ah, you will do just nicely,' Leilani said. She had found her way to the conversation between Melissa and Mr Sullivan from her new place of work. 'He is perfect - nasty, angry, troublesome,' Leilani said. Reaching forward, she sunk her hand into the picture and unbeknown to Mr Sullivan she took hold of him. She placed in his mind all she needed to, to get the young man she had seen, Alex, away from his mother, Melissa. A situation which she calculated would leave Alex vulnerable to her control.

'I shall leave this window open Lanny, but I need

more gold,' Leilani said. Without hesitation, Lanny, crunching the broken glass under his feet from the jar that had been thrown at him, made his way out of the room and back off to his store of gold. The gold that Lanny had brought in previously required replacing, as it had lost its energies, having been used by Leilani and her searching window. The gold that had lost its shining golden colour was now a clear liquid. It ran slowly from the tree trunk out through the tiniest of holes, small enough that the previously thick liquid gold could not have escaped. The clear liquid made its way out of the holes and on to the damp, cobbled floor, eventually disappearing round and down past the edges of the cobbles, returning itself to Mother Nature's earth.

Leilani, happy with her work so far, was confident that what she had put into action would play out just perfectly. Leaving the frozen image where it was, the window open, she followed her brother out of the room. Leilani had noticed something whilst looking through her window to Earth's realm. She had seen that the outside of Earth's Dragonfly Manor had shown signs of renewal. She wanted to see if her own Dragonfly Manor had such signs.

Stepping out from the old looking house, she was disappointed to see that nothing had changed. Earl, her furry companion, didn't fancy the chill in the air so he remained inside, watching as she went out of sight and the still old door swung closed behind Leilani with a bang.

'Well that's disappointing,' she said, not aware that Earl had preferred the cold of the house to the cold of outside and was not by her side. The night had fallen, the cold winds were beginning to pick up. The tall trees hiding her manor from the fields beyond were creaking loudly, breaking the silence that a remote home away from people provided. As with all Dragonfly homes, Leilani and Lanny's Dragonfly home was the only part of the realm of Heart that mirrored Earth's realm. The mirroring of each Dragonfly home was however stopped the moment the connection was broken. Each home became independent of one an other - changes in one would no longer be mirrored in the other. A change in Leilani's home that matched that of the Earth's realm home would have meant that the connection had been restored. Leilani's disappointment wasn't hidden.

Away from every Dragonfly home, all the land of the realm of Heart was lovingly looked after and in some places built on by its privileged visitors. Of course since Lanny's systematic destruction of all the Dragonfly homes in every village, in every town, in every city, in every country, on every island around the realm, its inhabitants disappeared from sight. Having either hidden to avoid capture, or been captured and used as slaves until their death, life was hard to find, it hid well. With no living being willing to be seen, the realm of Heart had been completely taken over by nature. Its animals, non human life, lived in the shadows so as not to be seen, captured and used by the brother and sister for their twisted experiments. They were enjoying Mother Nature's protection. The towns and villages that had been built by those that chose to stay and never return to the realm of Earth had been abandoned. Beautiful undulations of every colour from nature hid the homes that once stood above them, perfect places to hide for those who wish to be hidden! Not that Leilani or Lanny had looked for many years. Aware they had used up all they could, their age getting the better of them, they had just been waiting for death.

At Leilani's Dragonfly Manor, nothing had changed beyond its trees and gates for so many years. No town or street had grown up around her house, it was still very much a Manor House, on its own, hidden from all. She wandered down the old, uneven, rotten looking cobbles towards the gate hidden in the trees. She wondered if life may have returned to her land, with the light she had seen in the sky that morning, but no, as with her home, all was still the same - dried up, old looking fields and the dirt track leading off to Lanny's massive gold store, was as dead looking as a desert. The only structure that had grown from the ground in the last three hundred years, which had also lost its shine, the dust from its surroundings covering it, was Lanny's gold store.

Watching her brother walk back up the road towards her, his two Sun Bears behind him struggling with the new batch of liquid gold, she, unusually for her, got a fright. A loud crack of electricity came from behind her. Lanny, having also heard the noise, broke into a run. He arrived at the gate just in time to see a supernatural flash of light come from the closed door of their Dragonfly Manor. The crack was followed by an explosion of colours, followed by something else. Smugly, Leilani laughed and very calmly said,

'It's our dragonfly. Oh my, how you've grown.'

CHAPTER 14

'What should I pack?' Sophie asked as she closed the big red front door. Still young in her life experiences, a planned trip was something she hadn't experienced, let alone a trip with no destination or timeframe. Also, although she had now turned sixteen, she had the good fortune of having an upbringing with grandmother, which allowed her to be a child, act as a child and enjoy an element of innocence, despite her parents abandoning her and the life she lived within her dreams. Having always been a loner, Sophie had socialised more in that one night than she had most of her life. So much had happened. She knew her mind well, she knew it would replay the evening's events over time, but in that moment, her mind was occupied. In that moment she felt so alive, excited, full of anticipation as to what was to come.

'Not much,' was grandmother's response to Sophie's question. Having not left Dragonfly Manor in the three hundred years she had been waiting, grandmother did not know what the outside world would hold for her granddaughter. Her only experiences of the outside world came from her granddaughter's stories, the books she read and from the visitors. The visitors who had become non existent since Leilani and Lanny wiped the realms of Heart and Earth clean of all dragonflies and their key keepers. Since the Dragonfly homes reality turned into stories, legends and sadly were forgotten. What grandmother was sure of was that Sophie would be looked after. The day had started and ended with hope. Dragonfly Manor, as unexplainable as it was, had kept grandmother alive, well and supplied with all she needed, so she believed that the same would be true for her granddaughter Sophie. 'The less you have my princess, the less you need. The less you need my princess, the happier you will be. Pack a small bag and you will find that what is required, will find you,' were grandmother's wise words.

'Ok,' Sophie replied. A little confused as to what that all meant, she disappeared up the full of life staircase, followed by a bounding Anchor. Stepping on to the landing filled with a subdued but beautiful light, she stopped. Looking up to see where the light was coming from, her breath was taken away by what she saw. The ceiling was alive, full of stars, planets, colours, swirls of galaxies moving slowly. The light was changing as a new star came into focus and an old one left. Sophie, mesmerised by what she was seeing, was interrupted by a gangly Anchor, whose out of control legs once again failed to stop his charging forward motion as he crashed into the back of her legs.

'You will never change will you,' Sophie said to him. He looked up at her with his smiling eyes and dopey looking face full of happiness, his tail wagging, crashing off the banister. Sophie ruffled his head and headed for her bedroom. What she saw as she opened the door was far from her usual organised, chaotic room. All her belongings were still thrown across the floor but the walls! They were far from the old peeling paint, hidden by the posters that had covered them. Her room was a forest! The centre of her room was a clearing and every wall was covered in the most colourful trees. Trees, by the size of their trunks, that must have been hundreds of years old, to trees that were just showing their first signs of life. Sophie could smell the array of scents from the trees and the tiny flowers that covered the ground. She could hear water from somewhere. She spun round to see. On the wall behind her door, a fresh, clear brook trickled calmly off into the trees. Anchor barked loudly as he came into the room, not sure what to make of it all. His first reaction to anything, even before he knew what it was, was to bark.

'Anchor, you silly dog,' Sophie said. Playing around the water were the smallest, just alive, dragonflies. Each one had its own colours - purples, pinks, blues, greens, all glistened, creating a show of light that if focused on for too long, became a rainbow, rather than the many individual dragonflies. Sophie took a deep breath and closed her eyes, allowing all her senses to fully enjoy what her bedroom had become.

Bang, bang, bang, Sophie's eyes popped wide open. Crash... Anchor shot off out the bedroom door, the hackles on his back were up, giving him the look of being twice the size he was. Sophie followed as quickly as she could, but was no match for Anchor's speed, who disappeared down the stairs out of sight growling as he did.

'Grandmother!' Sophie shouted. Her feet hardly touched the stairs. Using the banister as balance, she cleared half a dozen steps, her speed and rapid descent causing her red hair to bounce and fly out behind her. Reaching the first landing, the growls from Anchor had stopped. They had been replaced with whimpers.

'They are going to take her.' Alex, out of breath, emotional, panicked, was once again standing in the hallway of Dragonfly Manor.

'Take who?' grandmother asked, appearing from the room full of books.

'My mum!' Alex said,

'Calm down, tell me what happened,' grandmother said, putting her hands on his shoulders and looking into his eyes as she did. Sophie, arriving at grandmother's side and stepping past Anchor, took Alex's hand.

'I don't know. Just these two policeman, some guy and woman appeared and said mum was being arrested. For child abduction.' Alex couldn't calm down. 'She told me to run. I didn't want to, but she pushed me. I left her outside the gate, I...' he couldn't talk, his emotions got the better of him, tears were pouring down his face. Alex had experienced a lot of emotional suffering during his short life moving from school to school, but Melissa, his mum, was always there. She was his foundation. He had never seen her look so scared. He had never been pushed away by her and he didn't like it. He had also never been in the presence of a police officer. The uniform, handcuffs, weapon attached to their belts, their army looking vests that made them look bigger than they were, all scary and intimidating. The man that shouted 'there she is,' he had an evilness to him that filled Alex with dread. And the woman who followed, she had a purposefulness to her walk that unnerved him. The whole thing happened so quickly.

'I think I may have done something bad. Everything just went blank.' Alex managed to force out the words before his emotions took over again. Sophie stepped closer to Alex, knocking grandmother's hands from his shoulders as she did, she wrapped her arms round him. She didn't say a

word. They stood together, with Anchor nudging
Alex's leg whimpering. Grandmother in the
meantime, had disappeared up the stairs to her
bedroom. She hoped to be able to see something but
she couldn't! So as quickly as she left, she returned to
where Alex, Sophie and Anchor still stood. She did
not want to leave Dragonfly Manor, but she knew she
had to.

'Where are you going?' Sophie said, as
grandmother opened the front door and took her first
step outside.

'Stay here, I will be back in a minute,'
grandmother said. Tottering down the path, she
couldn't help but be distracted by and admire the
flowers that had grown, flowers she remembered as a
child, full of variety and colour. Her home had truly
returned to its magical self.

Walking through the tunnel of bright green trees,
she recalled the fun she'd had chasing her brother and
the friends that would visit, there and in Heart. It had
been such a long time since she had allowed herself to
reminisce over the warm memories of her time as a
young girl. Three hundred years had passed, three
hundred years of not changing from the age she was,
waiting for something but not knowing what, hoping
for something but not knowing what.

As she stepped out of her tunnel of memories,
grandmother could see that the bright red front gate
was wide open. She smiled to see its twisting metal
design looking so new and alive. Then she looked
down at her wobbly cobbly path that was clear of
snow, to where the outside world met its bright
colour, the pavement beyond her garden a brilliant
snowy white. The uneven surface of frozen snow and
ice reflected the street lights, the shining undulating

surface creating shadows. Getting closer to the open gate, there was a shadow that didn't fit with the direction the light came from. It was in fact not a shadow at all.

'Oh,' grandmother exclaimed. What she saw was the forearm and hand of someone lying in the snow. Her pace slowed. What was she about to come across? Cautiously having arrived at the border to winter, she followed the hand and arm to its owner,

'Melissa!' Grandmother's voice echoed across the square. It was Melissa. She was lying on the floor in the cold, not moving. Grandmother looked up. What she saw caused her to step back into the safety of her spring like garden. From where Melissa lay was a circle of destruction. There were rings of snow lines which got wider apart as they moved away from her, snow lines that hinted at an energy explosion of great force. Its centre, its starting point, being just to the side of where Melissa lay. The cars that had been parked on the road side had been pushed out, they were laying on their sides and roofs. Snow piles had been pushed to the outer edge of the ripples. There was no distinction between the road and the snow covered grassed green area at the centre of the square. Gathering herself, grandmother peeked out from her garden again. She couldn't leave Melissa lying where she was. She looked to see if the area was safe. Looking up the street towards the home of Alex and Melissa, she saw that the garden walls to a few of Dragonfly Manor's neighbours were rubble. Only the wall of Dragonfly Manor still stood untouched. Then she realised that Melissa was not the only person lying in the snow. A few metres away were the bodies of two uniformed policemen, a suited lady and a weasley looking man, all of whom were in the same state as Melissa, showing no signs of life. It looked like they had been thrown some distance from whatever blast had hit them.

'Grandmother!' A voice shouted from the other side of the discarded cars. It was Vicky. She had come out of hiding having heard grandmother shouting Melissa's name.

'Child, are you alright? What happened here?' grandmother asked. Vicky appeared from behind someone's wrecked pride and joy with a startled looking Bart.

'It was Alex. They were trying to take Melissa away,' Vicky said, pointing at the scattered strangers.

'How are you standing?' grandmother asked. Vicky explained how Melissa had ordered Alex and her to run when she saw the police approaching, how Bart had not needed to be told twice, as he just about pulled her arm out of her socket whilst pulling her across the square. How when she had got about halfway across the square, she heard what she could only describe as the high pitched sound of thousands of flying insects, at which point she let go of Bart and turned to see Alex's eyes shining as bright purple as they had earlier that night. She described how everything suddenly went quiet and as it did, everything just exploded away from him. The noise of crashing cars and walls crumbing filled the air. Vicky described it as a war zone.

'I couldn't see what happened after that, as the pile of cars hid everything.' Vicky was shaking. She bent down to touch Melissa, with Bart by her side who had started licking Melissa's hand, hoping to see some sign of life. 'I didn't know what to do, I just stayed hidden. Alex, where is Alex?' Vicky asked, looking around and seeing the four others lying motionless.

'He is inside, he is fine. Come on, we have to get Melissa inside,' grandmother said. Both looked at the powerful woman lying in front of them, neither really knowing how they were going to shift her. Each took a hand as they tried to drag Mellisa into the safety of Dragonfly Manor's garden. After the first completely ineffective pull from grandmother and Vicky, Melissa gave them both such a fright as she woke up startled. She yanked her hands free and in the blink of an eye, stood up.

'Alex!' Melissa said loudly, her dark eyes wide open, frantically looking around trying to find her son.

'He is fine, he is inside,' grandmother said. Melissa looked at the bombsite that she had been in the centre of. Seeing the people who were there to take her from her boy, she took the decision to leave them where they lay, completely out of character for her. On her feet, her fight or flight state having taken over, she took no mind of Vicky or grandmother and she was up the path to Dragonfly Manor as quick as she had got to her feet. Grandmother, Vicky and Bart followed. By the time they had made their way through the tunnel of green, Melissa was in the house hugging Alex and Sophie. Her long, strong arms wrapped round both of them. Stepping in through the front door and closing it behind her, Vicky said,

'It would appear we are not allowed to leave this place tonight,' she said in her joking way, which on that occasion had the well needed effect of breaking the tension.

'Alex, what happened to you?' Melissa asked.

'Remember that time I told you about at school, in the canteen a few years ago, when I broke the tray?' Alex asked. Melissa nodded. She hated that story. She had taken him there, she had put him in the school that had taken away any confidence that her son had left from the continual moving from place to place. Her heart hurt to think of her son hurting the way he did.

'It was like that. I remember seeing those policemen coming to get you and everything went blurry, like I wasn't there. I got so hot I felt like I was going to explode. There was a noise, it was like a screaming. When everything went quiet, I sort of remember seeing you lying on the floor. The next thing I remember is being back in here. Mum I'm sorry, please tell me I didn't hurt you,' Alex said, stepping out of the embrace so he could see that she was ok.

'There is nothing wrong with me, look,' Melissa turned slowly so Alex could see that all was well.

'Vicky, oh Vicky are you ok?' asked Alex, remembering that she was also close by when whatever happened, happened.

'Will take more than you exploding to phase me. Bart on the other hand, he looks like he may take a little more apologising to,' she said laughing.

'What about the policemen and the other two?' Alex said.

'I don't know. We left them outside. They were still on the floor when we came in,' Melissa said. Knowing her boy was safe, her usual self returned. She wanted so badly to go out and make sure that they were fine. How could she? They were there to take her away.

'Mum, don't even think about it!' Alex knew the look in her eyes, 'You stay here, I will go and have a look,' Alex said.

'No! You are too important, we cannot risk you,'

grandmother said.

'We can't leave them. My importance is irrelevant if I cause pain to anyone. Sixteen years I have been hurt by others. If I am important in any way as you say, it will not be so others can feel as I have. I will not be as selfish as those who have done what they have to me and to so many others. If I am important in any way, I will not ignore the suffering of any.' Alex surprised himself. He had spent so many years trying to blend in, to hide in the crowd. As far back as he could remember, he had a connection with all around him. Many years of feeling feelings that were not his own, from being a young boy, to the young man that stood in the hallway. He had always tried so hard to block them out. Tonight not only had the dragonfly awoken, but the reality that he was different had begun the process of Alex's true self awakening. His true self had to know that those impacted by him were going to be well.

The compassion in the words that came from Alex, the love pouring from him, brought all who were listening to tears. They were silent tears of hope and love for a boy who had just appeared in their lives. The emotions took them all by surprise.

'I will go and have a look,' Sophie said. There was no argument from anyone this time. She silently crept her way down the wobbly cobbly path, through the canopy of trees. As she popped out the other side, she heard and could see that the night time air was filled with sirens and flashing blue lights, that were reflecting off the snow-covered lampposts that towered over the square. Stepping off the path, she carried on forward in the shadows that were being cast by the tall wall. The lack of snow and ice made it easy for her to silently make her way to the gate. As she peeked out, she could see one of the uniformed police officers was helping up the lady in a suit. All had their eyes open, all seemed to be ok. Seeing a queue of police vehicles speed into the square, Sophie dashed back to the house unseen.

'They are fine, but as you may be able to hear now, I think all the police in the world have just arrived,' Sophie said, closing the front door behind her. Alex sat down on the second step of the stairs. They were all fully aware that it was not going to be long before there was a knock at the door.

'Not sure how we are going to get out of this one,' Melissa said, looking at Alex, who didn't look as worried as she thought he would. 'Maybe I should just go out and hand myself in. It's me they came for after all,' Melissa said. No one responded for a few awkward moments. Finally Alex stood up and said,

'I assume there is a back door to your house grandmother?'

'Yes! What are you thinking?' grandmother replied. Alex was picking up on the panic coming from his mother and wanted to get her as far away as possible. His journey to the place he knew he had to find was going to give that distance between his mother and the authorities. His only issue was how were they going to get away, quickly. Clearly his mothers car was not an option and before they knew it, the police would be covering the streets looking for them.

'We need to get away from here. If none of us are here, none of us can be questioned' Alex said,

'And actually son, if none of us are here, they won't be getting into the house,' grandmother knowingly said. For a moment the hallway fell silent again. 'Come on, follow me.' Grandmother had an idea. The group of five did as requested. Along with their two furry companions, they all made their way down the corridor, past the kitchen door, past another two closed doors and round a corner to an old wooden door. The door looked like it hadn't been opened for about as long as grandmother had lived in the house. Surprisingly, it did however open with as much ease as a fully functional, well oiled, modern door.

'Come on, come on, quickly!' grandmother said, as she made her way down ten crooked steps into the back garden, that sat much lower than the house itself.

'I don't think the back garden has got its magic back yet,' Vicky said. Her limited eyesight in the dark could just about make out a mess of bushes, trees, old looking garden furniture and a swing, that was only held up on one side by a rotten looking piece of rope which hung from a tall tree. She was correct. The wave of awakening was still making its way round the property. It was actually a good thing the garden they were making their way through was as it was. Its dark and overgrown state helped in hiding them from neighbours and the track that ran to the rear of the properties.

'This way,' grandmother whispered, just loud enough for all to hear, waving her arm as she did. She was heading for a tiny gap to the far right of the garden. As they got closer, grandmother, even with her tiny stature, had to duck her head as she disappeared into the dark three foot high gap. The sound of the old dry leaves that were still attached to the dry looking branches, rustled as she couldn't quite bend down low enough to clear them all. Next to follow was Sophie and Anchor, then Vicky and Bart, leaving Alex and his mum alone.

'Are you ok mum?' Alex asked,

'I'm sorry for all that you have been put through - the moving, the schools, the uncertainty. I wish I could have told you more about how you came to be with me, but please, please believe me, I didn't steal you from anyone.' Melissa said the words with so much passion in her voice, desperate for him to believe her, for him to have no doubts, to love her like he always had.

'You are my mum. You have always been my mum and I have not and will not ever think that you stole me. I do trust you, but you will have to tell me everything about how we came together at some point,' Alex said. Comforted by his words Melissa hugged him, just for a moment, and then ushered him towards the gap that had swallowed up the others.

The two tallest of the group, Melissa and Alex popped out from the longer than expected, thick, sharp and noisy cave-like tunnel of bushes, trees and plants, into a very small clear space which only just fitted them all in. A reflection caught Alex's eye, the light was coming from inside another mass of branches.

'Alex, can you be a gentleman and pull all those off, please?' grandmother asked, pointing at the branches where Alex had seen something shiny. Doing as he was asked, Alex pulled hard at the first branch covered in dead leaves. It came away far easier than he had expected, clearing a large gap revealing the tall side of a van. Alex passed the branch back to Melissa, who placed it in the only space that was left - the tunnel they had arrived through.

'Oh wonderful, it's still here.' Grandmother seemed quite excited. Alex cleared more and more, revealing a very old camper van. Its panels were in surprisingly good shape for a vehicle that had clearly been there for some time. Nature and its carefully placed branches had protected the van well. The windows were cleaner than expected and with the whole side cleared, the back sliding door to its side, being opened by grandmother, did so without a squeak.

'Climb in everyone,' grandmother said. Anchor was the first one in, sniffing frantically, his hackles on his back up in protect mode. Bart was not so quick to jump in, he waited patiently, nervously, with Vicky. Grandmother was the first human to climb in. She made her way to the bench seat and made herself comfortable. With there being a lack of followers, she peeked her head out the door and said with a cheeky smile,

'Melissa, I assume you are the only one here who has a driving licence. I am sure the front door will open. No need for climbing over the seats and damaging anything!'

Melissa stepped forward and grabbed the handle of the front door. It was cold and had a sharp edge to it. Receiving a stab in her hand, Melissa let go. Pulling her sleeve down to cover and protect her hand, she took hold of the handle again. It opened as easily as grandmother had suggested it would. With it open as far as she could get it, she climbed in. She slid across the front bench seat, over to what looked like a huge, black, lorry like steering wheel. In its centre was a badge with the letters VW. It had been altered from its original state, painted in a rainbow of colours.

'Oh, I love these old vans. It's a split screen right?' Melissa asked, directing her question at grandmother.

'My dear, I don't actually know. It was left here in

the late nineteen sixties by a relative and was never picked up. I hid it from the neighbours as there was a man across the track who complained about everything, and a vehicle being where it should not be, I knew it was only a matter of time before he appeared at my door. Poor guy died. I always said if he smiled more he would have lived longer,' grandmother said.

'Ok then,' Melissa said. She was slightly confused by the story and the detail that wasn't really required in answer to her question. Meanwhile, Vicky and Bart had climbed their way into the back with grandmother. Sophie took the opportunity to stay close to Alex. The bench seat in the front had enough space for her slight self to sit between him and Melissa. With all in the camper van and the doors closed, Melissa could just make out through the branches that the van was pointing towards the track that ran along the rear of the square,

'So, what next?' Melissa asked.

'We get going my dear,' grandmother said, bouncing in her seat, clearly enjoying herself and the thought of a road trip. Melissa couldn't quite believe she was even going to try, but she did. There was a key in the ignition and she turned it.

'You can't be serious!' Melissa exclaimed, as the van's engine burst into life.

'Never underestimate what is possible,' grandmother said.

'But, this is not possible,' Melissa responded. Grandmother laughed and said,

'I think you would have said a few things tonight were not possible.' There was no reasonable explanation for a vehicle that had been sitting for so long to be as lively as it was, but grandmother was right again. Melissa smiled in recognition of the facts and decided not to question any further. Looking out the side of the van that was clear of branches, they could all see sensor lights in the gardens of the houses around them being activated.

'Melissa, now would be the time for you to show us how well you can drive,' grandmother said. Crunching the old van into gear, there was a jolt as Melissa put her foot on the accelerator and lifted her other foot off the clutch. Bursting free from the branches that hid the front of the camper van, Sophie screamed. Melissa had hit the brakes, throwing the passengers forward, almost off their chairs. The van was millimetres from hitting the stone wall on the opposite side of the track.

'Well that was close!' Melissa said. Managing to find the reverse gear, there were loud thuds and scratching sounds. The noise was coming from the branches that had been hiding the van. They had fallen to the ground as they burst free. Trying to reverse, not that she could see them, she was driving over them and pushing them back into the space the van had left behind. Having created enough space, Melissa said,

'Let's try that again.' Clear of the wall, she let the van as quietly as the engine would allow, roll down the track towards the main road. Arriving at the road's junction, the three seated in the front could see a mass of vehicles with their lights flashing. They were all stopped, blocking the road off to the left of them. Thankfully, a driver who was stuck in the queue that was getting longer and longer off to the right, the way Melissa and her passengers wanted to go, had courteously left a gap. It was just enough of a gap for the old camper van to squeeze through and leave the scene of Alex's explosion.

'So, who's up for some food?' grandmother shouted from the back.

'Food, grandmother? Only you could be thinking about food right now,' Sophie said. Anchor barked his response, along with his tongue hanging out and tail wagging, it was enough to translate his answer as a yes.

'Let's get away from here first,' Melissa said. Looking down at the dashboard, the dim lights showed her speed as being much slower than it felt and sounded. It also showed that the fuel left in the camper van's tank was not going to get them far. Heading out of town, the twigs and leaves were flying off the camper van, leaving a trail for whomever was looking to follow. They got less and less with every mile they drove. As did the fuel the camper van had. Nervous to stop, Melissa kept driving. Finally and thankfully, she and the old camper van made it to the motorway that was to take them on their northerly adventure. Five miles on to the open road, the engine began to cough and splutter. A service station was seen in the distance, just in time.

'A quick stop everyone. We can fill up the van and your tummies,' Melissa announced to the delight of the passengers sitting in the back. The evening had got late, but there was still heavy traffic on the roads and the service station reflected the amount of travellers. Melissa was pleased, as it meant they would be hidden in the crowds on the road and on their stop. On entering the service station, her comfort level changed. Although yes, they would be just more faces in the crowd, that also meant that there was a crowd of faces who may recognise them. One of the eating areas had a big screen television. It was playing the news, news that was being filmed live from the very location they had managed to make their escape from. There were words scrolling along the bottom of the screen which read, 'An unexplained explosion has caused the injury of four people, none serious. The area has been closed and residents evacuated for their safety.' Not only that, her picture was being shown along with her name as being wanted for questioning, no doubt given to them by the weasley manager. Melissa's heart sank.

'You know what guys, you go and sort the food, I am going to get the van filled up,' Melissa said. Pulling the hood of her coat up to help hide her face from anyone who may have been paying attention to the news, she went to walk away. 'You may want to stock up as it's going to be a long drive,' Melissa said. She left the group heading for the first shop full of bakery goods. Alex watched Melissa leave and wondered why she had left so quickly,

'Can you get me whatever, I think I will go with mum,' said Alex, directing his request and intention at Sophie.

'Ok, anything in particular?' Sophie asked. Alex didn't hear her, he was already a good distance away from the hungry group, running to catch up with his mum.

Melissa was already in the van as Alex pulled open the squeaking passenger door, just as Melissa was turning the key to get it going. The limited amount of fuel dragged from the bottom of the fuel tank, was just enough to get the old engine running. With a cough and a backfire, the van sprung into life and the two headed off to get some fresh fuel for the long drive.

Alex didn't, couldn't, say a word. Being alone

with his mum, having a moment to think without consideration of his fellow travellers, the enormity of what had gone on that day hit him. His mind returned to its usual place of self preservation, where it could not speak out loud, but was full of so many words. It was the place it had spent most of its life. His lack of confidence and fear of rejection did not come from a lack of care from Melissa, she was his rock. It came from the nastiness experienced from the frequent moves he'd had to make to different schools. From trying to fit in to places and social groups that had never accepted him. Over time, Alex learnt to stop talking to protect himself, in the same way he had learnt to shut off to the feelings and emotions he felt coming from those around him. After so many years of disappointment in the humankind he'd had the unpleasant pleasure of meeting, it was no longer Alex who made the decision to be silent. His mind, unconsciously, made the decision for him. Like a nightmare in which you can't speak, that was Alex's frustrating reality in these times. He had dared to hope that having survived the first weeks at his new school, having stood up to the bully and his strength in how he had coped with the evening's events, he would be free of his mental prison. But no. After the evening that had seen him unconscious, in pain, hallucinate, disappear, re-appear, be possessed by a dragonfly and finally cause some sort of energy explosion, Alex was back in his frustrating place of non-communication.

As silent as he was outwardly, his mind was anything but. Questions, he had many. Why had all that had happened, happened? Why was a man saying that his mother had abducted him? In his verbal silence, his head full of words, as much as he wanted to and as much as he tried, he was paralysed, trapped, unable to speak, for his mum, or anyone, to hear.

Silence reigned as Melissa stepped out of the van and began to get some well deserved fresh fuel into the van's, happy to receive it, fuel tank. Alex caught sight of her in the dirty, moss-covered wing mirror, shaking her head and talking to herself. Alex looked down at his phone. Its home screen, unusually for a sixteen year old boy, was a picture of his mother and him. The picture had been taken on one of the few days Melissa had off from work, a hill walking adventure which turned into a mountain climb. Taken having reached the summit, they were exhausted, proud of themselves and in awe of the view. It was a good day. The photograph was a reminder of a moment that seemed like a lifetime ago. Staring at the picture, Alex, as confident as he was that Melissa was his mother, wanted to know more of the hidden story. The honest and open relationship he thought he had with his mother, was clearly not completely that.

A thud from Melissa closing the fuel cap took Alex's stare from his phone. Melissa stepped into the van and sat back down onto the driver's seat. Breaking the verbal silence she said,

'So glad we can pay at the pumps, don't feel like making small talk right now.' Alex didn't respond. Melissa looked over and saw the picture Alex had been looking at, his phone still lit up from his reminiscing. 'That was a good day,' Melissa said. Alex, still trapped in his mind, smiled. That was enough for Melissa. She knew her son was still there, he would talk when he was ready. Equally so, she knew his mind was full and it was up to her to break the silence, whether he responded or not. As much as she was confused and worried, she had to seem strong for her boy. She had to work out what he could be thinking about, why he was stuck in his head and then talk about the relevant issue, until he could break free of his mind.

'Did you see the television?' Melissa asked. Knowing fine well he wouldn't answer, she didn't wait for his response, 'the big screen television in the restaurant when we walked into the service station, it had my picture on it.' That got a reaction. He stopped staring out the front window and whipped his head round to look at Melissa. 'Don't worry, no one got a chance to see me, that's why I left,' Melissa said.

Alex returned his gaze to outside the van. Looking through the trees, towards the restaurant and the shop part of the service station, he hoped to see Sophie, grandmother and Vicky.

'If that's not why you came after me, I guess you have some other questions,' Melissa said. Alex was screaming out the questions inside. As if they could hear him, the heads of Anchor and Bart who had been forgotten in the back, appeared at each side of Alex's head. Reaching over the front seat Alex received a loving lick on each cheek. He didn't turn round. He wasn't hugely happy about having dog slobber on his cheeks, but he appreciated their intention nonetheless. Reaching back with both of his arms he patted their heads. Their tongues back in their mouths, happy they had done their part, they sat back and joined Alex in looking out the window in anticipation of the returning shoppers, shoppers with food. Bart was also trying to get over being left behind by Vicky, it was very unusual for her to do so. On that occasion she forgot herself, she didn't think about Bart, she had made friends who had offered their hands without thinking. Enjoying that moment she went with it, leaving a poor unemployed Bart to wallow in his overthinking self-pity.

'I did not abduct you or anyone.' Melissa's words were repeated from the back garden of Dragonfly Manor. 'I have to be honest with you,' she paused. Her hands gripped the big steering wheel, her knuckles getting whiter with her tightening grip as she tried to control her emotions. 'As I said, I did not kidnap you, but I also did not adopt you. There are no papers. Honestly I don't know where you came from. You were left wrapped up in a blanket, in a small basket, on the steps of a hospital I was working in. Laying on you was a note that was addressed to me.' She went on to recite the words she read so many years ago, the words she knew so well, the words tattooed on her body. She released a hand from the cold steering wheel and reached down to the old metal key that was still in the ignition. As she did, Alex reached over and touched her hand, squeezed it once and as quickly as he did, removed his hand, leaving hers to do what it had intended. Melissa smiled, a smile of relief as she turned the key. The van fired up with a new lease of life from the fresh, full fuel tank. No coughing or backfiring this time, just the happy, gentle, distinctive rumble of the van's old engine working happily, and ready for its first trip in many years with its new unexpected adventurers.

Driving back round to the main building, Melissa, Alex and the dogs saw the three girls standing, waiting for their collection, weighed down with bags bursting full of goodies.

'Well, you took me at my word I see!' Melissa said as they bundled into the van. One of the bags gave up and spewed its contents over the floor, much to Anchor's delight. This time, Sophie joined her grandmother on the back bench seat. Alex was still silent, he hadn't even turned round to acknowledge their arrival. Sophie, sensing the change in his demeanour and not knowing him well, wrongly decided that keeping her distance, giving him space, was the right thing to do.

The dropped food having been picked up, joined the other full bags on the table that sat between Vicky, Sophie and grandmother. The feast began.

'What would you like Melissa?' Vicky asked,

'Just a bottle of water would be fine just now, thank you,' was her response. Melissa wanted to get back on the open road, away from eyes that may have seen the news report, back out on to the dark, wet, Friday evening busy motorway, heading north. With the hint of a wheel-spin, the group and their chariot were off. As Melissa exited the slip road and joined the traffic, in an excited voice she announced,

'Scotland, here we come!'

CHAPTER 15

Leilani watched as Dragonfly Manor's dragonfly and its trail of colours flew directly at her. Calmly, patiently, she waited for it to arrive into her hands, for her to be given the power of the dragonfly that was her birthright. The birthright that was lost to her, because of her and her brother's actions so many years earlier. Her calmness was not to last, as at the very last moment, millimetres from her grasp, the dragonfly's direction of flight changed,

'Noooooo!' Leilani screamed. All she could do was watch as the dragonfly and its trail of colours flew high above her Dragonfly Manor, far beyond her reach.

'Lanny, do not lose sight of that thing! It won't be able to get too far from the house, it has to come back so watch it, don't even blink,' Leilani shouted angrily, as she dashed back to her front door as fast as her creaking joints and wasted muscles would let her. Her intention was to retrieve a vile of blood from her stash in her damp, back room. Her reason for doing so was to have it ready to throw over the dragonfly she was sure would return. The act had worked on catching dragonflies over the years, so she assumed it would be no different with her own.

Swinging the door open she saw Earl. Appearing to have found his youth, he was running in circles. Leilani's focus was the retrieval of the blood and in her haste, she had completely missed the change that had happened instantaneously with the arrival of the dragonfly. With her first hasty step into the house she caught her foot on something. Looking down to see what it was, she saw roots crawling across her hallway, growing before her eyes. She stopped where she had almost fallen and looked around her old, worn, falling apart Dragonfly Manor. It was none of those things any more. The house's heart - the tree, was in full leaf. Its branches were thick, full of life. Her walls were like they were the day the house was built. The staircase leading up to the bedrooms looked like it had never been used, free from dust, chips and the splinters that Leilani, when she could be bothered, had pulled out of Earl's paws. The sparkling clean, stained glass window on the first landing, was full of colour that had been long since forgotten.

Leilani turned to look at the front door and its frame, the place that had lost its lights and life many years earlier. It had been functional to travel within the realm of Heart, but was tired. Now it was full of life, pulsing with light. The creatures and places lit up as they danced around its frame. The door's pinpricks of light were as bright as she could ever remember.

'Earl, we have to get that dragonfly,' Leilani said. She could feel the power of the house returning. Every wave of energy passed through her. Every part of her home was lit up with lights that came from the doorframe. It occurred to her that if the house was waking up, maybe she had already received what she had been waiting for. She looked down at her hand,

'Curses.' The return of the dragonfly had not given her the bite, the connection she had waited for since the day of her parents' murder. She was never told how to make the connection, her birthday being the day the secret was to be told to her. After one of the most horrific acts imaginable - the taking of her parents' lives, the privilege of becoming the key keeper being kept from her was a blessing for all who remained. Leilani had done everything she could to find out how she could make the connection, if her dragonfly did ever return. Many hundreds of hours had been spent torturing those within Heart - the people and every other living thing that she had captured from the Dragonfly homes in every village, in every town, in every city, on every island within the realm of Heart. Not just the ones that had connected with their dragonflies, but all that may have any knowledge. None gave her the answers she was looking for, not one broke.

Her anger growing, she refocused on why she had come into her Dragonfly Manor to begin with. The vile filled with blood. She knew she could not risk the death of the dragonfly with a more aggressive way of capture. She had learnt from her years of dragonfly capture, that the blood of an animal on its back created a heaviness that no dragonfly that she had ever captured, could fly with.

Earl followed as she made her way down the bright and alive corridor, to the door which led down to her room of damp, suppressive, darkness. The door was heavy, the door was cold. Leilani had expected, like the rest of the house, for it to have come alive, renewed. It had not. Stepping into her room it was as it always was. There was no lightness, no heart in the room. It was a black hole of misery. Leilani shrugged it off and collected what she needed. She chose a particularly old vile, the colour of its blood a deep, dark red, almost black.

'This will do perfectly,' Leilani said as she turned and headed back out into the warmth of the newly born house. 'Come on Earl, I may need your help with this one. He is a lot bigger than the ones we have

dealt with before.' Earl scurried past her. Having
made his way to the bright front door, he waited for
Leilani to arrive to let them both out.

'Where is it?' Leilani shouted at Lanny as she
made her way down the changing colour, wobbly
cobbly footpath.

'I don't know!' Lanny said nervously. The power
shift in their relationship had left him a shadow of his
former self when it came to dealing with his sister. 'It
went right up into the dark sky. There was no way of
being able to keep watching it, honestly, it's just
gone!' Lanny said, turning his head away from her,
waiting for the blow to come. On this occasion it
didn't. Leilani was distracted, she had seen something
move in one of the huge old trees towering above her
brother. She didn't want to act too quickly, or focus
too hard on the location of movement, incase it gave
whatever it was a hint that she had seen it.

'That gold your boys are holding has set. Useless,
just take it back,' Leilani said, knowing that the
direction of Lanny's store was past the tree she
wanted a closer look at. 'I shall come with you.' She
covertly slid the vile of blood into the pocket of the
worn dressing gown she wore at all times, other than
when she had climbed into her old bed and begun one
of her always sleepless nights. In a most unusual
action, Leilani bent down and stroked the head of
Earl. Her action was not a show of affection however,
it was for her to get close enough to whisper,

'When we get under the second tree to the left, I
want you to climb as fast as you can. There is
something there.' Leilani's whisper heard, the
sprightly Earl was more than happy to play the game.
Arriving at the tree, Earl slipped away from the group
and scurried stealthily with a youth-like speed up the

old tree's thick trunk. His eyes were wide open, searching for any hint of life. Three quarters of the way up having searched every branch on his way, he popped his head up and over a particularly thick branch. He found himself staring into a set of the darkest of eyes.

'My friend, please don't say a word.' A scared but very friendly voice spoke. Earl had stopped and the lack of noise from his movement, alerted Leilani to the fact that he may have found something. She did not look up, she just stopped where she was, letting her brother and his two bear companions walk off.

Earl had always been loyal to Leilani. She had come across him nearly two hundred years earlier, the friend of one of Lanny's torture victims, at a time when Lanny was very much in charge. Earl's loyalty had come from a place of fear, but something else as well. He saw in Leilani's eyes a sadness that showed she was capable of love. Years on, Leilani was far from love, her madness having taken over. The sadness in her eyes that Earl had witnessed had faded. Even with that knowledge, Earl chose to stay by her side. It was a decision that disconnected him from the realm of Heart's natural love, compassion and warmth. A move that found him torn on a daily basis. As time moved on and Leilani took control from her brother, Earl witnessed suffering like no one should. His desire to be at her side because of the hint of love he saw gone, he stayed, not out of loyalty, but now out of fear. The fear made every sick order he had been given easier to carry out. It was not long before his heart was as empty as Leilani's.

The light and energy that had filled Dragonfly Manor had not only awoken something in the house, but also within him. Looking into the eyes of the creature on the branch with him, Earl's instincts were to attack and knock whoever the dark eyes belonged to from the tree. But he didn't.

'Don't move until we are gone,' a squeaky voice came from the mouth of Earl. His discovery moved slightly, finding a sure-footed position incase he needed to run, or be able to stay, until he could leave. His movement exposed him to Earl. The light of the moon had moved from behind the clouds in the same moment, lighting up his face - it was a chimpanzee.

'You have found your voice,' the dark eyed chimpanzee said.

'Quiet, she will hear you!' Earl responded. One of the most wonderful of realities in the realm of Heart was that every creature, no matter how big or how small, from whatever species, was able to communicate clearly with all. There was no hierarchy. All in Heart were there in nature to exist together, for each other. To be heard by all and understood by all. To heal who needed to be healed, to be loved without any thought of self. Earl had not spoken for so long, he was as surprised as his tree branch companion to be able to.

'I will be fine Earl. I have not been seen or caught yet and I feel that this is not going to change tonight.' Having finished his words, he looked up.

'You know my name?' Earl said,

'Of course I do. As much as your lady looks for us, we have been looking right back and watching. As I said, we haven't been seen or caught yet,' the chimpanzee said, still looking up. Earl couldn't help but look where his new friend was looking. The light breaking through the branches gave hints of all kinds of movement above them. On closer inspection, Earl's eyes adjusting to the changing light, he could make out many silhouettes - humans, birds, four-legged animals and two-legged animals were everywhere.

'Look.' The chimpanzee pointed to the other trees. 'Now you have been woken from your poisoned existence in that house, you will once again be able to see what is out here.' Earl followed the pointing hand. In every tree, silhouettes appeared high up in the branches. At first they just looked like parts of the trees, but with the tiniest of movement he could see them all.

'Why are they all here? Are they crazy? If you have watched you know what she is capable of. And humans, I thought they had all gone?' Earl squeaked out.

'Yes my friend we know what she can do. Thankfully our human friends still exist here, they are few, but always full of hope. Did you see the sky this morning? All over Heart everyone saw it and are coming to this place. Word has spread. Those hidden are hoping for something new. We saw the largest dragonfly we could have ever imagined leave that house tonight. Friends who you cannot see here have already left, they are spreading the word,' the chimpanzee said in his unexpectedly deep voice.

Earl was worried. Not this time for himself and not for Leilani. For a wonderful moment, his heart was worrying for all the silhouettes and the strangers that would be heading for certain death if they arrived and were discovered by Leilani and Lanny. He was sure many had witnessed what evil things Leilani had done, but he was just as sure they had not witnessed what more she had learnt and could now do. If she took control of this last dragonfly and became the last key keeper, became the one to bridge the gap back to

Earth's realm, the new reality would be horrifying. Earl had been by Leilani's side with all her studies, experiments and magic that had come from sacrifice and death. He knew what her plans were, what her capabilities were. If all the silhouettes coming thought they knew pain and suffering, they did not. Earl left the branch and scurried back down the tree to the ground where Leilani stood waiting.

'You see nothing?' Leilani snapped at Earl. Not breaking his silence to her, he simply glanced up, shook his head, turned and headed down the path to catch up with Lanny. Leilani had no reason to question Earl, she was confident he would have exposed anything alive to her. With Earl's untrue confirmation, she no longer needed to keep up the facade of following Lanny to his store, so she turned and walked back towards Dragonfly Manor.

The moonlight was lighting up the front of her home. With her slow, purposeful walk back to the house and her senses heightened in anticipation of the return of the dragonfly, she could not help but notice the wobbly cobbly path was as bright as it once was. The front door was no longer worn, the windows were smiling at her and the most colourful of flowers had appeared everywhere she looked.

Leilani looked up at the dark sky with a scowl on her face, her cracked lips parted as she shouted out an order to the elusive dragonfly,

'Come to the one you belong to. Your power will be mine and all will be as it should be. All will be mine.' As Leilani finished her order, she continued her slow walk to the door the dragonfly, by her reckoning, would have to return to.

Born into all dragonfly homes with a visit from Shuing, the long life and magic that was found in every dragonfly came from its tree. If a dragonfly was to be separated from its tree for too long, its magic and long life would be lost and its lifespan would return to that of any other dragonfly, not born through Shuing. At the age of Leilani's and grandmother's Dragonfly Manor, their dragonfly would most assuredly be lost, turned to dust. Leilani was convinced that her wait for its return was going to be short. Her jaw, cheeks and the lines around her eyes actually creaked, as something appeared on her face that had not been seen in some time - a smile. Her youth, her power, her plans, they were all about to become her reality.

CHAPTER 16

Melissa was the only one awake as the colourful old van passed the sign welcoming the adventurers to Scotland. Used to the long hours and strange shifts patterns, her ability to stay awake and sharp was exceptional. The rear seat passengers on the other hand after filling their tummies, had fallen fast asleep less than thirty minutes after their pit stop, four hours earlier. Alex, silent, stayed awake longer. He spent three hours in his head, analysing the situation he found himself in, the situation that was to come and the people he found himself with, before finally succumbing to his dream-filled sleep.

Alex's dreams were as real to him as reality. The emotions within, spilling over into his waking life. Having met Sophie that evening, his ability to separate his dream life from his real life was only going to get harder. In his deep sleep on the front bench seat of the old van, Alex had just entered into a new dream. It was certainly not going to help his questioning of reality over dreamt fantasy.

In his dream Alex found himself in a field. Long, fresh green grass was ebbing and flowing like the ocean lapping against the shore. He could feel the heat of the sun bearing down on his back. He could smell the scents of a summer's day carried on a gentle breeze - the flowers, trees, animals. A hundred yards in front of him was a tree. It wasn't the tallest of trees, but its heavily leaf covered branches, reached far from its thick trunk and beckoned him into the shade they provided. Powerless to resist, he began his walk through the grass with his bare feet, every step cushioned by its softness. Getting closer to the tree, Alex could feel the temperature change around him. The hairs on his arms began to stand up, pushing out to protect him from the cold. The skin's efforts to trap the warmth failed in their task. Alex began to shiver. The comforting summer's day turned into a cold, grey, winter's afternoon. The soft green ground turned brown and coarse. The tree's shade still offered protection, but now it was not from the sun, but from the rain that was falling. Looking over his shoulder, Alex could see that the blue skies and summer's grass still existed behind him. The tree's efforts in pulling him in, to protect him from the rain now, were nowhere near as strong as the pull to return. Alex turned to make his way back to where the air was warm, the grass soft and green, but as he did, the ground fell away beneath him.

With an agonising crash, Alex's body, having fallen for some distance, found itself crumpled up on solid ground. Still only dressed in a pair of summer shorts, he managed to pull his aching body up. Getting to his feet, pain from his landing and the cold, hard, jagged rocks beneath his feet shot up through his body. Finding himself in an open cavern, Alex looked around to get his bearings. There was light coming from a hole he figured was about ten, maybe fifteen metres above him - the hole that he had fallen through. The light was enough to just make out where he was. He was in a cave, below the tree he had been walking towards. The roots covered the roof of the cave, spreading over its entirety, water dripping from their lengths. Each drop of water echoed as it joined the small, moss-covered stream that disappeared out of sight, into the darkness.

In the opposite direction of the water's flow was what looked like a possible escape, a tunnel. Its walls sparkling with an unnatural light, Alex's dream-self did not hesitate. Stepping off the rocks he had fallen on into the stream, its water was cold, but its moss-covered bottom provided cushioning for his sore bare feet. Ten steps up stream he could not stop himself from slipping, the stream was a stream no more, becoming more of an underground lake. Alex fell forward, splashing into freezing water, the sound of his impact drowning out the sound of the echoing droplets of water from the roots above. His arms outstretched, several feet down his fall was stopped by something, a corpse- like something.

'Sophie!' Alex screamed out loud, waking himself and all that had been sleeping in the camper van with a fright.

'Bad dream?' Melissa asked. She was glad to have someone awake and also that Alex had broken his verbal silence. Even if it was just one shouted word.

'No. Well er, yes, more one of my weird dreams actually.' The three ladies and their furry companions, now woken from their deep sleep and having brought their heart rates down from the scream, were stretching and yawning. Being the time of night it was their bodies were expecting far more sleep, so they needed that bit of extra oxygen a yawn provided to wake them properly.

'Where are we my dear?' grandmother asked Melissa.

'Just over the border with Scotland. I'm afraid we have a long way to go yet,' Melissa replied. Alex was going over his dream. He had often dreamt of trees, caves and dark tunnels, he had even begun to realise over that evening that he had probably dreamt about

Sophie, but landing on what looked like a drowned corpse was something new. Unpleasant and new.

'Are you ok Alex?' Sophie asked. As she did, she moved from the rear bench seat to the one Vicky had been sleeping on behind the driver, Melissa. She popped her head between Alex and Melissa as she got comfortable.

'Yeh, just a silly dream,' Alex said. He didn't want to tell her what he had seen.

'I know what that's like,' Sophie replied. Inside she had an overwhelming feeling of wanting to hug him, but was embarrassed at the thought of doing such a thing, for no real reason. She had been more affectionate with Alex than she had been with any boy, completely out of character for her, but it all seemed so natural to be that way with the bright-eyed saviour from her dreams. Melissa caught a glimpse of Sophie in the rear view mirror. She could see her looking at her son with affection in her eyes. Her face was blushing, filling her pale cheeks with colour. Melissa smiled to herself. Sophie moved closer to Alex, she had something to ask him. She whispered her question, if she was wrong, she didn't want to be both wrong and heard by everyone.

'Why did you scream when you saw me?' Alex was taken by surprise, only just missing colliding with Sophie's head as he spun round to look at her. His instant reaction told Sophie she was right to ask the question. She was somewhat freaked out at being right, but was also happy at the same time.

'Alex?' Melissa said in a questioning tone, curious as to what she had missed. The noise of the old van's engine was such that any quiet voice could not be heard and with Sophie whispering, there was no chance. Alex ignored his mum. Looking into Sophie's eyes he asked,

'How do you know I saw you in my dream?' quietly enough to frustrate all the others who didn't hear what he said.

'You know how!' was Sophie's cryptic response. Sophie had been dreaming, a dream similar to the one she'd had the night before her birthday morning. She was back in the tunnels being chased by a growling monster hidden in the shadows. The sound of its huge paws thumped as she tried to escape. The petrifying sound stopped as the bright eyes of her dream saviour appeared. Tonight's dream was different. This time, rather than finding herself trapped, her back against a wall, if she wanted to take it Sophie had an escape. The walls of the corridor she had run down were covered in shining gems. This time the end of the corridor was not solid, this time there was a cave, which was filled with an expanse of water, that shimmered with the light given by the gem covered walls of the tunnel. Sophie let herself fall into the water. Carried by its currents she was taken to the lake's edge and sunk to the bottom. Unaffected by being starved of oxygen, she lay, looking up through the water at the cave's ceiling. She could see a dark hole where it appeared the roots of the tree were growing out of, pushing out from the centre edges of the hole and across the ceiling. As she lay motionless, feeling the currents of the water wash over her skin, a single pulse of light dropped down from where the roots began. The small pulse of light hit her, but she felt no pain, instead her chest was filled with positive, calming, revitalising energy. The calmness she hadn't felt in a dream before was short lived, as a dark shape appeared over her, falling fast towards her, breaking the surface of the still water. Sophie was suddenly awake, woken just before she felt the impact of a figure whose darkness was broken by bright eyes.

'That place, wherever I was, I felt safe,' Sophie said.

'I didn't!' Alex responded. He turned away from Sophie and looked out into the darkness. The dull lights of the old camper van spreading across the road were not very effective. The light they gave was similar to the light at dusk, where the disappearing sun didn't provide enough light to see clearly, but it wasn't yet dark.

'What are you two lovebirds whispering about?' Vicky said whilst poking at Sophie's shoulder, always blunt and always wanting to know everything, she could not help herself.

'They are talking about being in each other's dreams,' grandmother said, from the back of the van.

'Oooo, love is in the air,' Vicky started singing whilst shaking a very embarrassed Sophie. With her song finished, she couldn't help herself as she went on 'you loooove him!' She got no reaction. Vicky reached over and turned her attention to Alex. Whilst prodding him she said, 'you loooove her!' Sophie, getting redder and redder in the face, turned back from looking over at Alex and sat in the seat facing her grandmother, who smiled knowingly at her.

That evening Sophie had hugged Alex, held his hand and not wanted to leave his side, all experiences alien to the red-haired loner. She felt something for him, feelings that she hadn't had before in her waking life, but ones she'd had in her dream life with every appearance of the bright- eyed silhouette. Alex also felt there was a connection, although at no point did he think it was anything other than the dragonfly, Dragonfly Manor and the location they were heading to that was creating that bond between them. He never assumed that anyone would have, or want, any kind of emotional connection with him.

The sound of vibrations came from a coat on the table. Bart jumped to his feet, indicating as he had been trained to. It was Vicky's jacket, her phone.

'Crap, I haven't let mum and dad know I was out!' She reached in her coat pocket and answered the phone. With the phone at its loudest setting, she could just hear who was on the other end.

'Hi, how are you?' Vicky said with her usual happy voice. A very clever girl, without any planning, Vicky covered up her absence with ease. 'Yeh, sorry I am at a friends, probably won't be back tonight. I may even stay the weekend.' Sophie could just make out a very anxious voice, which she assumed was Vicky's mum. 'No, what, are you ok?' Vicky's parents had not been able to return home to their house until just then, the square closed off because of Alex's reaction to his mum's arrest. They had assumed Vicky was at home safe and sound. Having got in and found she was not there, they had panicked. Vicky played the part of the unknowing very well. 'That sounds awful, glad you weren't home. I better go, will see you, well if not tomorrow then Sunday, but will let you know when.' Vicky hung up the phone.

'That was quite impressive. I would be most obliged if you don't pass that skill on to my son,' Melissa said jokingly, but serious. 'You guys should probably all get a bit more sleep, we still have a long drive ahead of us.' Sophie and Alex were glad of the loss of focus on their secret conversation. Sophie returned to the back seat next to her grandmother, hoping the subject wouldn't come up again. She pulled her coat over her shoulders, hugged her legs in and closed her eyes. Grandmother, who hadn't moved, was asleep already. She was so tired, fighting sleep was not an option for her. Vicky was joined by Bart, a warm, soft pillow which she used quite happily. Alex was wide awake. Part of him wanted to go back to sleep to see if he could find his way back into the dream. The other part of him was happy not to, his experience not being as calming as Sophie's.

The time of night meant the roads stayed quiet, even as they passed through Glasgow. Its city lights disappeared from the rear view mirror with every slow mile that passed. The road felt long, the drive longer than the seven hours they had been travelling. Having passed the last large town as they joined the small main road, the A9 heading north to the Highlands, the clouds cleared. The moon was low and full, lighting up the scenery in a mystical way. The mountains, hills, streams, rivers, reflected the light, casting shadows across the beautiful views.

'I didn't know the moon could give off that much light,' Alex said to Melissa quietly, so as not to wake anyone in the back.

'It's magical isn't it?' Melissa responded. Another hour passed and as good at staying awake as Melissa was, with the drone from the road, the sound of the old camper van's engine, the warmth provided by all the bodies crammed into the van and the old heating system, she was struggling to keep her eyes open. Thankfully a lay-by appeared and Melissa slowed down to turn into it,

'What's wrong?' Alex piped up.

'Nothing, nothing at all, I just need to rest for a bit before I fall asleep driving,' Melissa said. The van stopped. As Melissa pulled on the crunching handbrake, Alex jumped out into the cold air to stretch his legs. As quick as he closed the door, the van's engine fell silent. Melissa fell out of sight, making full use of the now empty front bench seat, asleep as soon as her head landed on the old cracked plastic.

The night time air was silent, not a breeze, not a drop of rain, or hint of a snowflake. The bright moon sitting large and low in the sky lit up everything like a desk lamp. Looking away from the road and into the valley, Alex's eyes followed the shimmering water of a burn to where it met with a waterfall. The mountains that were its origin towered above him, their peaks thick with snow, the moon sitting what looked like only inches above them. The night sky so crisply clear, was filled with more stars than Alex had ever seen. He felt as though he was looking right into and far beyond his own universe. Transfixed, hypnotised by its beauty, he began to feel his existence really was insignificant.

The outside silence was broken as the sliding door of the van opened behind him. Sophie stepped out. Feeling the coldness of the air hit her, she slipped her arms into the sleeves of the jacket she had over her shoulders.

'Wow, it's so amazing here.' Sophie had spent her entire life in a city with its street lights hiding the night sky. Green grass and colourful flowers were only seen in the small gardens she walked past. Huge expanses of land and fields were only ever seen in pictures, never experienced. The vastness of the space around her made her feel uncomfortable, vulnerable. A little way off from where they stood, the burn that Alex had followed with his eyes to the waterfall, formed by the water coming from the mountains far beyond, was enticing Sophie to investigate. She took Alex's hand and pulled him as she stepped off the tarmac on to the crunching grass. It was also an opportunity for her, for the first time, to get Alex alone and speak to him, if she could find the words. Sophie and her slight self had no affect on Alex. With his size, he wasn't moved from his spot with Sophie's pull.

'Come on, I want to see what's down there,' Sophie said. Her second pull on his hand was more effective as he gave up his stance and stepped forward with her.

'We are being watched!' Alex said, as they arrived at the edge of the burn. Standing proudly, some distance from them, was the largest of stags, regal looking with his head's raised position. He was not alone. Out of nowhere, with him, were more stags and hinds than they could count, all looking right at them.

'Oh, goodness.' Sophie stepped into Alex for safety.

'It's ok, I think.' Alex moved Sophie round and behind him, just incase. 'Maybe we should head back to the van,' Alex said. He didn't want to lose eye contact with his stalkers as they slowly stepped backwards.

'Ow!' Sophie, still behind Alex, had been stopped from walking backwards. She turned round to see what it was.

'Alex,' Sophie said firmly, 'look.' Alex peered over his shoulder. Behind them was a hind, her eyes, reflecting the moon, sparkled with life. She was also not alone, behind her were more stags and hinds as far as they could see. Their path to the camper van was completely blocked.

'Alex, we are trapped.' Inside, Sophie was

beginning to panic. Her instincts were to shout out for help to the occupants of the camper van. Before she did, she looked up at Alex. She couldn't make out the features of his face, with his back to the light of the moon he was in shadow, once again a silhouette. However, once again, his eyes were as bright as they were in all her dreams. Alex didn't say a word. He stepped round Sophie and towards the hind who was blocking their path.

'Stay with me, everything is fine,' Alex said to Sophie. Face to face with the deer, Alex's eyes changed from a bright white, to blue, to purple, at which point the deer slowly dropped her head and stepped to the side. The action was repeated by all the hinds and several stags that had been blocking their return to the camper van. A corridor of beautiful animals opened up before them, a path for their return. Slowly, Alex and Sophie climbed back up the verge to the lay-by. At the side of the camper van, the two turned to look back at what they had just passed through. They had gone, not a sign, not a sound. Any other day, either one of them would have reacted in shock, but today had not been any other day. The door to the camper van opened behind them and grandmother's head peeked out,

'Well that was a sight to behold, how wonderful. Are you two coming back in?' grandmother asked. Alex stepped to the side and let Sophie climb in first. He knew his mum was asleep on the front seat so he followed into the back and took a seat next to Vicky. With all four sitting comfortably round the camper van's table, a selection of food and drink spread out and no need for the inside lights due to the bright moon shining through the big windows, Alex asked,

'Can you tell me what the other place, the place

through Dragonfly Manor's door is like? Like, what did you do there? Who can go there? And why if it's so good, why would anyone come back?' Alex had lots more questions, but he decided the ones he had thrown out were a good place to start.

'Alex my boy, my Dragonfly Manor is just a small part of the amazing you would see,' grandmother quietly replied, trying not to wake a tired Melissa. Grandmother allowed her mind to travel back in time, reawakening the memories that she had locked away for so long. The three watching, saw her face light up as she danced through happy, wonderful, magical memories. Reflecting back on Alex's questions, she put her own personal memories to the side, instead she began to talk about the people who were lucky enough to visit the Dragonfly homes.

Every unexpectedly, splendidly, wonderfully perfect Dragonfly home greets each visitor with its lovingly made red iron, flower-covered decorative garden gate. The same gorgeously red wobbly cobbly footpath, each wobble and cobble framed by the most unexpectedly, splendidly, wonderful display of flowers with every shape, colour and smell your mind could conjure up. The same friendly, perfectly formed incredibly inviting bright red front door, with its completely oppositely crooked windows that give this unexpectedly, splendidly, wonderfully perfect home its most inviting of smiles. The thing is, not everyone could see its unexpected, splendid, wonderfulness. The answer to one of Alex's questions, was that the ones who could see its magic, were those in the greatest need of it. Those that could not see a Dragonfly home's magic would see a house with all its quirks, its flowers, its cobbles, but would never see its inviting smile. They would see the garden's seasons as they would their own, unlike those who could see, who were always greeted with the garden in full bloom, bright and new.

Dragonfly homes and their link to the realm of Heart, were for the healing of those that needed healing. Requiring healing whether physical, mental or something else, those with a spark of love in their hearts, despite their pain, their suffering and living in the broken world they did, could see the welcoming smile of that special place found in every village, in every town, in every city, on every island. Those whose hearts were engulfed in selfishness, hate and the suffering of others would never be so lucky.

There was another type of very special person. These people whilst in Earth's realm could see hints of Heart, often not realising it when they did. It was no accident that Vicky found herself stumbling into the lives of the group that night.

Grandmother went on to describe that when the images, pulsing in colour and light, began dancing on the doorframe, if the door handle was turned in its anticlockwise direction, with the key of course, the dragonfly, a very different Earth would show itself on the other side of the door once it was opened - Heart, a shadow of Earth's beginning. Balanced, respected, loved. A place where every human, animal, plant, droplet of water or soft breeze was respected as one. No rulers, no one person in charge, no selfishness, just a place where the Earth realm could be truly understood without the poison of lies, greed and destruction created by the human race, just nature and all its magic lived there.

Heart was a place where the sick would be well, the bullied uplifted, the hurt would be loved, the lost would be found. Heart was a place of learning, smiling, healing. A place to bring the balance needed for Earth to survive. There were some who visited who never returned to Earth's realm. The thought of returning was too painful a thought, instead they would become part of Heart, no better or worse than any other living thing that called Heart home. However the majority did return to their homes in Earth's realm. Loved ones, human or otherwise being their pull. What they had learnt and experienced they would share, maybe not in word but certainly in action, helping to bring balance back to Earth. Until that is, a brother and sister, trapped in Heart a couple of hundred years earlier by their actions, began the spiral that finds our Earth in the state it is in today. A place where humans assume they know all, assume they know best, by their arrogance having taken Earth to the brink of the end once again. But this time, the end is approaching faster than at any other time in Earth's existence.

Once the lucky few had stepped through any Dragonfly home's doorway, the first thing that every single person was confused by was talking. Every living thing was understood by all, a fact that was also true in Earth's realm, if only humankind stood down from its pedestal. Have you ever wondered why a cat will sit on a person's knee who does not like them, why a dog seems to know what you want without you saying, why an elephant will rescue a lion, a dolphin will appear and help a drowning human. The self importance of human life does not mean that all other living things on Earth cannot understand us and each other, humans are just not listening. When stepping into Heart, that first reality becomes magically and wonderfully clear. For as long as any visitor to Heart stays, they are welcomed. They learn and understand that nature and its plant life, give everything that could ever be needed by all human or other life forms, whether it be food or medicine. It's all there, as it once was, and could be again on Earth.

New friends are made. Days are filled with playfulness. There is an awakening to the reality that magic is just nature, nothing mystical or wrong with it, it's in all of us. It is just a reality that has either been forgotten, or arrogantly dismissed because it's not explainable. Every day fills every visitor with the joy of living.

'You know what, there are things that are possible that even in your wildest dreams you could not think could be,' grandmother said.

'Well, I wouldn't have said a tree would grow out of nothing inside a house in minutes, or that I would explode, so I think my mind is pretty open,' Alex said with a smile.

'I shall finish my story right here. All you need to know and remember is that from my memories and experiences of Heart, it was a place that words cannot truly describe. A mirror of Earth but a reflection of its best self. It is a place full of possibilities. It is a place that at this very moment in time, is more important than at any other time in Earth's existence. I do not know what is going to happen in the coming hours, let alone days. I do not know young man what you are truly capable of. I do not know what the connection that you and my Sophie have. What I do know, is we are going to find out!' grandmother said, finishing with a knowing nod. The group were left with plenty to think about. The three young ones had more questions they would have liked to ask, but respected grandmother's conclusion to her story.

There was a breeze picking up outside the thin metal walls of the camper van. The noise created a gentle hum as it brushed past the old rubber seals round the windows. As the breeze grew in strength to a wind, the camper van began to rock, nature acting as the parent, rocking its cherished baby in its crib. The group, still tired from the day's events and the early hour, had no chance at fighting the inevitable - within minutes, all were fast asleep.

CHAPTER 17

The old engine happily fired into life as the passengers were brought round from their dreamless sleep,

'What time is it?' Alex asked his mum, whilst lifting Vicky's head off his shoulder.

'About 6 o'clock. Sorry to wake you all up, but I think it's a good idea to get back on the road,' Melissa responded.

'That was quite a good night's sleep, everything considered. Alex your shoulder is very comfortable, I can recommend it to anyone who is looking for one,' Vicky said. She was on form as quickly as she was awake. The passengers in the back couldn't see anything outside the van. The cold night and the warm sleeping bodies had caused the windows to mist up. The moonlight was blocked and the only light in the back was from Vicky's phone, who, as quickly as she had sat up, began checking what was going on in the outside world.

'Hey look, we are trending,' Vicky said whilst showing all an article on her phone.

'Well, we are far away from there, so we have nothing to worry about,' grandmother said confidently. Although the hour was such that many would be heading for work, the darkness of the winter's early morning was indistinguishable between the midnight hour and the early morning hour they woke to. The long A9 road that wound its way up through the Scottish Highlands was deserted. The traffic from the town they had passed and the town they were heading towards, having only just started their day's travels, was far from the middle of the A9 where the adventurers had stopped for their sleep.

'We do know exactly where we are going don't we?' Melissa asked from the front, whilst clearing the thick condensation from her front and side windows with the sleeve of her jacket.

'Yes, yes we do,' said Sophie, speaking for the first time that new day. She had seen exactly where the pinprick of light on the Dragonfly Manor front door was. It shone brightly to the very north of the British Isles. With the smallest amount of research, she had discovered that there was only one village anywhere near where the light indicated. It also happened to be the very village a scientist, several years earlier, had discovered as being the point that over two billion years ago, had been struck by one of the largest meteors to have ever hit the earth. The village, only one hundred miles from where they left their A9 lay-by, was called Lairg.

'We should be there by about eight o'clock, by my reckoning,' said Sophie, showing off her geography skills. It was a subject she had always taken great interest in, the natural world being a great escape from the people world.

Sophie was absolutely correct. At two minutes past eight that morning, after enjoying the winding roads and the light from the sun's rays appearing from behind distant hills, throwing a pink light across the sky, the camper van's headlights dimly lit up the sign welcoming them to the village of Lairg.

'So here we are,' Melissa said. Slowly they drove along the side of a loch. In the distance was a dam, whose lights were being lost in the morning light. A small waterfall was crashing down from its highest point into the calm waters of the loch. At the foot of its visible wall, it sent out ripples that spread across the loch's entirety, coming to an end as they gently bounced into the grassy banks.

'Not the busiest of places!' Vicky said sarcastically. At that time of morning, they were all used to traffic jams and work. They were truly in the rural Scottish Highlands - not a single person was seen. Continuing on the road, within a minute they found themselves out the other side of the village. 'And there we go,' Vicky said laughing.

'Yes, not the biggest of places. But my goodness it's beautiful,' Melissa said. Alex climbed over the seat, into the front to join his mum. He had stayed in the back, with Sophie. As much as he would not say or act on it, she was already more than just another one of the group to him.

'So what are we looking for grandmother?' Alex questioned whilst looking out, trying to see through the trees. He felt odd calling her grandmother, it was a word he had never called anyone. As odd as it felt, it gave him the feeling of belonging to something.

'My boy, I honestly do not know. I feel that we should return to the village and try to find some signs of life,' was grandmother's response.

Melissa found a forestry road closed off with a big green metal bar, with just enough space in front of it for her to turn. As they came back into the village, they saw lights on in a shop. Slowing down to look, no life could be seen inside or out, so they kept driving, back towards the loch's side. Vicky started laughing,

'Look, do you think that's what we are looking for?' She pointed to the tiniest little island, with what looked like a dolls house sitting on it, a small tree and a windmill. They all started laughing. It was the cutest thing, but not really the size grandmother had pictured when thinking about the stories she had read about the legend's beginning, Shuing and his dragonfly.

'Glad you can all see it, thought my not-so-great eyesight was playing tricks on me!' Vicky said, still laughing.

'Melissa, I think we should have a drive round all the little streets and backroads. There is something here somewhere. We just have to find it,' grandmother said. She knew if there was a Dragonfly home she would see it and if there was, it would undoubtedly be of some help to them.

It didn't take them long to navigate round the very few streets and the single track roads that weaved their way round the outskirts of the village. There were some lovely looking cottages, a couple of very large houses, beautiful views, but there appeared to be no Dragonfly home.

Their early morning investigation was not very covert in their old, brightly coloured, noisy camper van. Someone was taking an interest in them. Alex had noticed a woman at one of the large houses they had passed. A gap in a row of tall green conifer trees gave Alex a split second which all the others missed. Behind the trees he saw an open field, with a big house at its far end. Standing at its open front door was a woman, he couldn't make out any features, just that she had very long blonde hair. The line of trees came to an end and the single track road led them past a long, tree- lined drive, which Alex figured must have lead up to the big house. They continued past and up the single lane road. After about a mile they came to a dead end, so they had to return back the way they had come. Back past the same long drive. Alex, remembering where the hidden drive began, was ready to have a good look when they passed by. Even with the slow speed Melissa was driving at, he only had a split second to look. As he did, he saw the woman he had previously seen at the front door, standing at the iron gates set back just a little from the road, watching them pass.

'There are alive people here then!' Vicky said, having seen the woman watching them. No one commented. No matter which road they took, they ended up back at the road that ran along the loch, in front of the dam. Since passing the big house up the dead end road, they had found themselves back at the loch four times. On the opposite side of the road to the loch was a small wooded area. In it was a burn that made its way under the road and out into the loch. Every time they passed it, after having seen her at the big house, Alex saw the same woman hidden slightly by the trees, watching them. As odd as he found it, he didn't say anything.

'Why is that woman watching us?' Sophie spoke up. She had noticed her on their second passing of the wood.

'What woman?' grandmother asked.

'The woman in the woods,' Sophie responded.

'It's the same woman we saw on the driveway on the way back from the dead end road,' Alex said. Melissa hadn't seen her, Vicky was struggling to make most things out in detail as they were driving about and grandmother had also missed the interested party.

'She is definitely watching us. It's weird!' Sophie said. Melissa got to a point where she could turn the camper van round and headed back to see if she was still there. She was.

'Excuse me, but can you help us?' Melissa, having stopped and wound down her window shouted, to the not-so-well hidden woman in the woods. The woman didn't respond, she also didn't move from where she stood. Melissa crunched on the handbrake, opened the door, climbed out the still running van and made her way over to the fence, which separated the road from the woods.

'Sorry to be so blunt, it has been a long night. But do you have a problem with us?' Melissa asked. The blonde woman looked angry as she responded,

'Why did you bring him here?'

'Sorry, what?' Melissa replied, surprised and confused. The blonde woman left the place of slight cover from the trees and shadows and stepped towards Melissa.

'Melissa, I left him with you to keep him safe!' The woman's words created an instant reaction in Melissa. Her body tensed, she was in a fight or flight state. She looked around frantically to see if there was anyone else nearby and if there was any reaction from the occupants of the van. Thankfully the answer was no to both. Was it a trap, did this woman just recognise her from the news, was she waiting for the authorities to arrive. No, that made no sense, her words were very specific. Melissa's heart was racing, her chest rising and falling in dramatic style as she tried to take in more oxygen to keep her alert. The woman stepped closer. Fully out of the shadows and on the other side of the fence, she took hold of Melissa's shoulders, looked her right in the eyes and said,

'My son, Alex, Alex Hugins, why did you bring him here?'

'Oh my god. No, that's not possible.' Melissa broke free from her grip, turned and ran back to the van and sped off.

'Mum, what's wrong? What did she say?' Alex asked. The van's engine revved loudly. Melissa was pushing the poor old van to its limits and far above the speed limit of the village. She didn't respond to Alex. She was trying to get her own head straight, was that actually possible? This was the only question that kept going round and round her fuzzy mind. She kept driving. Leaving the village, she headed out the road beyond the trees that followed the loch as it opened up, away from the dam.

'Mum!' Alex raised his voice. Her driving, her face, her silence was scaring him. Still she did not respond. The road broke free from the trees and the loch opened up to the side of them. Alex turned to grandmother,

'Please, can you get her to stop?' he asked.

'Young man, I think she will stop when she wants to stop,' was her response. Her wise head knew, whatever was happening would be what it would be. There was no point in intervening. The dogs were standing to the side of the seats, they were looking out at the loch, tails wagging, they liked what they saw. No one said a word. Everyone but Alex, who could not take his eyes of his mum who seemed to have forgotten how to blink as she stared into the distance, was taking in the incredible view. The meteor strike had truly caused the most beautiful of natural water features, if the place they were seeing was actually where it had happened. The loch's expanse of water was so calm, reflecting the pink from the morning's sky. There was a light mist at various inlets, ground level clouds that seemed to be stuck where they were. All kinds of wildlife could be seen for those that tried - rabbits and hares darting about, trying to find the freshest blade of grass, birds hovering, dropping out of the sky, sitting on sparse tree branches, and the occasional ripple appearing from the loch, as an insect would land or a fish would pop up from the depths. The hills and mountains were many miles away, but seemed close enough to touch. Ten minutes past, it felt like thirty to Alex.

'What is that?' Vicky shouted the words, giving the catatonic Melissa such a fright, she got out of her head and slammed on the brakes. Everyone looked around trying to see what had caused such a dramatic response from Vicky. No one could see anything that fitted her exclamation. All was as they would expect - beautiful, remote, alone, nature-filled. Then grandmother clicked,

'Vicky, your eyes are not so good here, but they are there. Tell us what you see,' grandmother said.

'There, there is an island, it's beautiful,' Vicky said. She was pointing out to the widest part of the loch. In its centre was an odd patch of mist hovering above the water, a thin layer that was clear below and clear above. 'I don't understand, it's there, I can see it clearly!' Vicky said.

'Remember how you could see Alex when none of us could, how you said you could be of help to us because you could see him?' grandmother said,

'Yes!' Vicky replied,

'You were right, you were so right.' Grandmother took a satisfied deep breath and sat back into her seat. Vicky, in her excitement at what she was able to see, clambered in a very unladylike manner across Alex, flew open the sliding door of the stopped van and jumped out to get an unrestricted view of what she was seeing. What she was able to see was crisp, clear. Her failing eyes were not failing in that moment. She could see so clearly in fact, that for many years she had only been able to see that clearly in her dreams. Alex was a bit confused, he thought he would be able to see what needed to be seen, to find what needed to be found. In his mind he was questioning if it was that easy. Had they actually found, in such a short time, the very place they were searching for? Had they found where they needed to be?

CHAPTER 18

'There, look, there. That's her!' Leilani's excited words echoed around her dark, damp and smelly room, that's sole purpose was for spying and manipulating others through her golden window to Earth.

Leilani and her brother's night, had felt as long as it did for the group heading north, back in Earth's realm. She had a patience that could usually out-wait most and the long night had tested it, to its fullest. Many hours earlier, prior to her exclamations of finding someone of relevance through her gold and crystal opening window, her calculations about the dragonfly having to return back to Dragonfly Manor were to come true.

An eye on the sky at all times, Leilani sat contently on the top step of the steps leading up to her revitalised front door. Lanny stood at the bottom of the steps looking up at the house. He had sent his bears back to the gold store with the liquid gold, seeing as Leilani had no use for it at that time.

'Sister, looks like new doesn't it?' he said, studying every brick, window frame, piece of glass and tile of their Dragonfly Manor.

'It does brother,' Leilani responded. Her response surprise Lanny, causing his examination of the most unexpectedly, splendidly, wonderfully perfect of homes to stop. It had been some time since she had called him anything but an insulting name. To hear her call him brother, that was a sign a softer part of her still existed. Softness was a trait Lanny had never had. He knew that if it continued to grow in Leilani, it could be a turning point for him, for him to once again hold the power. Lanny turned away from the house and his sister. Looking into the garden and the trees beyond, he tried to hide the wicked smile that was growing on his face.

Earl, Leilani's steppe polecat companion, was acting slightly out of character. He was not staying at her side. Instead, he kept disappearing down the cobbly footpath and out of the iron gate. Leilani, her focus elsewhere, had not noticed. Lanny's two loyal sun bears, Gregg and George, on the other hand, had. Sitting as they always did, one each side of Lanny, they watched curiously, hoping to get a hint at what he was up to. They hoped for some insightful information that they could give to Lanny and in return, receive the rare praise they both longed for.

The trees beyond the garden gate and its walls cast shadows across the dirt track. The shadows also fell across the in-bloom garden, creating plenty of hiding places for any living thing that was confident enough to take the chance of being that close to the brother and sister.

'There are things moving tonight,' Lanny said.

'Clearly they are you stupid man. Look at the plants growing in front of us. Try not to state the obvious. Idiot!' Leilani's soft moment, was definitely just a moment.

'I see that, I am not talking about that! There are things moving, non plant shapes, all around us,' Lanny said. She took her gaze from the sky and began to focus on the shadows in front of the two of them.

'Earl, you are sure there was nothing in that tree earlier?'

She spoke quietly, assuming her companion was

where he would usually be, by her side. Instead George was happy to reply,

'He's not here, he's there.' He lifted his paw and pointed his long claws towards the gate as Earl appeared, scurrying through the shadows. Thinking his disappearances were still unnoticed, he slunk back to Leilani's side. As he made himself comfortable, a blow came out of nowhere. It sent him falling down the steps.

'What have you been up to?' an angry Leilani asked the cowering Earl. Thankfully, the buzzing in his head did not stop him from coming up with an acceptable answer, very quickly.

'Checking, I was checking the trees like before. I thought maybe the dragonfly could be there. Just checking that's all.' His response was acceptable to Leilani.

'Fine. Stop acting so pathetically you silly old man, or you may find your usefulness does not continue,' Leilani said threateningly. She was however still curious as to what her brother was seeing move. He wasn't likely to be lying to her, he wanted the power as much as she did, he wanted the ability to return and have control of the realm of Earth, with all his gold. She knew he wanted to leave her in Heart, his statement had to be fact. Although, she was also confident that no living thing that she and Lanny did not control, would come near them. After all, every living thing knew that she would use them for whatever purpose she decided, if seen and captured, which if seen, they surely would be.

'Lanny, go and take a closer look.' Leilani's order was spoken calmly. He did as she asked, happy to leave her presence. Siblings they were, but close they were not, they hated each other.

Lanny made his way out of the gate, George and Gregg on all fours bounding off into the distance in front of him. Having made his way across the dirt track, he stopped at the edge of the tall trees and waited. Closing his eyes, he listened for the slightest rustle.

'Boys, will you shut up!' His sun bears were scratching and climbing, making it hard for him to hear. George and Gregg stopped where they were, five feet off the ground. Each had their claws deep into the trunk of the tree they chose to investigate. A couple of minutes passed then George saw something. No matter what he had been ordered to do, his instincts, well trained into him by Lanny, was to attack. He shot up the tree to the first branch, his speed taking a crow by surprise. George's claws swiped the poor bird from the tree. The force was so perfectly controlled, he did not kill the bird, just injured it. Stunned, it fell to the ground, right at Lanny's feet.

'Good job George,' Lanny said, looking up to where his loyal bear was sitting, very pleased with himself. Lanny was not looking at him for long, as the attack had brought all that had been hiding in the shadows to movement. The whole tree was moving, there was not a branch or leaf that did not have some sort of life on it.

'Leilani!' Lanny shouted as loud as he could. 'Gregg, move, go and get the rest!' The rest Lanny referred to, was the rest of his bears. George and Gregg were his generals and they controlled his many thousands of bears, scattered around the realm of Heart, ready to act when asked. Several hundred of them occupied space in and around his gold store. Gregg leapt from the tree and in a cloud of dust, disappeared down the dirt track. George, alone, high up in the tree, was himself suddenly knocked from where he sat, hit from above by a human. The human had been hiding along with the many species of living creatures, all unexplainably led there having seen the mystical lights in the sky that morning. George landed with a thud, on his feet.

Leilani arrived at the gate to see a sea of living things appear from the shadows. Having been taken by surprise and without Lanny's army of bears, there were far too many for her to do anything about them. For the first time since being a young girl, since the time she was party to the lives of her parents being taken, she felt fear. Wave after wave of life fell from the trees, disappearing off into the woods and scattering across the fields beyond.

'Humans, there are humans here, why? How? Lanny, your bears, get your bears!' she screamed at her brother. Lanny had stepped back, his back against the garden wall he yelled back,

'Already done!' Coming back up the dirt track was Gregg and behind him, an army of his savage bears.

It was at that very moment that the distraction gave the magical insect a chance. From behind Leilani and Lanny, high up in the sky above Dragonfly Manor, the trail of colourful lights appeared once more. The bright moon caused the body and wings of the large dragonfly to cast a shadow on to the blooming garden. The dragonfly was heading back to its home in the tree.

'Aaaaaaaaa!' Leilani screamed. The area had never heard such noise - all the animals, the people, the bears bounding up the track, Leilani's scream was lost in it all. Lanny, too focused on the escapees, did not hear his sister's scream or see her fast movement back to the house. He was completely unaware of the dragonfly's attempted return. The speed in which the dragonfly fell from the sky made all that were still hiding high up in the trees watching, feel confident it would be safe. Leilani, just entering back into the garden screamed again, as the dragonfly was only feet from the smiling bright red front door,

'No you don't!' With all her strength, she threw the vile of blood she had kept concealed, with supernatural accuracy. The thin glass of the vile smashed as it made contact with the dragonfly's hard and colourful back. It had been only millimetres from safety. The thick, crimson blood fell around the dragonfly's sides as it fell to the floor. Small shards of glass protruded from the sticky red substance, giving the back of the dragonfly the look of armour.

Leilani stopped her run and began to laugh. The sound was so horrifying all movement behind her stopped. Those running to attack, those running to escape, they all froze. Over the many years of hunting and capturing dragonflies at all the Dragonfly homes in every village, in every town, in every city, on every island around the realm of Heart, Leilani and Lanny had never experienced one the size of the one that lay weighted to the floor, no matter how hard his wings tried to fly. Maybe he was going to return to his normal size, maybe not. Maybe it was the blood that had not only captured him, but had also stopped whatever transformation in size may have happened. Either way, Leilani had captured the largest and surely the best life-giving dragonfly that they could have possibly imagined.

Lanny abandoned his army of bears, who knew not to enter the gate of Dragonfly Manor without express permission from Leilani. Arriving at Leilani's side, together they walked slowly, cautiously, to where the dragonfly lay.

'Lanny, this will be different from before. We must not waste this opportunity for the sake of youth. This is, could be, our only chance to get our door active once again. Do not touch it, you will leave this dragonfly for me to do what is needed.' Leilani's clear and concise order was said in a calm, but threatening tone, leaving Lanny under no illusion that he would have no say in what was to come.

Lanny stood back, joined by Earl and the two bears whose no entry rule was waived. The wings of the dragonfly were losing their strength, their blur becoming a slow movement, eventually coming to a stop. Leilani standing over it, said,

'Now we shall see. Now we shall learn. Now you will know the pain that all your family have known, the ones that I took, the ones that you abandoned by never returning. Your absence caused the death of every dragonfly in this and Earth's realm. Know that, as you suffer and give me what I have patiently waited for.'

The energies, the magic that had appeared that day, were not diminishing with the dragonfly's capture. Dragonfly Manor continued to become more alive than it had been for those hundreds of years since the dragonfly's escape. This fact was not lost on Leilani as she bent down, grabbed its tail end, opened the house's red smiling door and dragged it inside.

'I think I shall show you to the room that has made all this possible. The room, my research, my sacrifices, have born a new type of magic that is mine. There we shall see how quickly you will give me what I want, how quickly this door you are being dragged through will work for me. Of course if you fight me, if you don't give me my open door, I will take from you something else my prehistoric friend. That youthful, life-giving loveliness you have, it will be mine.'

Leilani, victory running through her old veins, gleefully pulled the dragonfly over the roots that had sprung up in the newly invigorated hallway, down the corridor and past the kitchen. The door being open, Leilani could see its cupboard doors were no longer mouldy and hanging loose, they were as quirky, colourful and snug fitting as the day they had been created. She carried on down the corridor to her room. Leilani stepped in through the doorway and down on to the first step with Lanny, Earl, George and Gregg following close behind. With the renewal of Dragonfly Manor, the potent smell of death was more obvious than usual.

'Noooooooooo!' Leilani's calm demeanour was lost, not for the first time that day. Her hand, wrapped round the tail end of the dragonfly, had hold of it no more. As she pulled him into the room, her hands were no longer filled with the hard shell tail. Her hands were filled with dust. She fell to her knees, trying frantically to scoop up the dust that she did not catch,

'Get in here! Help me! The dragonfly is still here, look, it's not gone, we can use this.' The respect commanded by a strong, powerful Leilani was in question from the onlookers, while they watched an old mad woman, clutching at dust. Lanny turned and walked away.

'Get me gold!' she screamed after him. Composing herself, she tried to pour what dragonfly dust she had in her hands into an empty jar she had taken from the nearest shelf. 'Another way showed itself to us today, get me gold!' Her uncontrolled scream had turned into an assertive shout. Out of sight Lanny nodded his head,

'She is right boys, let's get the gold,' Lanny said to George and Gregg who, having been on their back legs for the victory walk into the house, were back down on all fours and moving rapidly out of the open front door. Earl, he wasn't sure what to do. Was this his opportunity to run? Of course he hadn't been looking for signs of movement earlier, the reason he gave to Leilani for his lack of being by her side. Fully aware of their presence, he was in fact conversing with who was causing the movement. He was making friends, waking up from the nightmare he had been living in for far too long. Lanny out of sight, the bears already along the dirt track, Leilani distracted with the dust, Earl decided that it was indeed his time to escape. Confidently, he made his way down the wobbly cobbly path, out the gate and to freedom.

'Oh!' He had forgotten about the sun bear army, silently waiting for their next order. He knew that nothing he would say would get them to leave, the orders had to come from Lanny, George or Gregg. Equally so, Earl knew that they wouldn't follow him without an order. So, having got over the little surprise, he continued his confident walk. Walking into the woods, through the woods and off into the fields that the silhouettes and shadows were still making their escape across, he took a sigh of relief to have made it.

'I set that weasley man on to them earlier, he must have them by now,' Leilani said. With Lanny and his bears not having taken long to return with the gold she needed, Leilani had quickly filled the cauldron with the liquid gold, placed the crystals and was waiting for the window to open.

'No, no, no, no. How is that possible?' The window open, Leilani watched the woman she was hoping to get control of and saw the moment she was about to be arrested. The same moment Alex exploded with energy. She followed Alex through her window as he ran back into the garden and into Dragonfly Manor. Her exclamation of "no's", was because a familiar face was leaving the front door of Earth's Dragonfly Manor,

'How can she be alive?' It was grandmother. Her grandmother. Looking now older than the day Leilani saw her, watching her and her brother from the upstairs window whilst they took the life of their own mother, grandmother's daughter. 'There is more going on here than even I thought was possible,' Leilani said. Lanny just watched, didn't say a word, his emotions being kept well in check. Leilani continued watching as grandmother left the garden. Stepping out into the site of the explosion she met with a girl, whose eyes caught the light in quite an unusual way. As the light hit her eyes, they reflected it with a mirror-like effect. Leilani watched as the two turned their attention to a body lying on the floor. The woman, after suddenly waking up, joined the two and they all quickly disappeared into Earth's Dragonfly Manor. Then nothing, she could see nothing. She forwarded through time, right up to the very moment the police swarmed the square. She watched as every house was searched except for Dragonfly Manor! Wall lights, street lights, torches lit every part around the grounds of Dragonfly Manor, but still she could see no sign of the ones she needed to see. Going backwards through time, Leilani checked over and over again, was there something she missed?

'Stop, go back a bit. Look, something is not right.' Lanny had seen something. She paused the picture as requested. The view was from above, looking down onto Dragonfly Manor. 'Those bushes moved, those branches fell, but there is nothing there.' He was right. The place he was looking was exactly where the adventuring group had climbed into the old camper van and made their escape. Focusing on the spot her brother had identified, Leilani, again, began spinning back through time, watching, looking for the slightest change.

'There you are!' Leilani smugly said. She had gone back many years, to a time when the old camper van was not so old and the bushes were not so tall. 'That's how they got away. But how could we not have seen it?' Leilani questioned out loud. 'It doesn't matter, we just have to find them!' she said. Searching every angle she could, she watched for an invisible vehicle. A space that didn't make sense in the traffic, a direction of travel hinted at by the slightest thing that was out of synchronisation with its surroundings.

Grandmother, her wisdom and knowledge about how the Dragonfly homes worked, had a thought just before heading out to the camper van with her group. The house and its true self was not seen by all. Its magic came from the tree that had been given its status by a visiting Shuing. The parts of the tree she had used in the building of Sophie's dolls house birthday present, showed that there was magic in the tree even if removed, so before leaving, she took a small branch, a stick really and hid it in her coat pocket. Her intention and hope was to be cloaked from anyone, public or police who where looking for them. What she didn't realise, or didn't even know she needed to, was that by her action, she had in fact cloaked them not only from prying eyes on Earth, but more importantly from the searching eyes of Leilani.

Finally, Leilani found a pattern that made sense, her patience had paid off,

'There it is!' Leilani said. She could see the camper van quite clearly. Grandmother had made a mistake. It hadn't even crossed her mind that when Alex and his mum left the group to fill up with fuel, her Dragonfly Manor stick was separated from them, which meant they could be seen. Leilani and Lanny gleefully watched as the camper van returned to collect the shoppers.

'Who is that?' Lanny said. The van had stopped and grandmother, unseen, had got in first. As soon as she did, the van began to fade from view leaving Sophie and Vicky outside, visible to the watching pair but only for a moment - as soon as they stepped in they were gone.

'She looks familiar!' Leilani said. She had turned back time and stopped the image where she could see the two girls standing outside the disappearing van. She zoomed in. 'Yes, she looks very familiar,' she said looking at Sophie. With the picture playing again, even with the camper van and its occupants gone, she could follow them. The direction they were heading became clearer and clearer with every break in traffic and movement of vehicles around them. Leilani stepped back from her window.

'Lanny, I know where they are going.' Having watched and calculated where they would be, she caught up with them. The window showed her a view from high up in the sky. She was looking down on the village she had come across connected to the name Hugins, some time ago, the name she had missed. As she searched the picture, a glint, a reflection of light caught Leilani's attention. From outside the village just a short distance along the loch side, the eyes she had seen outside Dragonfly Manor's garden, outside the van, the reflecting mirror eyes, could be seen again.

'There, look, there. That's her!' She could only see Vicky, but she knew she was not going to be there alone. She knew that she had found them all. Zooming in on the moving picture with precision, she said, 'She is looking out at something. If that boy is the one I have been looking for, if they are where I think they may be, hahahaha, oh, the fools, this is a good day.' Leilani turned to her brother. 'It's ours brother, it's all ours.'

CHAPTER 19

'What are you seeing? Tell us.' Sophie had stepped out of the camper van and joined Vicky. Anchor and Bart had become best friends on the long drive. Bart, most out of character and training, ignored Vicky, as he and Anchor ran amongst the bushes, dashing backwards and forwards across the small patch of sandy beach that Sophie and Vicky were making their way down to. 'I still don't see anything,' Sophie said.

'Girls, don't go into the water, it will be freezing cold!' grandmother shouted from the camper van. She was not quite as quick as the girls, but was making her way out through the open sliding door. Alex had stayed seated, his legs throbbing from Vicky who had clambered over him. Melissa had shuffled across the front bench seat and was watching out the passenger's window, looking out to the motionless water that filled the massive hole created by the meteor, now a loch.

'It does feel different here doesn't it,' Melissa said.

'What do you mean?' Alex asked,

'I can't put my finger on it but there is just something different. I don't just mean that the air is actually clear and fresh to breathe, unlike at home, but there is an energy, I feel lighter. There is a positiveness which is uplifting,' Melissa replied. With the camper van's window closed and Melissa being so close to it, her breath began to steam it up, restricting her view.

'Come on Alex, what are you waiting for? Let's

find out if we can see why Vicky was in such a hurry to get out,' Melissa said. The place they found themselves was not the only thing that felt lighter. The usual, quite intense demeanour of Melissa was changing. There was a freedom to her aura that was quite different to what Alex was used to. Alex's hesitation on leaving the camper van came from a fear of not knowing what was going to come next. Everything that had gone on the night before, was obviously leading to something unexplainable, and he was to be at its centre. He did not feel the need to rush straight into the unknown, just yet. He didn't want to let his mum down, he didn't want to let the group down. He especially didn't want to let Sophie down. He watched as she stood at the water's edge, her red hair looking even richer in the morning's light than it did before. He could see her breath as it hit the cold air and slowly drifted away from her, eventually evaporating, becoming one with the damp, fresh, morning air that was filled with an electric energy.

Alex got out.

'Ok Alex, do your thing,' Vicky said. She was looking backwards and forwards to him and the island that only she could see. 'Come on, it's there, seriously it's there. If I can see it, it must be real!' She laughed as she said it, always finding herself the funniest person in any room. Alex looked across the beautiful loch. As hard as he tried - eyes wide open, eyes squinting, closed then reopened, he could see nothing but the still waters and eery mist that hovered above the place Vicky was looking.

'I don't understand. If I am that important why can't I see it?' Alex asked grandmother. Sophie moved over to his side and took his hand. The moment she did, Alex's chest filled up with a heat, a burst of energy which caused him to take a step back. Sophie's reaction to his movement away from her was to let go, but she couldn't.

'Alex, what is it?' Sophie asked. He couldn't get his breath, he couldn't answer her as much as he tried. The heat and energy was spreading throughout his entire body. The sand beneath him began to vibrate, sending ripples out across the loch towards the mist. 'Alex!' Sophie said louder, still unable to let go. Alex closed his eyes. Not only could he feel the heat and energy building inside him, he could feel Sophie. He could hear and feel, every cell in her body. With his eyes still closed, he turned to her, let go of her hand and pulled her in close to him, a full embrace.

Melissa, Vicky and grandmother stood back and watched the show. From the two of them a light began to shine. Starting from Alex, it engulfed them both. It wrapped them up as Alex's arms wrapped up Sophie. As quickly as it had begun, it ended, at which point Alex let go of Sophie.

'Well Sophie, well young man, it would appear that you are just meant to be aren't you,' grandmother said, pointing across the loch to the island that was now visible to her. 'I assume you can all see that?' Alex, Vicky and Melissa turned to look. They could, all of them could see it. The dogs had seen the island's appearance before any of them and were already swimming, ten metres from shore. Protruding from the mist was an island, a beautiful, life-filled island.

'Don't! Please don't! If you go there she will have won, she will get what she has wanted.' A stern voice came from behind them. The long blonde haired woman who had been watching them at the loch side in the village, the woman who had spoken to Melissa like they had met before, was seated on top of a heavy breathing horse. With chestnut coloured legs that rose up to a chestnut chest, falling back to a light coloured and spotted hind, he was a stunning, muscular looking horse, with the friendliest of eyes.

'Please stop, all of you!' she pleaded again. Anchor and Bart in the distance had not heard her. However, having realised that they were going to struggle to make it all the way out to the island, they were already on their way back. Melissa knew the answer to the question Alex then asked,

'Who are you?'

Having jumped down from her tall horse, the blonde woman walked down to join them. Her mode of transport followed closely behind.

'It's not important who I am. What is important is that I know who you are and that by you being here, you are risking everything.' She looked over at grandmother. 'You should have known better. You have seen what they are capable of.' Grandmother was taken aback. How could she know who she was and talk so knowledgeably.

'My dear, at this point you have the advantage, you should answer the boy's question,' grandmother said, giving her a look that showed she meant it.

'My name is..' she hesitated and shook her head. She knew that telling them her name would tell them everything, 'my name is Alexandria.' As soon as the name made its way to Alex's ears, his heart began to race. He had noticed a familiarity to her face on their first meeting.

'You are my birth mother!' Alex said without any hesitation. He knew it to be true.

'Woe!' The surprised single word came from Vicky, which pretty much summed up everyone's feelings. 'So, you are the reason for this big chunk of loveliness,' Vicky said, her words lightening the moment and bringing a smile to Alexandria's face.

'Yes I am.' Looking into Alex's tearing eyes, she said, 'My heart has been broken since the day I watched Melissa lift you from the steps I had left you on, for her.' Melissa had stepped next to Alex and put her arm around him. She pulled him in close, to protect him, something she had been happy to do all his life.

'Why?' Alex asked.

'If you have come here, having met with Patricia and undoubtably been in her Dragonfly home, you probably already have the answer,' Alexandria said.

'Who's Patricia?' Vicky piped up. 'Oh, it's you,' she said looking at grandmother, who with all her knowledge, was still confused as to how and why this woman knew so much about her.

'Your grandchildren, they still live. Your grandchildren, they came so close to discovering me and my boy. To have come here you must know how valuable my boy is. That is why he must not be here,' Alexandria said.

'Yes I know how valuable I think he could be. But I do not know why he shouldn't be here.' The tone of her voice changing from curious to stern, grandmother said 'his meeting with my granddaughter tonight started something. My dragonfly, which I had not seen since that awful day many years ago, which you clearly know about, it awakened. It came back to my Dragonfly Manor last night, because of him. It joined with him.'

Alexandria interrupted,

'It's joined with him!' She dashed over to Alex, went round to his back and pulled his clothing down from the back of his neck.

'It's not there. It joined with him when my granddaughter and he were close, but it left,' grandmother said.

'Oh no, please no, it left where?' Alexandria asked.

'It left into the door,' Sophie spoke up.

'Did it come back?' Alexandria asked. Sophie shook her head. 'You, don't know what you have done!'

'I know very well what has been done young woman and at this point, as important as I feel that you are to what has been and what may be, it is about time that you woke up to the fact that this day had to come,' grandmother confidently said. Alex, still hugged in close to Melissa, took his gaze from Alexandria and his eyes fell to the sandy floor. Alexandria let out a sigh and spoke again,

'My life, its only reason for being, is to protect what my bloodline was gifted. That is what I am trying to do. I can see what you are all seeing. The island now visible from the shore has never been visible and should not be. I and my bloodline have known of its location from the beginning. Knowing its location we would go to it, love it and use it. But until today, it only became visible once we stepped foot on it and it would be visible to just us. I saw what happened when you and this fiery haired young woman came together, the light that came from you Alex, how it wrapped round you both. I have never heard, read or seen anything like it. Something is very different here today. The island being seen, that could bring them to us. They can see more than you know Patrica,' Alexandria said, bringing her speech to an end.

Grandmother, as much as she knew about the legend of the dragonfly, as much as she knew about her home, as much as she knew from the stories she read about the beginning, what she knew very little about, was her grandchildren, the brother and sister. Over the years, until all fell quiet, some stories had got back to her. She knew about the consuming of the dragonflies, the slavery of Heart's inhabitants, the violence and death they together had subjected the beautiful place to, the beautiful place that was for healing and bringing balance. But how they did it and what Leilani and Lanny knew, grandmother did not.

'What do you mean by they can see more than I know? And how would you know? How can you know?' grandmother asked. Realising there was no point in hiding any truth from them now, Alexandria filled in the missing parts to the story. She told them that she was a direct descendant of Shuing, the one and only human that had been given the gift by the dragonfly. The gift that made it possible for Shuing to create Dragonfly homes all over the Earth. Each Dragonfly home with its tree, its doorframe, its doorway into a beautiful version of what Earth could and should be, created to help those who needed it. An escape from bullies, an escape from suppressors, an escape from abuse, an escape from the pain of illness, an escape from war. Alexandria explained that although she did not have the gift of Shuing, she could travel to and from Heart, not just through a Dragonfly home, but from the island. It was with that ability, passed down through her generations, that Alexandria had travelled back and forth, as recently as the morning of the day before and how she had seen more pain and suffering than she could cope with.

The one blessing for her was that Shuing had been the first, and last, to hold such a connection with all that surrounded him. Alexandria and all her descendants were not empaths, so thankfully with all that she witnessed, she did not feel as Shuing would have, as Alex would have!

Alexandria had never known Heart in any other way than it was under the rule of Leilani and Lanny. She had been told stories of how wonderful it once was, by her own mother and by the ones living and hiding in Heart. She had been brought up with the knowledge of her descendants. Out of all the knowledge she had been given, the one piece, the most important piece, was that she should never allow the opportunity for the doorways to be open.

'Your granddaughter, Leilani, she has discovered a way to see to Earth. She has also found a way to manipulate people on Earth as well. The day I discovered it, was the day, with a heavy heart, I destroyed the dragonfly tree that was at the centre of my family's Dragonfly house. My actions took all the magic from my home. It was also the day I began my search for a safe place and a protector for my baby boy. I could not risk her seeing him, here, here with me,' Alexandria's emotions began to get the better of her. Alex had heard enough. He stepped away from Melissa. Grabbing Sophie's hand as he passed her, he walked towards the water.

'We are here now. She said it, together we are different. I think we should go to the island,' Alex said quietly to Sophie.

'Yes, but how?' Sophie asked. Alex looked around for something, a boat, a log, something that they could float out on. He figured grandmother's warnings earlier about the temperature of the water would be correct. Swimming was probably not really an option. As they stood, the sound of heavy thuds hitting the sand came from behind them. Before having time to look to where the sound was coming from, the huge horse that Alex's birth mother had ridden up on stepped beside them. He bent forward, down into a bow.

'Please let me help you.' A voice came from nowhere, heard only in Alex's head,

'He wants us to get on!' Alex said to Sophie. Neither having ridden a horse in their lives, they hesitated. The horse shook its head, its mane falling to the side that the two stood.

'Hold on to me, I won't let you fall.' The voice in Alex's head was as clear as Sophie's voice that was speaking at the same time as the horses,

'If we grab that, we should be ok,' Sophie said pointing at the mane. Alex smiled. Not answering either of them, he threw his leg over the back of the horse. Once up he reached his hand out for Sophie, who gladly took it. With one pull from Alex and a small jump from Sophie, she was sat up behind him.

'Alex, what are you doing?' Melissa asked. She was concerned that they were about to do exactly what they were about to do.

'Troy is talking to him,' Alexandria said in a soft loving voice. She recognised the look in her horse's eyes. 'Alex, is communicating with an animal, how is that possible?' Alexandria fell back and sat on a rock. 'Patricia, he is different to all that have gone before.'

'No, they are different to all that have gone before,' grandmother replied as they watched Troy, Alexandria's horse, and his two passengers, wade out into the loch.

'Where are they going?' Leilani asked. She had been closely watching in excitement as the group all exited the van and had been joined by Alexandria. She was so focused on them, she had completely missed the fact that the island had become visible to all.

'You're the one with the window, you tell me,' Lanny sarcastically replied, slightly forgetting himself and his place in the excitement of finding the group. Finding them in the place where Leilani had calculated it could have all begun, she spun her crystal, blew on it gently and the picture pulled back up into the sky.

'That's it, that's it, look!' Leilani squealed. What Alexandria was scared of was now reality. Alex's return to the place of his ancestors, his return with Sophie, had indeed given Leilani exactly what she wanted. She too could see the island.

'The door, quickly!' She grabbed her gold covered crystal, a small vile of the liquid gold and the ashes of the dragonfly and sped out from her dingy room into her fully alive Dragonfly Manor. 'Look. The light is dull compared to the others, but we know where and what that is don't we,' Leilani said gleefully to Lanny and his bears who were very close behind her. Leilani was still completely oblivious to the fact that Earl had still not returned.

'Right, we need to get there.' As much as she tried, the process of touching the light and the sequence of door handle turns she was sure would work, did not. However the door was lit up with more lights than she had seen for many years.

'We should try the next nearest light,' Lanny intelligently said. Leilani didn't acknowledge him, but did exactly what he suggested and it worked instantly. Her Dragonfly Manor door flung open. She could see beyond it, into a garden that was not her own.

'This is quite a distance from where we need to be. Hurry, we must move fast. We must get to that island before they do.' Leilani flew out the door with a youthfulness not seen in her for many years. Her tired creaking legs were moving as fast as they ever had. George and Gregg had gone on ahead, looking for an animal that would be used to transport their master and his sister.

'Sister, the island, will it be here on Heart?' Lanny asked. Leilani was convinced it would be. She figured there was a high chance that there would be a doorway on it like the island itself, unseen before, between Heart and Earth. She had to be the first one to it. She had to be the one to take full control, or at the very least be there to take control of whatever may come through it.

'Sophie, you be careful,' grandmother shouted out across the loch.

'If she is watching she has seen, she will be coming,' Alexandria said.

'Let's just hope whatever is meant for those two out there on the loch, it happens quickly,' Melissa said.

'Not really very fair though is it?' Vicky said,

'What isn't?' Melissa asked.

'Well, we come all this way, I find the island and we are sat here on the beach. It's a nice beach of course, but still the one on that island looks nicer,' Vicky said, Bart at her side. Anchor was sitting at the water's edge, contemplating following. He contemplated a long time, so long he eventually sat down, then lay down and fell asleep.

The water had got too deep for Troy to keep his hooves on the ground. It did not stop their forward motion. The energies provided by the site of the meteor strike, created a drop in the gravitational pull that would normally be experienced. Troy floated quite well and his kicking legs provided the forward motion they needed. It still took some time, longer than those left on the beach, who knew the race was most probably on, would have liked. Finally, once again, Troy found ground beneath his feet - slippery rocks, turning into soft sand. Alex and Sophie's feet rose out of the water as Troy victoriously stepped up and on to the small sandy area, just before the start of the greenest and lushest grass any of them had ever seen. Alex jumped down and caught Sophie as she did the same. As soon as they were on the grass, the island vanished from the sight of those left on the loch's shoreline. The onlookers, this time including Vicky, could only see the still waters of the loch, with its thin layer of mist hovering over where the island was.

'Look, there's a house,' Alex said as he walked away from the water and the grass into an area of trees. Sophie followed close behind. Troy stayed to enjoy the grass, a nice change from the dry hay he had been eating being winter back home.

'This must have been his home,' Sophie said.

'I guess so, how is it still standing?' Alex asked,

'You are being funny right?' Sophie said with a giggle. Alex stepped into the shadow of the tree that was growing up through the old, rustic, wooden home. It created a canopy above all the other trees, bushes and plant life that was thriving. Arriving at the door, Alex hesitated to touch the handle. Sophie did not. She stepped forward and took hold of it, turned it and threw open the door. Stepping inside, she found one large room, in the centre of which was the tree. Alex, having hesitated, was about to enter the house when Sophie disappeared.

'Sophie, Sophieeeee!' Alex shouted. Alex stood for a moment, nervous to take another step incase he was also taken. Looking back out of the entrance door, he could see Troy happily filling his tummy on the lush grass, which he realised looked familiar,

'It's the dream,' Alex said out loud, although no one was there to hear him. He stepped into the cottage expecting to be taken wherever Sophie was. He wasn't. He stood looking around. There was no furniture, no belongings of any kind, just a fireplace on the far wall. The old cottage was a circle, not a corner in sight. The curved walls were alive with pictures. Different places all blending together, changing with every second that past. A natural window into Heart itself, the reverse of Leilani's pain-made window.

Alex couldn't waste any time. He had to get to Sophie. He thought he knew where she may be, but how could he get there? He walked up to the trunk of the tree and walked round it, looking for some hint of how his rescue could commence. Maybe there was a door in it he thought. No, there was not.

'Sophie, can you hear me?' he shouted, he got no response. Thinking back to his dream, he remembered that he fell through the field, so he headed back out of the cottage. He searched the ground for some sort of indentation, or hole, with no luck. Standing next to Troy, Alex reached out and started to stroke his head. A calmness came over him as he spoke to him, 'You know big fella, I have no idea what I should do.' The grass looked as inviting to Alex as it was to Troy, so he sat down, then lay back, allowing the soft grass to surround him as he fell back into it. Looking up at the sky through the branches of the leaf covered canopy of trees, he began to sink. Having had the feeling before, this time he did not panic. The ground slowly opened up around him and he fell.

'Hello!' A new voice, this time not in his head. It echoed around the cave he found himself in. He had not fallen as he did in his dream, Alex was being lowered slowly to the rocky, slippery cave floor below. 'There was one before who was worthy of help to heal a world so torn. Once more, there is one, this time joined by another.' The cave went quiet as Alex landed softly on his feet. As quick as his feet touched the ground he was running up the small underground stream he had been placed next to. He knew exactly where he was going. Slipping in his haste, he found himself at the edge of the lake from his dream and there, motionless under the water, she was. This time Alex did not fall into the water and on to Sophie. This time Alex stepped into the water. The moment his feet touched the water and caused a ripple that slightly distorted his view of Sophie, her eyes opened. Looking up at him through the water, she smiled and raised her arms up to him.

'Go to her,' the echoing voice said. Sophie took hold of Alex's arms and with her tiny body, managed to pull Alex into and under the water with her. A light shot out from between them, twisting, swirling through the water. The gems that were in the walls sparkled from the reflection. The droplets of water falling from the cave's ceiling and the tree's roots, shone like a galaxy in space. Alex could feel a new kind of energy, a loving energy wrapping around him, passing through him, pushing the two of them out into the middle of the lake.

'Together you are strong. Together you can be all that is needed once more.' With that, the cave filled with light, a trail of colours coming from the one whose voice Alex had been hearing. From the centre of the tree above, the hole where the roots grew, came the first. The dragonfly that started it all. It dropped from the ceiling, its wings tucked in. It hit the lake with such force that the water was pushed out, crashing off the walls into the streams that went into and away from the lake. The noise was like a thunderstorm, tornado and hurricane all at once. Alex and Sophie's ears felt as though they were going to burst, the force of the impact making them feel as though their skin was being ripped from them. Suddenly everything fell silent.

'Are you ok?' Alex asked Sophie. Still holding each other tight, they found themselves on the hard, damp bottom of the lake, its water thrown out to everywhere but where they were. They could hear the trickles of cold, fresh water, returning from the streams that had cut their way through the rock walls over many thousands of years. Over time they would refill what had been emptied.

'Yes. I feel like I shouldn't be, but yes. I feel wonderful. And y…' she stopped as she was about to ask, as having opened her eyes, she was face to face with the colourful eyes of a dragonfly.

'Alex, can you feel that?' Sophie softened her embrace. Alex couldn't see where she was looking,

'What is it?' Alex asked.

'It's the dragonfly,' Sophie responded. Alex let go of Sophie and rolled away from her, trying to see what she was seeing.

'Where?' he asked.

'It's like before, it's on you. I mean in you,' Sophie said. Alex stood up and as he did, he felt a heaviness that pushed him back down to the lake bed.

'Alex. The weight of the world is on your shoulders. The weight of all that are suffering. The first time I appeared there was pain, there was suffering. Now it's not just humanity that is in pain. Earth, the very nature that makes Earth a paradise is nearing its end. No one person could hold that weight. I have stayed hidden, I have stayed watching, I stayed hoping that the ones who were worthy would one day come, come in time. Together, always together.' Alex forced his way to his feet and reached his hand out to Sophie who was still sitting in the damp. Hesitantly, she placed her hand in his and Alex pulled her to her feet with ease.

An energy-filled light fell on to them from where the dragonfly had been hiding. In each other's arms once again, the dragonfly that had made its home in Alex, reached it's wings around him and down his arms. Together they felt everything, the pain that Alex knew well, that he had learnt to block out was being felt not only by him. Sophie couldn't help herself, she burst into tears. She had spent her life a loner, been abandoned, been bullied, spent her life hiding, she thought she had felt pain and suffering. She had not. Not compared to what she was feeling in that moment.

'Alex, how have you been able to,' she couldn't say any more. Wrapped up in his arms, her head on his chest, she was to feel one more thing. The dragonfly placed on her a bite to the back of her neck, the same bite that Shuing had received and Alex had had all his life on his hand. The connection was complete.

The pain blissfully began to subside. They squeezed each other tight, each closing their eyes to fully enjoy the connection. The enormity of their beginning and of what was to come was sinking in. As they stood together, they felt a movement which made them feel slightly dizzy. Opening their eyes to see what it was, Alex and Sophie found themselves back in the cottage, standing with their backs to the tree, looking out the open door towards Troy.

'Grandmother!' Sophie shouted. Letting go of Alex, in an instant she ran from the cottage. Alexandria had uncovered a rowing boat she had hidden in the trees, the boat she used quite regularly. She had loaded the adventurers up and taken them all across to the island, which, as with every visit she made, became visible to her and those who accompanied her, as soon as they stepped on to the small sandy beach.

Their arrival coincided with the very moment Alex and Sophie returned from the cave below. The cave, created by the meteor, which shared its energies and jewels with Earth as it impacted with it those thousands of years earlier. Sophie ran across the grass and gave her grandmother the tightest hug she had ever given. Alex followed in a much slower fashion, patting Troy as he passed him. He walked up to his two mums and put his arms round both of them. He felt at home, he felt the love between all three of them, of family.

'Yes, fine, always the third wheel!' Vicky said. She wasn't left for long as Bart and Anchor, unable to control their excitement at the return of their friends but unable to get to them, decided that their happiness should be directed at Vicky. Whimpering loudly, they jumped all over her and licked her frantically.

'Sophie, what is that?' Grandmother saw the bite that Sophie had been given. Growing from its centre was every colour imaginable, pouring out, covering her shoulders, back and up her neck.

'Grandmother, life will return to all of our homes again. Alex and I, we have been shown everything. Grandmother, the first dragonfly, it has awakened.'

THE END

Printed in Great Britain
by Amazon

84253965R00171